EMILY'S HOLIDAY HAS STARTED BADLY.
STUCK WITH HER MUM'S BEST FRIEND,
SHE HAS NO TECH, NO BFF AND NO CHANCE
OF THE GORGEOUS TOBY ASKING HER OUT.
NO ONE UNDERSTANDS HER WOES . . .
LEAST OF ALL HER MUM.

BUT WHEN SHE FINDS HER MUM'S OLD DIARY,
EMILY IS STUNNED TO DISCOVER THAT
HER MUM WAS ONCE A TEENAGER TOO!
A NINETIES TEENAGER CALLED LILA MACKAY
WHOSE WORLD IS FULL OF WEIRD FASHIONS,
TV SHOWS AND MUSIC EMILY'S NEVER
HEARD OF. BUT THERE ARE BOYS.
AND EMILY SOON BEGINS TO WONDER
IF PERHAPS SHE AND HER MOTHER ARE
NOT SO DIFFERENT AFTER ALL . . .

GILL SIMS

GILL SIMS IS THE AUTHOR OF THE HUGELY
SUCCESSFUL PARENTING BLOG AND FACEBOOK
SITE 'PETER AND JANE'. HER FIRST BOOK
WHY MUMMY DRINKS WAS THE BESTSELLING
HARDBACK FICTION DEBUT OF 2017,
SPENDING OVER SIX MONTHS IN THE TOP TEN
OF THE *SUNDAY TIMES* BESTSELLERS CHART,
AND WAS SHORTLISTED FOR DEBUT NOVEL
OF THE YEAR IN THE BRITISH BOOK AWARDS.
HER GLOBALLY BESTSELLING WHY MUMMY . . .
SERIES HAS NOW SOLD OVER A MILLION COPIES.
THIS IS HER FIRST YA BOOK.

First published in Great Britain in 2025
by Electric Monkey, part of Farshore

An imprint of HarperCollins*Publishers*
1 London Bridge Street, London SE1 9GF

farshore.co.uk

HarperCollins*Publishers*
Macken House, 39/40 Mayor Street Upper,
Dublin 1, D01 C9W8

Text copyright © 2025 Gill Sims
The moral rights of the author have been asserted

PB 978 0 00 851378 8

Printed and bound in the UK using 100% renewable electricity at
CPI Group (UK) Ltd
1

A CIP catalogue record of this title is available from the British Library

s book contains FSC™ certified paper and other controlled
sources to ensure responsible forest management.

or more information visit: www.harpercollins.co.uk/green

GILL SIMS

LILA MACKAY

is very misunderstood

EMILY

CHAPTER ONE

My mother hates me. I have spent some time trying to work out what has happened to me, and how my life has gone so very wrong, and that is the only conclusion I can come to. I am only fourteen years old, and my mother hates me. She must hate me, because why else would MY OWN MOTHER purposely, selfishly, *cruelly* set out to ruin the life of her only daughter, other than because she hates me and she ONLY THINKS OF HERSELF.

On the first day of the Easter holidays, I should be at Poppy's house, making get-ready-with-me TikToks. If we were at my house, Mum would be there, and she'd ask what were we getting ready for, we're only going to the park? But at the park is Toby Cooper who I am sure is JUST ABOUT to ask me out, and that is why I must be ready at all times, because the first time the love of your life talks to you is a really important moment that I will remember forever. If I was old and sad like Mum, I would probably say it is totally #**memories**.

Of course, Mum doesn't understand about that, which is hardly surprising because she doesn't understand anything. If she knew about Toby, she'd be all, 'You're too young to think about things like that, don't waste your time on boys, you can't possibly be in love.' I don't think Mum has ever been in love, so how would she even know whether I'm in love with Toby or not (I definitely am though).

But now, instead of being in Poppy's bedroom pooling our MAC collection, with TayTay on repeat, so I look my best before Toby sweeps me off my feet and everyone thinks I am the coolest girl in our year for dating Toby Cooper, who is the best looking boy in our year, I am destined for the CRUELLEST OF CRUEL SUMMERS!

Well, technically it's the Easter holidays, but it is quite warm today, and Taylor Swift hasn't written a song called Cruel Easter Holidays.

I am en route to my destiny, away from Poppy, away from Toby, away from all that brings hope and joy to life, by way of a train, where there is a woman sitting opposite me on her phone watching recipe videos with no headphones on and laughing loudly, for reasons that escape me – why is macaroni cheese so funny? There is a man reading the *Sun* on his tablet sitting next to me, and another woman across the aisle playing what sounds like *Candy Crush* which I didn't even realise was still a thing, and an annoying child behind me, kicking the seat every ten seconds, watching *Paw Patrol*, and the whole carriage is filled with people enjoying lovely, beeping, dinging, singing, mind-rotting electronics courtesy of the train's free WiFi – all of them . . .

Except me. I have nothing to do but stare hopelessly out the window as the train hurtles me further and further north, away to the bleak moors of Emily Brontë and far from all I have ever known. It will serve my mother right if instead of Toby, I take up with a dark and brooding Heathcliff sort I meet on the moor and run off with him and die of the consumption after getting my feet wet and forgetting my shawl.

I said all of this to Mum (apart from telling her about Toby) as she put me on the train, and she gave me an unsympathetic look, and said that I had no one to blame but myself since I had left my iPad at Dad's house, and I was the one who had smashed my phone.

I didn't *mean* to smash my phone. The way Mum said it sounded like I'd taken a hammer to it in a fit of rage, rather than what had actually happened, which was that I'd dropped it down the stairs last night when I was trying to SnapChat Poppy at the same time as bringing down all the dishes in my room because Mum said I was a disgusting skank and also that she had no crockery left. Harsh. And *that* was when I realised I had left the iPad at Dad's when I had been there the night before to say goodbye before I was cast adrift into the wilderness because my own parents don't want me. Like a Victorian orphan.

Maybe I'm more Jane Eyre than Cathy Earnshaw. Maybe I will marry a massive red flag like Mr Rochester, and *then* Mum will be sorry. And Dad. But mostly Mum, because all of this is *her* fault for deciding that she wanted to go on a residential writing course to finish the novel she claims to have been working on for years. According to her, it is her 'dream' to get it published. And it's all very well, her chasing her dreams, but what about me, her only daughter, while she does that?

What about me, indeed?

I was quite excited at first when Mum told me she'd had a last-minute offer to go on the course. I am such a kind and loving daughter that before I realised Mum hated me, I was really happy for her, because she said it meant a lot to her, and she would love to actually finish this novel instead of writing dozens of poorly paid articles about top cleaning tips and mystery shopping reviews and 'stealing her style'. The course was paid for by some old dead millionaire who wanted to further the cause of women's fiction (personally I could think of better things to do with my money if I was a millionaire but each to their own). Mum could never have afforded something like this herself.

I was happy for me too, because I thought it meant I would get to have that time at home all by myself, being grown up and having parties and sleepovers and doing whatever I wanted all the time, and I would find some way to just casually mention this in Toby's hearing and he would think I was really mature and sophisticated and how could he possibly resist that?! But Mum had other ideas.

Initially, she said I could go and stay with Dad, but that didn't work because Dad is spending the Easter break on an archaeological dig with some of his students (including his new girlfriend, which I Do Not Approve Of) in a desert somewhere, and the site does not allow under eighteens, and even though I said I could clearly pass for eighteen even though I'm only fourteen, everyone agreed that I couldn't go with him and sit around a hotel all day by myself.

I offered again to stay at home on my own. I looked very noble, and slightly pained, as I suggested that it would be a sacrifice I was willing to make, but Mum told me not to be so silly, and then asked me if I had a stomach ache as I looked very peculiar. It is not my fault she can't recognise Noble Suffering when she sees it! Mum was looking fairly Nobly Suffering herself, and saying she'd have to turn down the course, because so many people were also away over Easter, when she came up with a brain wave, and rang Uncle Tom to see if he would mind having me for a couple of weeks.

I was pretty sure he would say, 'Absolutely not' – asking someone to look after your child for the holidays when you are not a feckless parental character in an old children's book is a fairly big ask of anyone – but to my astonishment, he said yes! Uncle Tom 'dabbles', as he puts it, in property developing and he has just bought another house that he is doing up, and he said I could make myself useful while I was there, helping him decorate and get the house straight, and why didn't Mum come and spend a few days after she finished the course too?

Once I got over the initial surprise, and some horror, I didn't *hate* the idea. I thought maybe I could start a house reno TikTok and go viral as the youngest interiors inspo account in the UK. I had plans to tie fetching scarves around my hair and show people how to create quirky, original yet affordable looks for their room. But that was before it all went horribly wrong and I forgot my iPad and broke my phone.

I had been quite hysterical at Mum about what was I supposed to *do* without a phone ALL HOLIDAYS as she very unreasonably refused to replace it, or even to pay to have it repaired, insisting that she was always telling me to be more careful with my things. Her solution was to point out I could get my iPad back from Dad in a couple of weeks and to give me an old Nokia phone she had in a drawer – one with *buttons*, ugh! And no data. I demanded to know what use this would be, and she said I could ring people on it. Actually make *calls*, like I'm some sort of *animal*. And when I said what I am supposed to the rest of the time, when I'm not talking on the phone like it's 1850, Mum said that Alexander Graham Bell didn't invent the telephone until 1876, LIKE I EVEN CARE when phones were invented. I tried to send a text with it, and it was impossible. I don't think Poppy even *gets* texts, anyway. She certainly hasn't replied and this phone is so old and hideous that it doesn't even have old people messaging apps like WhatsApp. I never thought I'd see the day I would feel grateful for WhatsApp. Mum suggested I could write letters to people, and when I asked how I would send them, if Uncle Tom would be providing me with carrier pigeons or something, she laughed and said there was such a thing as the Royal Mail, and people would probably love to get some proper letters.

I don't think my friends would even know what to do with a letter. I would be highly suspicious if I got a letter. Mum claims that when she was young, you had penpals in other countries and you wrote to each other about your lives and sometimes you met up or went to stay with them, and frankly that just sounds like grooming and Stranger Danger to me. How on earth can Mum lecture me with a straight face about not talking to strangers on SnapChat when she was writing off to Jean Michel and oooh-la-laing all over his stamps?

But I had three hours to kill on this train, so in the end, in despair, I tried to write a letter to Poppy. Mum said just think how useful my letters could be one day to my biographer if I end up famous for something. What could someone like me be famous for, though? I don't think a letter that only says 'Dear Poppy' would be very helpful to anyone, because that is as far as I got before I got stuck. What do you write in a letter? Aren't you supposed to be all 'Good morrow, kind sir, I trust this finds you not dead of the plague or other disgusting olden day poxes, I have sent to my cousin in the country for some apples forsooth.' What interest would Poppy have in that? Snapchatting is so much better than letter writing.

The Train of Doom finally pulled into Leeds, and Uncle Tom was there as promised to meet me. I had wondered what would happen if I didn't get off, but just carried on, and ran away to Darlington or somewhere and was never heard of again, and no one could find me because they couldn't do Find My iPhone. I could change my name and get a job and live a double life. But what if I didn't like Darlington? And what sort of a job could I get, with no phone to apply, when I'm only fourteen, even if I lied about my age? Also, it occurred to me that Mum would probably blame Uncle Tom and this isn't really his fault, and I didn't want to get him into trouble.

Uncle Tom started telling me about the house as we drove there. It was quite a long drive. Mum had claimed that Uncle Tom lived in Leeds, but Uncle Tom laughed when I said this and told me that at best it could be called 'Leeds adjacent'. I had been envisaging Uncle Tom and I creating some sort of ultra cool urban living space, me popping out for fancy coffees, maybe going to some swanky shops that Poppy will not have heard of, and coming home looking completely different. I would probably BE completely different: mature and sophisticated and cultured after my sojourn in a big city, instead of our small provincial town. Toby Cooper would be bowled over by how grown up and exotic I seemed, and would be unable to resist my charms. Maybe I wouldn't even fancy him any more – I'd find him too childish and foolish, and would want someone older, more on my wavelength. How was any of that going to happen though, in the 'Leeds adjacent' ancient old rectory on the moors Uncle Tom was telling me about?

'Your mum thought you'd love it!!' Uncle Tom said. 'It's very Brontë-esque and I believe *Wuthering Heights* is one of your favourite books?'

'I mean, yeah, I like *Wuthering Heights*,' I wailed. 'But I don't want to *live* in it.'

What I want is for someone to fall in love with me, as passionately, as hopelessly, as death-defyingly as Heathcliff loved Cathy. But I could hardly say that to Uncle Tom. And I definitely didn't want any of the other parts, like the lonely old house and the mad inhabitants. What if *I* went mad living there, before my life has even started? And I returned to Poppy and Toby wild-eyed and frizzy haired, fit only to be locked in the attic out of sight, what hope would there be for me then?

I did suggest this to Uncle Tom, who just laughed and said I was confusing my Brontës, that was *Jane Eyre* and the first Mrs Rochester I was thinking of, and he didn't think I could be driven to such extremis in the two weeks I was staying with him.

'My hair could turn white,' I muttered gloomily. 'I will be squandering my youth, alone, on the moors. What will become of me?'

Uncle Tom told me to stop being so dramatic and that I never knew, I might have fun. I did know though, because when grown-ups say things like that, you are *definitely* not going to have any fun at all.

CHAPTER TWO

So far, my premonitions about how little fun these weeks would be have been proved correct.

When I arrived on Thursday night, I thought maybe I had been overly pessimistic in the car, and that things wouldn't be so bad. Obviously not being able to talk to Poppy would be bleak, and, cut off from communication with the outside world, I could be sitting in blissful ignorance thinking about how much I love Toby and he could be going out with someone else without me knowing. But on the other hand, perhaps it's true and absence will make the heart grow fonder, and when I get back, even if I haven't completely reinvented myself as a Leeds cool girl, Toby will see me and realise that I was the key to his existence that he had been searching for. Or at least think I am quite hot and worth spending some time with.

That first night at the rectory, I felt like an adult. Uncle Tom and I cooked dinner together (pasta) and he talked to me like a grown-up and not like a child, and really seemed to listen to my opinions and everything, and although I don't have my phone or my iPad, I do have a TV in my room that I can get YouTube on and Uncle Tom has subscriptions to literally *everything*, though I don't know what the point is watching anything if I can't SnapChat Poppy while we're watching it, and if I can't then watch all the memes people make out of it afterwards and send them to my friends so they know I'm cool and that I get the jokes.

After dinner I showed Uncle Tom my broken phone and explained the pits of despair I was sunk to, and how life is no longer worth living without it etc, and he said to cheer up, it could probably be fixed and we could take it into the Apple Store next time we're in Leeds. But I pointed out that that would cost a fortune and how was I going to pay for it, and so he said maybe if I worked really hard helping him with the house renovations, so he could get it ready faster and back on the market, because he is an evil capitalist property developer, then he would pay for the repairs for me.

Although I don't approve of capitalism, I suggested that perhaps the best thing to do would be to get my phone repaired *now* and then I could work off the debt, and we could go into Leeds in the morning and go to the Apple Store. Uncle Tom laughed and said why would he disincentivise me like that, and that no one would do anything if they already had the rewards of their labours up front. I explained that that was *exactly* the sort of attitude that summed up what was wrong with capitalism, and that that was why I didn't believe in it, and Uncle Tom said he hadn't believed in capitalism when he was my age either, and I should go to bed as we had a busy day ahead of us tomorrow. Which rather spoilt the feeling of being treated like a grown-up.

The Doom and utter lack of fun began the next day. Uncle Tom is taking advantage of my phoneless state and need for repairs, and he has been working me *relentlessly*. I have spent hours and hours scraping about a million years of paint off about seven hundred doors! I asked him why he had bought a house with so many doors, and such *painty* doors, and he said those were High Victorian original features I was complaining about, and did I know how much value they would add to the house when they had been fully restored.

I don't know why some doors add value. Everyone needs doors, obviously, but why whether they are covered in paint or not makes them more valuable seems silly. Uncle Tom disagreed though, and told me to wear a mask in case I was breathing in lead fumes.

Lead fumes!

He might as well send me down the mines.

I thought once it was the weekend, we would at least we would get a day off, but Uncle Tom had me up at 8am! On a Saturday in the holidays! I told him over breakfast that I could in fact take this to the UN, that child labour was not allowed, and it would serve him right if I reported him. He said he thought making a fourteen-year-old get out of bed in the holidays to do some light decorating probably wasn't high on the UN's agenda, but I could always phone ChildLine if I really felt he was being unreasonably cruel. I asked what ChildLine was, and he explained it was a phoneline you could ring up if you were being abused in any way by your parent or carer.

'What, like *call* them?' I said doubtfully. 'Like, dial a

number and *talk* to someone? *Talk* talking to someone? Couldn't you text? Or even email? Don't they have an app?'

Uncle Tom considered. 'Well, they probably do now,' he said. 'Back when your mother and I were young though, you called them.'

'But Mum always goes on about how she didn't even have a mobile phone when she was my age,' I said.

'We used landlines,' he explained. 'And a lot of people would call ChildLine from a phone box.'

Now I was really confused. He explained that the phone boxes I saw by the side of the road had been in regular use when he was a boy, and if you needed to make a call when you were out the house, you put in 10p and called the number.

'But how did you know what the number was?' I asked.

Uncle Tom beamed. 'You remembered them!' he said. 'Everyone remembered each other's numbers. I still remember your mum's. And your Aunty Kate's. I could still call my best friend from school's number if I needed to, though I haven't seen him in twenty years. Not that he'd be there, his parents retired to Tenerife and sold the house. Our generation has all sorts of skills born out of necessity that you Gen Zers will never know or understand!'

I rolled my eyes and said 'OK, boomer!' which got me treated to a lengthy lecture about how Uncle Tom is NOT a boomer and is, in fact, Generation X, which according to him is the best generation, and 'Gen Z could never understand how much better it is to be a Gen Xer'. I decided not to tell him about the iPad babies, it might blow his old boomer mind.

CHAPTER THREE

Uncle Tom does at least permit a lunchbreak, which I suppose is something. Though, since obviously I am still phoneless, I have nothing to do in my lunchbreak but contemplate the grinding misery of my very existence. The amount of work Uncle Tom is wringing out of me, I think I might have grounds to renegotiate for a brand-new latest model iPhone instead of just getting mine repaired. He needs to learn capitalism works two ways and the workers will not be exploited any more!

After the weekend's brutal work schedule, Uncle Tom said today could be our rest day, while he waits for an electrician to arrive, but it is not proving very restful, as he suggested that if I wasn't doing anything else (apart from RESTING!) I could sort through some old trunks he is planning on using as coffee tables and side tables. Once we had established this was not, in fact, a joke, Uncle Tom explained more about what he wanted me to do with the trunks.

'They look great in old houses as small tables,' he said, 'but I've not looked in them to see what's inside for years

– never had time. Every time I move them, I think, I really must sort these out, they'd be a lot easier to move if they were empty. So maybe you could do that for me, while I give Pete the electrician a hand?'

'But how will I know what to do with everything?' I wanted to know.

He waved his hand airily. 'If there's anything that looks valuable or useful, put it to one side. Same with anything interesting, like old photos. Sort them into piles for me to have a look at. If you just find things like my old A-level coursework, then chuck it in the burn pile.'

I sighed and trudged up the stairs. I wished I could message Poppy and see what Toby was up to. Or *who* Toby was up to. I wondered what Poppy was doing too. Something more exciting than sorting through boxes of old rubbish, I bet. I kept reaching into my pocket to check my phone or message her and realising there's nothing there. I wonder if this is what that phantom limb thing is like, when people lose a hand but they still feel sensation in it, and sometimes forget it's not there.

I have taken to composing SnapChats in my head. They are really witty. Probably wittier than anything I've ever actually sent. I tried to tell Uncle Tom this last night, as I attempted to persuade him that, after three days of ceaseless labour, he really owed me those phone repairs and that he was probably causing untold psychological harm to me because I was getting phantom phone syndrome. Had anyone, I demanded dramatically as my closing argument, ever *studied* the traumatic effects on teenagers of being denied phone access?

Uncle Tom had laughed and said, yes, only for *every teenager* for millennia though, so maybe they needed to conduct a longer study with a bigger sample. I kicked myself for my basic mistake in saying it was the lack of phone that was causing me distress, and realised I should have said it was depriving me of social interaction with my friends that was causing the harm. After all, once upon a time, we'd all have been hunting woolly mammoths together or something. Or whatever it was that Uncle Tom and Mum did when they were young.

Not that it was the same for them when they were young. Everyone knows the boomers were never *really* young like we are young now. Uncle Tom said if I called him a boomer one more time, I would be stuck playing Snake on the rubbish Nokia forever. I was very tempted to reply, 'OK, boomer,' again but there was something in his eye that told me he meant it, so I decided I had better be quiet.

I sighed, and wished I could send Poppy photos of what I was being forced to endure, and opened the lid of the first trunk. It was, as Uncle Tom had predicted, full of loads of old folders of schoolwork and textbooks. I piled up the folders on one side and the textbooks on the other, because the textbooks had given me a cunning idea!

Downstairs, I heard Uncle Tom going into the kitchen to put the kettle on, while he and Pete took a break, and I dashed down to implement my plan. It was infallible!

'Uncle Tom!' I said brightly. 'Hello Pete-the-electrician,' I added politely. 'Uncle Tom, I've sorted the first trunk, it was mostly old schoolwork, so that's in the burn pile, but also there were some old textbooks.'

Uncle Tom looked up from the mugs. 'Well done. I think the textbooks can go out as well, though they probably can't be burned.'

'No, but I've had this really good idea!' I informed him, with my best Emily-is-super-helpful smile that Mum falls for every time. 'You see, the textbooks are *vintage*. And vintage books are worth a lot, so you could make loads of money selling them on eBay! And it will be no trouble to you at all, because I could do all that, I could research how much they're worth, and list them and organise the whole thing. At least I could . . .' I trailed off hopefully.

He didn't take the bait.

'If only I had a phone to do it on . . .' I said.

Still nothing. I had no choice but to go ALL IN.

'But if you took me into Leeds tomorrow and we got my phone fixed, then I could do that for you, and you would probably make so much money selling the old books that it would more than pay for the repairs, so really, it would be financially *irresponsible* of you not to go and get my phone fixed,' I said. 'I mean, what if you've got a book up there that's worth thousands and thousands of pounds, like happens on *The Antiques Roadshow*? Which I don't watch, by the way, Mum has it on sometimes and I see bits. But just think, Uncle Tom! You could make so much money you wouldn't have to be a property developer and sell your soul to capitalism any more, and you could just retire and maybe in your spare time be a second-hand book dealer with a little shop in Paris selling rare things and antiquities and you would be living in *Paris*, like Emily.'

'Emily? Emily who? Emily you? Emily Brontë?'

'Noooo, Emily in *Emily in Paris*, obviously!'

Uncle Tom looked blank, and muttered something about too damn many Emilys, but I was not to be dissuaded. 'And literally *all* you have to do to make this happen is to *get my phone fixed*!'

I was pretty sure I had clinched it with the dream Paris scenario at the end, I could see Uncle Tom was wavering, but no. No. He was shaking his head and laughing at me.

'You nearly had me there,' he said. 'A little bookshop on the Left Bank, a bell jangling above the door, a ginger cat asleep on top of a pile of antique sheet music on a chair in a shaft of sunshine . . .'

He looked wistful. I held my breath.

'But sadly,' he carried on, 'I don't think the sale of a pile of old A-level texts is going to enable that vision. Believe me when I say I wish it was that easy. So I'm afraid you'll have to wait for that phone repair, because apart from anything, I simply don't have time to take you into Leeds tomorrow.'

In vain did I plead and beg and cajole. I wept that no one understood me, and Pete-the-electrician took his tea and a packet of chocolate digestives and sidled out the door, while Uncle Tom sighed and said I was wrong, that it is the very nature of teenagers to believe they are misunderstood, and I sobbed that no, no one knew what it was like to be *me*, or what my life was like, and I really *was* very misunderstood, and he didn't understand me, and neither did Mum, Mum especially didn't understand me, I didn't believe Mum ever *had* been a teenager, so much did *she* not understand me, because she was always saying things like, 'I know how you feel, Emily, when I was your age . . .' and then she'd tell some really boring story that had nothing to do with what we had been talking about, so I *knew* no one knew how I felt and NONE OF THIS WAS FAIR.

Eventually I was cried out, and Uncle Tom sighed and said, 'You're right Emily, you're absolutely right. |I *have* forgotten how hard it is being a teenager, and if I'd remembered, I would never have bloody signed up for this. But we're both here now, and we need to make the best of it, and agree that while you may sometimes find me a little unfair because I no longer have my finger on the beating pulse of teenagedom, you need to cut me some slack, because I have no idea about this parenting thing, and frankly tears and tantrums wasn't how I saw this going, but I'm not going to let your mother down now, this is important to her, and I'm not going to let you down either. We both need to make the best of this situation, so how about this? Let's both work really hard this week, and next Saturday, I'll take you into Leeds and we'll get your phone fixed, maybe go for a pizza, maybe even, depending on how much the phone repairs cost, we could go shopping or something? Where do teenage girls shop these days? What about TopShop? Is TopShop a cool shop? Miss Selfridge?'

I sniffed, and gulped that I had never even *heard* of these shops, and suggested some others, and did I really have to wait till the weekend?

Uncle Tom was adamant. He didn't have time to take me in before then, and he wasn't letting his dearest friend's only child loose on the public transport system in a strange city. I said I was *sure* Mum wouldn't mind me going into

Leeds on my own on the bus. Uncle Tom gave the ultimate adult brush-off, 'We'll see' (i.e. NO), and suggested I finished sorting out the trunks if I wanted my phone fixed at any point.

The second trunk appeared to be mostly history essays, and then I found some folders of old photos. I wondered if it was OK to look through them, or if I was prying, but then I reasoned Uncle Tom had told me to sort through the trunks, and that was what I was doing, and really if I was to properly sort things out, I had to look at them.

It is so *weird* looking at paper photos. Mum said you only got one chance at a photo because film was so expensive, and when the film was finished you had to take it to Boots and get it 'developed' and you didn't know what the photos looked like until then. And selfies hadn't even been *invented*.

The clothes people were wearing in the photos were unbelievable. Like, some of them could've been nice, if they weren't so tragic. And the *hairstyles*. Didn't they have mirrors in the nineties? I decided to ask later who all the people were. I put the photos to one side, and took all the old essays for burning out to the back garden where Uncle Tom has an old rusty bin thing full of holes he says is an 'incinerator', but is definitely a bin, and then boxed up all the textbooks and put them in the utility room to go to a book bank or charity or the dump, whatever he wants.

It was nearly dinner time when I started on the third trunk, which was more of the same. How on earth had Uncle Tom written SO MANY essays? Is this all that lies ahead of me when I get to sixth form? I thought it would be a lot of sitting round drinking iced coffee and not wearing uniform, but Uncle Tom must've spent every waking hour writing essays. I added, 'How many essays did you actually write?' to the list of things to ask him at dinner, along with my questions about the photos.

I was hauling the last load of paper out from the bottom of the trunk to go down to the incinerator when I found a small fat notebook tucked into one corner. It looked totally different to all the A4 pads of notes Uncle Tom had told me to chuck out, and I opened it, intrigued. I only had time to glance at the first page and realise it was someone's diary, when Uncle Tom yelled up the stairs that dinner was ready. I scrambled up, grabbing the notebook and the envelopes of photos, and hurtled downstairs.

Uncle Tom looked at me in horror as I dashed into the kitchen. 'Go and wash. You're filthy.'

I dumped the notebook and photos on the kitchen table and grumbled off to clean up. When I came back, he had the notebook in one hand and was flicking through the photos on the table with the other.

'You found one of Lila's diaries,' he said in astonishment, waving the notebook at me. 'I'd forgotten all about them!'

'Lila?' I said. 'Lila as in . . . my mum?'

'Yes, Lila as in your mum. She was always scribbling in one. She loved her diaries.'

'Why is it in your trunk?' I asked. 'Why doesn't Mum have it?'

'I suppose I forgot to give it back to her. She gave me her diaries to look after, the summer before university, when she was going travelling with Kate and Jas.'

'What, you mean Aunty Kate and Aunty Jasmit?'

'Who else?' said Uncle Tom. 'She'd developed this morbid fear that for some reason she would die a tragic death on her grand tour of Europe, perhaps flinging herself in the Seine for reasons unknown, or succumbing to fever in Naples – I'm not sure, she was quite dramatic about it all. But anyway, she entrusted me with her diaries to . . . I don't know. I think she had some vague idea of them being published in the event of her death and the world finally recognising her genius. Anyway, obviously she didn't die, and she came home and I gave them all back, but I must've missed this one.'

'Are you sure this is *Mum* we're talking about?' I asked again, very dubious about Uncle Tom's recollections of my mother, because it all sounded most unlike sensible, boring Mum, who was forever telling me to stop letting my imagination run away with me and not to be so dramatic.

But he had put down the diary now, and was looking though the photographs properly, laughing and smiling and shaking his head. 'Look at us!' He grinned, waving a picture. 'There's your mum and me, Kate and Jas and all the others.'

I looked more closely at the photo. Three laughing girls, three beaming boys, all with their arms wrapped around each other, frozen in time, looking like they were having the time of their lives and thinking they would be young and beautiful and laughing forever. Uncle Tom pointed out who everyone was, but none of them looked like anyone I knew. Even my own mother didn't look like my mother. I said as much, and he said, 'Well, why would she?

She wasn't your mother then. She was just Lila. Lila MacKay.'

I wasn't sure I liked the idea of Mum not being my mum. Of there being a time when she was someone else. She was my mother. Surely, she had always been my mother. That's what mothers did. She had absolutely no business going round the place being all 'Lila MacKay' when she was supposed to be being *my mum*.

CHAPTER FOUR

Uncle Tom's iPad buzzed after dinner, and he jumped, and said, 'Talk of the devil. Lila! Emily's right here. Say hi to your mum, Emily!'

'Hi,' I said sullenly. I felt very aggrieved with Mum for having the cheek to have had a life before me, on top of the fact she had now entirely abandoned me to go off and have a life of her own. I took some satisfaction that her background appeared to a rather dingy hotel room. At least she wasn't staying somewhere super fancy without me.

'Emily!' Mum looked genuinely thrilled to see me. 'How are you getting on? Are you having fun? Uncle Tom not working you too hard? I'm missing you so much, sweetheart!'

I saw my opportunity and decided it would be a shame to waste such valuable maternal guilt and launched into an explanation of how I really *really* needed my phone fixed and I was earning money working for Uncle Tom but he wouldn't give me anything up front because *capitalism* and he wouldn't let me get the bus into Leeds on my own either because he thought I'd get lost or kidnapped or something, but I totally definitely wouldn't, I'd be fine, but if Mum could just transfer me the money to get my phone fixed *now*, I could pay her back when Uncle Tom paid me, and also if she said it was OK to let me go into town by myself then Uncle Tom would have to let me, because she was my mother, even if she rather seemed to have forgotten that fact right now.

I was aware of Uncle Tom raising his eyebrows in the background as I poured all this out, but I had started and I didn't seem able to stop, until I ran out of breath and finished, 'Please, please, Mum. Just say I'm allowed to go into town on my own and lend me the money for my phone, please Mum, PLEASE, I'll never ask for another thing as long as I live!'

'I very much doubt that is true,' said Mum. 'I'm sorry, Emily, but Uncle Tom's in charge. If he's not comfortable with letting you go into town on your own, then I have to agree with him. I'm not undermining him, when he's been kind enough to look after you at such short notice, *and* to pay you for helping him. It will do you no harm at all to wait for the weekend to get your phone fixed. Delayed gratification always makes the reward better, you know.'

'OH MY GOD!' I shouted. 'Why does NO ONE understand me? This is all so unfair, I HATE you. You have no idea what it is like to be me. I don't think that's even you in Uncle Tom's photos because if you had ever been young or had friends or BEEN IN LOVE YOU WOULD KNOW WHAT IT IS LIKE and YOU WILL NEVER UNDERSTAND!'

'In love?' said Mum. 'Who are you in love with, Emily?'

'You couldn't *possibly* understand,' I repeated, with all the dignity I could muster, and then burst into tears and ran out of the room as the iPad squawked, 'Emily? Emily?' and I heard Uncle Tom say, 'Lila, calm down, don't worry.'

I stamped upstairs and then thought of a lot of other things I had to say to Mum if she was still FaceTiming Uncle Tom. I stamped back down to tell her that I hoped she was *happy* with how she had ruined my life, and would *enjoy* seeing her only child live a lonely, barren existence, but I stopped outside the kitchen door.

I could hear their voices still talking. Then I heard Mum say in a funny sort of choked-up voice, 'She's just so *difficult* right now. I don't know where I went wrong with her, I feel like she hates me.'

'She doesn't hate you,' said Uncle Tom. 'Don't you remember what it was like being a teenager?'

Mum sniffed. 'Of course I do. It was wretched. That's why I've always tried to so hard to make sure Emily knows I understand. But she just sees me as her aged mother who knows nothing of what she is going through.'

'BUT YOU *DON'T* KNOW ANYTHING ABOUT WHAT I'M GOING THROUGH' I wanted to shout, as I turned and fled back up the stairs again. I could hear Uncle Tom saying, 'But Lila, I know you hate the idea, but that's exactly why I think this would be so helpful to you both . . .'

I didn't care what Uncle Tom thought would be helpful. How could he possibly know? How could *anyone* possibly know what could help me, what I needed, what my life was like? None of them knew. None of them cared. I burst into furious tears and sobbed bitterly into my pillow until I gave myself a headache.

When I had finished crying, I got up and sat in the window seat in my room, which seemed a good place to be pathetically woebegone and broken-hearted, staring wistfully out the window at the moors. You had to crane your neck a bit to see the moors, but they were definitely there. I had considered running out the door to roam them, and try and come to terms with my misery and draw metaphors with the bleakness of my own life and the moors, like Emily Brontë, but it was raining. That probably wouldn't have stopped Emily Brontë, but also she did end up dying of the consumption, and I shouldn't think running around in the rain on the moors helped with that.

It would serve everyone right if I caught my death of cold out there like Emily Brontë. Maybe that's all she was trying to do, just make everyone a bit sorry for not seeing how she suffered. Would it take my own tragically early death for my mother and Uncle Tom to understand how badly they had treated me? I hope not, Emily Brontë was quite old when she died, at least thirty, and I am far too young. And how can I die without knowing if Toby likes me? Or without ever having been kissed by *anyone*, let alone Toby?

CHAPTER FIVE

I was still staring gloomily out the window when Uncle Tom knocked and came into the room. He put Mum's old diary down on my bedside table. I glared at him.

'Emily, we're worried about you,' he said gently. 'Your mum's worried about you. About how you think no one understands. And what you said about being in love? Do you want to tell me about it?'

I shook my head, and then somehow found myself telling him all about Toby, and how he will probably ask someone else out, and how *miserable* it is, being in love for the first time, and how I just *wished* I could make Mum understand.

'I think maybe she understands more than you think,' Uncle Tom said. 'We had a long chat, your mum and me. She said you've been saying for a long time she doesn't understand, and she doesn't know how to show you she does, but I think we've come up with a way. We've agreed you can read her old diary.'

I was horrified. 'That's, like, so *cringe*. What if she's got, you know, *icky* stuff in there?'

'Well,' said Uncle Tom, 'if you're mature enough to be in love, surely you're mature enough to deal with the idea of your mother being an actual human being with feelings as well? Just . . . take a look, Emily. I think it would help you both, a lot. Or you could come downstairs and watch TV with me, I've got a lot of episodes of *Gardener's World* to get through?'

'NO! Thank you,' I added, as he was trying to be nice. 'I might just watch some TV up here.'

He shrugged. 'Just think about looking at the diary, yeah?' he said and left.

Mum's diary was sitting on my bedside table and looking at me. I shut it in the drawer and tried to watch an episode of *Bridgerton*, but it was no good, I couldn't fix my mind to anything.

I wondered what Emily Brontë would have done, faced with the same situation. She was barely more than a baby when her mother died, so she probably would have happily read her diary to find out more about her. Also, Mrs Brontë would not have had rudeness in her diary. Nothing but wholesomeness in Mrs Brontë's diary, all about going to church and what the dairy maid said to her, and what the many Brontë children had been up to.

Mum's diary is probably a very different kettle of fish. I have seen some nineties films like *Heathers* and they were all obsessed with *sex*. What if Mum has written about things like that? What if it describes her *doing* it? I can't think about my mother and such things, much less *read* about them in her own words. It would be very traumatising for me. How could Uncle Tom and Mum even think about doing such a thing to me?

I picked up the diary and went downstairs, where Uncle Tom was indeed watching one of his many episodes of *Gardeners' World*, and I handed him the diary.

'I can't read this,' I said. 'I just can't. The idea of what Mum might have written about. I can't read about my own mother and her . . . her . . . RUDE THINGS!'

Uncle Tom turned off the TV and said, 'Emily, would it help if I promised that there will be no sex in this diary?'

I could feel my face burning at Uncle Tom even saying that word. What if he decided he needed to have a Talk with me about How Babies Are Made and Staying Safe? It had been cringe enough when Mum did it, I would actually die on the spot if Uncle Tom broached such subjects. How could he just sit there and say 'sex' without being deathly embarrassed? Especially at his age. It's one thing for me to talk about it with Poppy and my other friends, quite another to have such conversations with Mum and Uncle Tom. They are much too old for such things.

Uncle Tom shook his head as I stared at him in speechless mortification. 'Emily, if you are immature enough to be embarrassed by me saying "sex" then you probably are too immature to be in love,' he said.

'I am *not*!' I burst out. 'I am not immature. It's just *gross*, hearing you and Mum talking about things like that.'

'Sex isn't gross, not when it's between two people who care about each other,' Uncle Tom said. 'But I don't think I'm quite up for having that chat with you tonight, when my mind has been pondering dahlias and sweetpeas rather than shenanigans.'

I definitely wanted to die, I just wanted to die right there and then. At least 'shenanigans' was better than 'sex'.

Uncle Tom handed the diary back to me 'But like I said, if I promised there was nothing like that in there, would that help?'

'How can you be sure?' I demanded suspiciously.

'Because it says 1996 on the front. And I know for a fact that in 1996 she wasn't doing anything like that. It wasn't till late 1997 that she –'

'LALALALALALALALALALALALALALALA!' I stuffed my fingers in my ears. I had no need to know what my mother did in late 1997, or what Uncle Tom knew about it, THANK YOU VERY MUCH!

'OK, OK!' Uncle Tom held up his hands. 'I won't say any more about it, other than that I guarantee there is nothing like that in this diary. So you'll be quite safe.'

'I still don't think I want to read it,' I said sulkily.

Uncle Tom sighed. 'Fine,' he said. 'I just thought it would help you see that your mum does know how it feels to be young, that she does understand, that you are not as alone as you think you are. You know,' he added, 'it wasn't easy for Lila to agree to let you read this. These are her private, innermost thoughts. It took a lot of courage. And it's a sign of how much she loves you. But if you don't want to read it, I can't make you. You might as well put it in your bag, so you remember to take it with you and give it back to Lila. Now, isn't it about time you thought about bed?'

I was going to argue that I wasn't a baby, and it was only 10.30pm, but I was afraid of what else Uncle Tom might try and talk to me about tonight if I stayed up, so I just nodded and said, 'Good night, then.'

I lay staring at the ceiling for what felt like hours. I heard Uncle Tom come upstairs and go to bed, and still I couldn't sleep. I tried reading one of the books on the bookcase in my room, but it didn't help. I didn't want to wake up Uncle Tom by watching TV. I lay there for a while longer and then I gave up and went and pulled Mum's diary out of my backpack.

At least if I *tried* to read it, then Mum and Uncle Tom couldn't be all, 'Well, Emily, if you'd only read that diary, you wouldn't feel like that' next time I reminded them how they could not possibly understand anything about what it is like being me.

I was under no illusions that this was going to provide any great insights into the meaning of life. But it might shed some light on whether or not Mum had really named me after Emily Brontë, like I hoped.

LILA

CHAPTER SIX

Oh God, oh God, oh God. Jas is sleeping over tonight, and we went shopping today for all our essentials for starting at actual sixth form college on Monday. Not essentials like Mum says are essentials like sensible school bags and what she calls 'proper' shoes. No, we got the things we really need, like lipstick and mascara and a Wonderbra. Well, I got a Wonderbra, Jas didn't because she is ideologically opposed to push-up bras. It makes my boobs look amazing though.

I can't believe we are finally going to be in a school with boys. Real boys. All these years, we have been shut away in an all-girls school, and boys were a distant dream beyond the railings, as we stood in the playground watching the boys from the mixed school up the road, who always had lucky girls in tow.

I mean, some of the girls knew boys, obviously. The popular ones with important hobbies like amateur dramatics or tennis.

It wasn't like Jas and I haven't tried having hobbies. We did go to the amateur dramatic society once, but everyone knew each other, and horrible Rachel Kemball was bossing everyone around and said she didn't think we were really the right sort because we didn't have any experience, and we said that was why we were there, to get experience, and she huffed and said we could help with the wardrobe, but all the clothes smelled a bit like old lady wee, and there were no boys in the room with the old lady wee clothes, so there wasn't much point really.

We had such high hopes for tennis too, but we couldn't go back after I fell over wearing my tennis skirt and I'd forgotten to put my gym knickers underneath and everyone saw my pants. I mean, I did want the boys to see my pants eventually, but not like that. And I wanted them to see my good pants, from Knickerbox, not the M&S ones with the days of the week on them. It was even worse that I was wearing Tuesday pants on a Saturday, and next time we went to tennis everyone started calling me Tuesday, so that was the end of that. It was very loyal of Jas to quit with me though, even though she wasn't very supportive of my BRILLIANT IDEA for ultimate coolness for starting college, which is changing my name!

When I told Jas, on the way home from the shops, she said, 'What are you changing it to? What's wrong with Beth?'

I pointed out that Beth is a Good Girl's Name, and that Beths aren't cool. Beths are the ones who fuss over everyone and are unappreciated and then just die and everyone is sorry *then* but that's not much use to Beth, is it?

Jas reckoned there's other ways to be a Beth than Beth from *Little Women*, but I don't think there is. That's the Beth that everyone immediately thinks of when they hear 'Beth', don't they? Poor, tragic, put-upon, dead Beth! So, I don't want to start college with everyone immediately thinking I am a goody two shoes, dying early, doing virtuous deeds sort of person! I want to be *cool*! I want to start college like Olivia Newton John at the *end* of *Grease*, when she was all big hair and stilettos and black leather, showing John Travolta who's boss. We want to rule the school, not be the meek little Sandies in our pastel frocks and Alice bands! We've just had four years of that. And 'Beth' doesn't fit with that image!

I told Jas I wanted to be called Lila instead and she was very rude about it, and said it sounded like a lilo and had I just made it up, which I haven't at all, it's just another short form of Elizabeth. OK, an *unusual* form, but one day I bet there'll be loads of girls called Lila and I will have been a trailblazer. Jas still thought I should have gone for something more obvious, like Lizzie if I was shortening Elizabeth, but that is no better. People hear Lizzie and think of Lizzie Bennet. What's the point of trying not to be one of the *Little Women* if all I do is turn into a Jane Austen character? Jas did say that Lizzie was the cool one, who got the rich hot guy, but Mr Darcy was a grumpy idiot who didn't deserve her, and in my opinion Lizzie should've told him where to stick Pemberley and stayed a sassy spinster.

Jas said Lizzie would probably have been burned as a witch or something then, because unmarried women were shunned, and that that was why we've got to overthrow the patriarchy. To be honest, I would like to get a boyfriend before I start on the whole overthrowing the patriarchy thing. Jas claims she doesn't want a boyfriend, she is just going to take lovers and use men for her own pleasures. I'm not really sure how that even works, they haven't covered it in *Just Seventeen*, but Jas has read a *Cosmo* article on it.

Mum wasn't much more enthusiastic than Jas when I told her about my brilliant name change plan. She kept saying Beth was a beautiful name, and she didn't know what I was talking about, Beth in *Little Women* was a lovely character and not feeble at all. But when I asked her what Beth actually did, she looked vague and couldn't come up with anything other than, 'Well, she died?' Weird Nicky had sidled into our kitchen for some reason and he also voted in favour of Beth, probably to suck up to Mum.

Ugh. Weird Nicky, from next door. Why couldn't we have someone normal live next door, why did it have to be *Weird Nicky*? And what was he even wearing? Was . . . was he wearing overalls? Combined with his glasses and his tufty ginger hair that was always messily in need of a cut, but never in a sexily tousled way, it was not a good look. Mind you, you could put Weird Nicky in a designer suit and it still wouldn't be a good look. He'd still look like someone you'd cross the road to avoid, he'd just be wearing a suit.

Then we had a row because I told Weird Nicky no one had asked him and Mum told me not to call him Weird Nicky and that he had kindly come over to cut the grass and she said he should stay for a cup of tea and could chat with us all about starting college, and Weird Nicky looked hopeful and started to sit down. I gave him my best glare, the same one I used when I gave him a Chinese burn when we were six, and he paused, bum halfway into a chair, and stood up again and said he'd better go and that he'd see Mum on Monday.

I asked Mum what he meant after Weird Nicky had shuffled out the door, very much hoping it did not mean what I feared it did. But no. Mum had only offered to give Weird Nicky a lift to college on Monday morning when she dropped Jas and me off. Why? Why would she do that to us? Mum insisted that having made the offer, she could hardly take it back. I pointed out the many *many* reasons that arriving with Weird Nicky would spell instant social death before we had even got started, including the fact that he had wet his pants when Mum misguidedly invited him to my fifth birthday party, thinking she was being 'neighbourly' when in fact, it had RUINED my whole party.

Mum dismissed my fury by saying that was nearly twelve years ago and I reminded her it was actually only eleven years. But Mum went on and on about how Nicholas had been so kind, coming over to cut the grass and help with the garden every summer since Dad left, and he was feeling quite nervous about starting college, so Mum had thought how nice if he could go with us, and then at least he'll have someone he knows.

Mum just doesn't get it. Coming and doing our garden every summer is weird in itself. That alone would be enough to make him Weird Nicky, quite apart from the fact he's JUST VERY WEIRD! Mum insisted it wasn't weird, it was very kind and said she couldn't go back on her offer.

I CAN'T BELIEVE SHE IS DOING THIS TO ME!'

Truly, I reflected bitterly, of all the issues inflicted on me by my father's decision to run off with his secretary and leaving me to bear the shame of coming from a Broken Home, being forced to associate with Weird Nicky was by far the worst and most unjust.

Mum did at least let Jas and me eat our dinner in the sitting room, watching my video of *Clueless* for the forty-third time to get inspiration for our first day, and to come up with a plan for ditching Weird Nicky, because it was already bad enough that we were starting college as virgins who couldn't drive, we could not take any more shame! Although we had high hopes for soon rectifying at least one, if not both of these situations!

MONDAY 2ND SEPTEMBER

Well. That, quite frankly, could not have gone any worse. OK, it could have gone slightly worse, but only if we hadn't managed to persuade Mum not to drop us off in the college car park, and instead to let us out round the corner, so we were at least able to give Weird Nicky the slip. But seriously, the only thing that could have made today worse was if people had thought he was with us.

We tried *so hard*. How did we get it so wrong? We had planned our outfits with so much care. We had watched all the films: *Clueless, Heathers, The Breakfast Club, Pretty In Pink*. We *knew* how you were supposed to dress to be the cool kids in a school environment with no uniform. We had spent hours in River Island and Top Shop nailing our look. We were literally the reincarnation of Veronica Sawyer at the start of *Heathers*. All we needed was a croquet mallet and a psychopathic boyfriend and a trail of bodies. Well, maybe not the bodies. But any sort of boyfriend would be good.

When he got in the car, Weird Nicky's eyes nearly popped out his head and he said, 'Wow!' With hindsight, that might not have been a flattering wow. Because when we walked into the registration, everyone else was wearing jeans and T-shirts and trainers or Doc Martens. Except us. We froze in horror by the door, wondering what we should do. Jas's suggestion was that we just ran away, whereas I had some hopes we might be able to style it out and set a trend.

Then Jas reminded me that we had never managed to style anything out, or be trendsetters, because we have never been ahead of the curve. Whether it was the class obsession with making pom poms, or the great troll doll swapping game, or switching from magazines like *Smash Hits* and *Just 17* to the more sophisticated and frankly terrifying publications of choice such as *Cosmo*, Jas and I have never been the ones to lead the crowd. In fact, we are invariably late to the style party. There was *no way* we could 'style out' our little miniskirts, tight jumpers over crisp shirts and thigh high socks with clumpy loafers in a room full of Adidas, 501s and a sea of Oasis and Blur T-shirts.

It wasn't *fair*. We looked amazing and we had put so much effort into it! Jas had even had me iron her hair straight, which is not as easy as you might think it is. I might have ruined the ironing board when Jas's hair mousse reacted with the heat and left a huge stain. Mum will not be impressed.

We backed out through the doors we had burst through so triumphantly a few seconds earlier and hurtled across the foyer and into the car park. Never, ever, ever had I been so relieved to see Mum getting out of her car. She was waving Weird Nicky's lunchbox at us and wanted us to give it to him. Of *course* Weird Nicky brings a packed lunch and can't go to the canteen like everyone else. Probably because he only eats slugs and snails and puppy dogs' tails or something.

I leaped into the car, rapidly followed by Jas, and demanded Mum took us home to change, but she just kept saying why did we want to change and that we both looked very smart as I desperately tried to explain that we looked WRONG and that we couldn't go in there like we were and that no one else was dressed like us and that everyone would think we were weirdos. Like Nicky.

Mum refused to take us home to change, saying she didn't have time and would be late for work, and then Jas remembered that there was an Oxfam on the high street, only five minutes away.

A stream of jeans and T-shirts passed us as we continued to cringe in the car and argue with Mum until we finally convinced her that our outfits might bring about our actual deaths through shame. Grudgingly, she drove us to the charity shop and even more grudgingly gave us each a fiver to kit ourselves out, with strict instructions we both paid her back and took Weird Nicky his lunch since we had made her so late. I didn't have time to argue about what shameless advantage she was taking of her only daughter's emotional distress and had no choice but to agree.

Right up until we set foot in the door of the Oxfam shop, I had harboured wild hopes that it might have suddenly become some sort of amazing vintage thrift shop, with racks of faded T-shirts emblazoned with the names of bands so cool and obscure no one would have heard of them, and thus we could sneer at the sheep thronging the corridors of the college in their *sad* and *mainstream* Blur and Oasis tops and loftily say that we just didn't think bands nowadays were political enough or had enough gravitas for *us*.

Jas had questioned the wisdom of this, pointing out that knowing our luck, if we did find such T-shirts, the first person we ran into would probably be that group's Number One Super Fan and we'd have to answer all sorts of questions we couldn't answer.

Jas needn't have worried though. As soon as the bell on the door jangled, and the angry old Oxfam lady looked up from where she was arranging a display of half used balls of wool and knitting needles that looked like they may actually have been used to poke someone's eyes out, the same pervasive smell of wee and stale Yardley's lavender toilet water that had lingered so persistently in the wardrobe room of the amateur dramatic group hit us, and we realised we were never going to find anything even remotely stylish in here.

We were in despair, as the woolly lady harrumphed through her whiskers at us and we wondered if we could cobble together some kind of quirky unique style from the offerings before us, even though we had never managed to do that even with the entire range of Miss Selfridge and TopShop at our disposal, let alone the Worst Oxfam Shop In The World and a fiver each. Anyway, I didn't want my own style, I just wanted to look like everybody else.

Jas said it literally didn't matter *what* we looked like, as long as we didn't look like we were going for a job interview in a life insurance company.

Looking at the options before us, picking up a drab tweed skirt with a drooping hem, I couldn't help but think that I was going to end up looking like my gran, or an Anita Brookner heroine. I had borrowed Mum's copy of *Hotel du Lac* over the summer, reading it lying in the park, initially hoping it might be rather racy, on account of its French title, and eventually just hoping someone would see me reading it and think me intense and intellectual and intelligent and therefore fall in love with me on the spot.

The only person who had sat down next to me in the park and attempted to discuss it with me was Weird Nicky, though, and he'd had spinach in his teeth. I had told him to go away, *now*, because I was 99.9% sure if he hadn't appeared when he did, a really cute boy with floppy, dirty blond hair who was sitting on a bench across from where I was trying to lie languidly under a tree was about to come over and talk to me. But by the time Nicky and his wretched spinach had shambled off, the blond Park Boy had disappeared.

This was quite disappointing. I had already jumped ahead from him coming over to me and being impressed by my great cleverness and borderline Frenchness, to him asking me for a coffee and walking me home and kissing me tenderly, and then within a mere matter of days, declaring his hopeless, abiding, everlasting love for me, while staring into my eyes with his own sexy sea-green eyes. I didn't even know what colour his actual eyes were though, thanks to Weird Nicky, who ruins everything. Sea-green would have been jolly nice though. I have never met anyone with sea-green eyes. I probably never will if Nicky and his spinach-green teeth have anything to do with it.

On top of all that, I found *Hotel du Lac* rather boring, just a lot of old people moping around in a depressing hotel. Mum said that perhaps I was not old enough to appreciate its subtleties, which was rude, like at sixteen I cannot understand what an adult book is about.

Maybe I could cobble together some sort of French chic from the contents of the charity shop? Some sort of black ensemble, involving a polo neck, and maybe I could quickly cut myself a fringe and put on loads of eyeliner and an air of ineffable *ennui*? I suggested this to Jas, but she was unconvinced. What would I cut my fringe with? she wanted to know.

Why can't people just go with my Vision, when I have one? Why must everyone put problems in my way? First Jas tells me to be quirky and find my own style, and when I suggest a style to quirk in, she squashes it. Will no one ever understand me?

Jas smashed my French Dream like the gates of the Bastille by pointing out that there weren't any black polo necks. Scary Old Lady offered up 'a vairy nice *taupe* polo neck,' and brandished a horrific beige number, and I was too feeble to say no as she bristled at me menacingly, and said I'd definitely keep that in mind.

We were running out of time. The official Induction Talk began at 10am, and it was now 9.37am and it would take us a good ten minutes to get to the college, even if we ran. I was in despair, and facing no option but to buy the Taupe Polo of Doom, as we could not now leave without purchasing anything. The shop woman would probably put a hex on us. We did *The Crucible* last term, and I could see a basket of corn dollies behind the counter which looked suspiciously like Salem 'poppets'.

Then Jas gave a shriek from the back of the shop and summonsed me to her. I dashed through the racks of polyester pussy-bow blouses, hope rising in my heart, as the witch shushed us. Blimey. It's not a library.

Jas was standing by a rail tucked away at the back of the menswear section, excitedly rifling through a rack of old shirts. I was deflated. I thought she'd found something.

I should not have doubted her though. She flung a lumberjack shirt and a pair of enormous looking men's jeans at me and told me we were going GRUNGE.

Witchy Wendy huffed at us to mind our language and told us that it was a respectable shop.

Jas hustled me behind the curtain in the corner that did service as a changing room as she explained the plan: that in our baggy jeans and plaid shirts we would be transformed into hip and cool grungsters, instead of tragic try-hard wannabes. It was, she assured me, the perfect solution. When I asked what to say if someone asked me my favourite band, she told me just to say Nirvana and then say I didn't want to talk about it, because I was, like, too sad about Kurt Cobain.

I didn't think this was going to work. But then I looked in the mirror and grabbed a brush out my bag to tone down the slightly over-moussed Big Hair I had spent so long on that morning, and decided that maybe I could have Angela vibes from *My So-Called Life*?

'Oh my God, *yes!*' said Jas, and then she told me that if I had red hair, I would look *exactly* like Claire Danes.

We had to go. We chucked Mum's fivers on the counter and dashed out, relieved that our massive jeans were covering our snazzy high-heeled clumpy loafers, as there had been no time, money, or indeed options for other shoes. We limp sprinted back to the college, and paused outside, hot and gasping for breath. I took a deep breath, as did Jas, and we looked at each other in despair. The body heat generated by our mad dash had triggered something in our new shirts. So near, and yet so far.

We smelled like dead people.

I rifled furiously through my bag and came out with a can of Impulse and a bottle of Excla'mation perfume, and doused us liberally in both. Now we smelled like people who had died of drinking peach schnapps. But we couldn't have everything.

Jas and I followed the last stragglers into the lecture theatre.

Oh, what bliss, to be in a *lecture theatre*! How much more mature and adult than having to go to the assembly / gym hall and listen to the head teacher droning on while staring at *The Apparatus*, as the bizarre collection of ropes and bars attached to the wall of the hall was known, which was apparently something to do with gym, but we were never allowed to use or even to touch, as it was VERY DANGEROUS, which led to me spending many hours when I should have been listening to improving speeches wondering why, if *The Apparatus* was so VERY DANGEROUS, someone had seen fit to pay to have it installed in a school?

There was no Apparatus in the lovely lecture theatre. There were tiers and tiers of tippy-up seats, like in a theatre, and Jas and I attempted to casually sashay in at the back, except we were the last people in, so all the seats were taken, except the front row. There is no sashaying to the front row. Only shuffling in shame.

As we trudged down the shallow steps to the saddest seats in the house, we heard an all too familiar voice crying, 'Tom! Tom! Tom, HI!'

I didn't want to look round. Maybe it wasn't her. Loads of people sound just like other people, right? But involuntarily, I found myself glancing to the side, and saw the despicable Rachel Kemball, waving wildly at *none other* than the gorgeous blond boy from the park, who may or may not have sea-green eyes.

What was Rachel doing here? A distinct lack of Rachel Kemball and her ilk was a big part of why Jas and I had lobbied so hard to come here for A-levels. Of course, we had said things like 'more diversity' and 'better course options' and 'good life experience to get us ready for university' but what we'd really meant was 'boys' and 'no more popular people looking down their noses at us'.

Obviously, we knew that there would be popular people here too, but they wouldn't be people who'd known us since we were awkward adolescents with braces and frizzy hair. We were meant to be reinventing ourselves. How could we do that with Rachel here? She had made a massive song and dance at the end of the last term about how *she* would not be doing anything so mundane as mere A-levels, but would in fact be going abroad to take the International Baccalaureate. And now here she was, large as life and twice as smug. And she already appeared to *know* people and be surrounded by admirers, cementing her status as the most popular person to ever be popular, including of course, *my* Park Boy, whose name, I had to now assume was Tom. He was sitting in the row in front of Rachel, and obviously was so delighted to see her that he was leaning over the seats to say hello to her.

By mutual consent, Jas and I picked up our pace and scuttled to the front in the hope of plonking ourselves down with our backs to Rachel, before she spotted us and made one of her catty remarks dressed up as a friendly comment, along the lines of when she had called my school dance dress 'fun' at the end-of-year dance with St Bartholomew's. I had been attempting to exude mystique and seduction, in the hope one of the St Barts boys would actually notice me and ask me to dance; I had not been attempting to exude *fun*.

Obviously, no one noticed us at the dance except Weird Nicky who had come over and tried to sit with us, and even suggested dancing, but I was not that desperate. At least if we were sitting on our own, then we could pretend we were just aloof, or too cool to want to dance, or that it somehow offended our feminist principles. But to dance publicly with Weird Nicky – ugh. That was admitting that I was on his level. That I, too, was aboard the Loser Cruiser, destination *Sadsville*.

Rachel Kemball was still busy loudly and excitedly filling in Park Boy Tom on her *thrilling* summer. 'Yah, yah, so I did some work experience in my dad's law firm, and then I went to Greece with Mummy and Daddy and then I had a girls' trip to Ibiza, oh my god, no? You were in Ibiza too? How did we miss each other?'

'Because it's a bloody big island, maybe?' I muttered to myself.

I studiously avoided Nicky's enthusiastic waves and gestures that apparently he had saved us a seat, and we finally made it to the safety of the front row, which in the last thirty seconds had changed from the worst place in the world to a longed-for comfort zone.

A bored looking dad-aged man stumped on to the platform in front of us and yelled at us to SETTLE DOWN. He then told us his name was Mr Pritchard and that he would be extremely mean and treat us like the horrible children we still were and that everything we'd heard about cool sixth-form teachers was wrong.

'Don't bother coming to me about extensions, I'll say no,' he told us, before threatening us not to come up with excuses about Mummy and Daddy getting a divorce or our hamster dying, then directing us to Miss Jackson, the Pastoral Deputy Head. 'She won't care either, but it's her job to pretend to.'

A flustered looking lady with a lot of scarves and artistic spectacles scurried on to the stage as Mr Pritchard stumped off. She told us to think of her of as another mother, she was here for us (unlike Mr Pritchard), whatever we needed. Then she introduced Mr Lorrimer, the head of the college.

The lugubrious Mr Lorrimer proceeded to recite a speech he had clearly given a thousand times before, about how we must remember that we would get out what we put in etc. We paid as much attention to his talk as he had put into writing it.

So far, sixth-form college was looking like a bit of a let-down. Yes, there was a 'lecture theatre' and no Apparatus, but other than that, it was all looking and sounding suspiciously like school. There were common rooms, and boys, which were both exciting novelties, but the rest didn't sound so different. What had I *actually* been expecting?

I had mainly seen myself rushing busily along corridors holding armfuls of books and leaning against lockers and tossing my hair sexily at Park Boy Tom types, or sitting in a room that had desks and a whiteboard but definitely wasn't a classroom, having earnest and important discussions led by a *cool* adult, who treated us like equals. If said adult had teachery vibes, then they were more like Robin Williams in *Dead Poets Society* than Mr Pritchard and Miss Jackson (who I decided was definitely the Teacher Most Likely To Cry In Class Before The End Of The First Week) and Mr Lorrimer, who I suspected would spend the rest of the year hiding in his office pretending to be busy and important. How could I sit prettily, perhaps with my hair pinned up in a loose tousled bun, using a pencil as a hairpin to show I was very clever and didn't care about shallow things like appearances, and contribute intelligent and witty comments to arguments about the dystopian themes of capitalism in nineteenth-century French literature with someone like Mr Pritchard or Miss Jackson at the helm?

More importantly, how would anyone fall in love with me in such environments?

Because in truth, that is all I want. More than I want to fit in with everyone else, and be a popular person, and live the sort of ordered and organised life that people like Rachel Kemball did, I just want someone to fall in love with me.

Oh God, Lorrimer had finished, and everyone was getting up and making for the door. I hadn't been listening. What were we supposed to be doing now?

I asked Jas and she scolded me for daydreaming again then told me we were picking up our timetables and our locker numbers and then it was break time and then it was orientation tours till lunch time and then after lunch we had our first classes, but they were just to get to know each other, the course work didn't start till tomorrow and how had I not got any of this?

We ducked behind a group of girls who all seemed to be friends already as Rachel reached the end of her row and glanced in our direction. Unfortunately, hiding from her put us right in Weird Nicky's path. He beamed in delight and said he'd hoped we could've sat together, but maybe we didn't see him, and then he looked confused at our outfits and asked why we had changed, he had really liked what we had been wearing. Frankly that was as good a reason as any to not wear those clothes ever again. He also wanted to know if I happened to have his lunch.

I thrust his lunchbox at him and stalked off as he trailed after us, still wittering about what subjects he was taking and who did we think would be in our classes, and did we want to sit with him if we were in any of the same classes, and could anyone smell something, was there a funny smell, he could smell something, it was a bit like peaches and maybe dead mouse. Luckily he didn't seem to put two and two together and realise that it was us, because then he suggested I could sit with him if we were in the same history class, and I snapped that no, I didn't think so.

Nicky just stared at me through his horrible thick glasses. God, even his eyes were a weird colour. He finally got the hint though and said he'd maybe see us later, and left us alone, to my relief. After he left, Jas said she thought I'd been a bit mean, and that Nicky was harmless, and would it hurt me to be a bit nicer to him?

I did my best impression of what I thought a mirthless laugh would sound like. Jas asked if I was all right and I said, 'I don't want to be nice to Weird Nicky who definitely cuts up frogs in his bedroom and stuff!'

Jas looked doubtful about this claim, but you just have to look at Nicky. He *looks* like someone who cuts up frogs in their bedroom. And it's all very well Jas saying we should be nice to him, but this is *our* chance to reinvent ourselves. It's going to be hard enough with bloody Rachel swanning round like the Queen of the Universe telling everyone about Daddy's law firm and Ibiza. If we're nice to Weird Nicky, we're going to get stuck with Weird Nicky. And if we end up having to hang out with Weird Nicky, everyone is going to think we are like Weird Nicky. We'll be the weird freak gang. Everyone will think *we* cut up frogs in *our* bedrooms. We'll never get boyfriends. It'll be just us and Weird Nicky FOREVER. And the dead frogs.

I asked Jas if that was what she wanted and she recoiled in horror, saying that she hadn't thought about it like that and that I was right, first impressions count and Nicky wasn't the impression we wanted to make. We'd got to the common room to collect our timetables by then, and Jas went off to the other end of the room because they were laid out alphabetically.

I curse the Roman alphabet. I curse it unto hell and back. Lucky old Jas with her nice safe surname beginning with a C got to walk off the opposite way into the sunset. I, however, was saddled with my stupid father's stupid name of stupid MacKay and thus I had to run the gauntlet to the Ms which was, of course, only one stop on from the Ks and thus Rachel Fudging Kemball. Who was, of course, standing holding court with Park Boy Tom and a couple of other handsome popular looking boys. There was no avoiding her this time, and she gave a start of surprise, which I was fairly sure she was putting on, and cried, 'Beth! Beth MacKay, what on earth are you doing here?'

I gritted my teeth. I could not even begin to explain to her that actually I was *Lila* now, and *Beth* MacKay was as dead as her *Little Women* namesake. Not in front of these boys, as Rachel pretended to be confused and unable to understand why I was now Lila, when all I had wanted was to just start off as Lila, cool, funny, interesting Lila, 'Have you met Lila? Oh, she's amazing, you must meet her, she's brilliant, is

Lila.' And now I was going to have to be Beth. Drab, nice girl Beth. You need someone to help with the bake sale for the orphaned sloths? Beth will do that. Beth will sew on buttons and minister to the unfortunate and go to church and sing in the choir and live a life of unfulfilled repressed passion. Lila can't do any of that, sorry, she's too busy being an international rock star, but Beth can definitely help.

I ground out a bitter 'Hi Rachel' and asked her what she was doing here, pretending I couldn't remember where she was supposed to have gone.

Rachel shot me a look of pure hatred and tossed her horrible shiny hair before wittering on about changing her mind about her International Baccalaureate in France because, according to her, you have a higher chance of being accepted at Cambridge with A-levels, and Daddy had been all stressy about maximising her chances, so she'd changed her plans. I said something vague and untrue about it being nice to see her and catching up later and hurried away before she could call me Beth again.

I decided if I could only introduce myself to people as Lila first, then if Rachel kept calling me Beth, I could explain with a casual little laugh, that I had in no way copied from Rachel herself, that Beth was a silly baby name from primary school and it was just a little joke between Rachel and me. Better yet, I could just avoid her for the next two years. Even better than that – my preferred scenario, in fact – I could pray for her to be hit by lightning, just enough to, oh I don't know, wipe the specific part of her memory that made her remember who I was. Maybe it could give her some nasty habits, like picking her nose in public too. See? What more evidence is needed that I am a Lila at heart and not a Beth? A Beth would never wish such a thing on someone.

As I searched for Jas among the throng in the common room, I wondered if I could go back to the Oxfam shop and get the terrifying woman in there to hex Rachel?

Jas and I finally fought our way back to each other, only to find we had been allocated different groups for our orientation tours, and we weren't taking any of the same subjects, as Jas was doing all the sciences and maths, due to her ambition to be a Nobel prize-winning feminist scientist, though she hadn't quite decided what sort of scientist she wanted to be, apart from a feminist one, and I was doing English Literature, History and French, on account of my own ambitions to be a deep and meaningful writer, living on the Left Bank in Paris (hence my foresight in taking French) and probably being the youngest person to ever win the Booker Prize.

I hadn't actually told anyone about these desires ever, as they seemed too pretentious for words. Which was ironic since putting things into words was exactly what I wanted to do. Even Jas didn't know. I have never shown anyone any of the stories I write in my bedroom, when I'm not writing this diary. It just seems such a *Rachel* thing to do, to go about announcing I think I'm all that, and that I think I'm good enough to write real books that people would want to read.

I don't think I am good enough, anyway.

All the girls in books who write books always have enormous self-belief. Look at Jo March in *Little Women*. She never really doubts that she will be published one day. Perhaps that is what comes of being a Jo and not a Beth. Maybe if I hadn't spent my life until now being Beth, I would have more confidence in myself. Hopefully my new incarnation as Lila will help and I will become a swashbuckling, ass-kicking paragon of certainty in my own abilities.

In the meantime, I had to negotiate the 'orientation tour' on my own, without Jas, and the rest of the afternoon too. It dawned on me that Jas and I were not going to get to spend as much time together as we had until now, due to our wildly differing subjects, but we put our best Brave Faces on and agreed we would definitely be fine and anyway, we'd see each other at lunch, as I trudged off to find 'Blue Group' and Jas went to find 'Yellow'.

Blue Group was led by a swishy-haired and very grown-up girl from the upper year, who obviously turned out to be best friends with Rachel Kemball. So keen was Rachel to demonstrate her deep and abiding friendship with Upper Sixth Sarah that she even abandoned Park Boy Tom, who was also in our group, along with Weird Nicky, which was less good. Nicky tried to sidle over to talk to me, but I gave him a stern look, and he unsidled.

To my astonishment, when Park Boy Tom and I found ourselves standing together at the back of the language lab, as Sarah waved her hands at the banks of headsets with an air of sophisticated ennui and Rachel did her best nodding-dog impression, Tom *spoke* to me.

'Cool shirt,' he said, gesturing at the Oxfam lumberjack number.

I automatically glanced behind me to see who he was talking to, but there was no one else there. I goggled at him for a moment in what must have been a very unattractive way, then gathered myself and gulped, 'What? This old thing?' as I attempted a nonchalant laugh.

He grinned at me. God, he has the most lovely smile, even if it turns out his eyes aren't sea-green, they're a sort of grey-blue colour. Perhaps, the colour of a *stormy* sea? 'It's nice to see a girl looking original. Not dressing like all the others.'

Wow. Obviously he was not a Channel 4 viewer, and had no idea my 'original style' was a copycat of my favourite ever programme *My So-Called Life*. That was a good thing though. Clearly he *liked* it. As long as he didn't get close enough to smell it. There was still a lingering whiff of dead people. Also, a thought hit me. If he thought I looked cool and that this was a deliberate style choice, did that mean I would have to keep dressing like this? Would I have to go back to the scary witch lady and plead with her to set aside all consignments of flannel shirts and baggy jeans for me, so I could continue to wow Tom with my originality?

Tom introduced himself and I tried to look interested and surprised by the news his name was Tom, like I didn't already know from Rachel shrieking it at the top of her voice across the lecture theatre so we all knew *she* knew the hot boy. 'Lila,' I said, with my most normal smile.

Tom looked alarmed and asked me if I was in pain. I muttered I was fine, hastily losing the normal smile, which obviously wasn't doing the trick, and going for an attempt at a sultry and moody look. Tom was all concern though, rifling through his bag offering paracetamol if I needed it.

Rachel noticed from the front of the group that Tom, who she had clearly decided was her personal property, was daring to speak to one as lowly as me, and barged over demanding to know if Tom had heard what Sarah was saying about the lunchtime French study group and was he up for it, not that Rachel needed to do it, because according to her she was practically bilingual, but she thought she could probably help with it, give the poor non-bilingual proles some useful tips.

Tom shrugged and said he might be up for that, and then turned back to me and said, 'What about you, Lila? Do you fancy a lunchtime French group?'

'Sounds a bit saucy,' I said without thinking, and clapped my hands over my mouth in horror. To my relief, Tom laughed, as Rachel scowled at me.

Sarah led us on, looking more and more bored with each revelation she shared. Rachel's attempts to dazzle her with the famous scintillating Kemball wit and tales of Ibiza and work experience at Daddy's law firm did not appear to be making Sarah look any less depressed about her morning leading these wet young puppies around the college.

'So, like, yeah, this is the computer lab.'

Sarah by now sounded so utterly bored with life that I was genuinely concerned we might have to administer CPR. I whispered this to Tom, still lurking at the back with me, and was highly gratified when he laughed again. Sarah was talking about the computers though, and explaining that, wonder of wonders, they were connected to *the Internet*.

Ooooh. The *Internet*. Was this going to be the earth-shattering, life-changing thing everyone said it was? Was I finally going to be able to experience its mysteries, and enter the twentieth century?

The Internet had been a thing of forbidden wonder at school. We most certainly had not been allowed it, as our teachers viewed it as Dark Magic, and in fact warned us repeatedly against it. The Internet, as far as they were concerned, was an evil up there with DRUGS! Curiously they never specified anything particular to be aware of with DRUGS, such as the ill effects of various types, or how to know if your drink had been spiked, or what to do if you thought someone you were with had taken something or too much of something. We were simply told repeatedly that DRUGS were bad. So very bad.

The warnings against the Internet were equally vague. I was unconvinced any of our teachers had ever used it, as they seemed unable to offer any explanations about why it was so terrible, other than it was 'no place for young girls.' But they seemed to think that was the case for anywhere other than church or school. We had even been warned against the evils of hanging around the Woolworths pick 'n' mix counters, which were SPIKED WITH DRUGS BY NE'ER-DO-WELLS, apparently. Though why these NE'ER DO WELLS had nothing better to do with their drugs than add them to the cola bottles and flying saucers was anyone's guess.

Jas's parents had recently had the Internet installed at home, and we had ventured into the mysteries of the World Wide Web, but we had never had time to find anything interesting before Jas's mum was shouting at us to disconnect because she wanted to use the telephone. Mum was highly resistant to the idea, telling me it was just a fad, that it would be a waste of money because people would have forgotten all about it in a few years' time. Even Dad had failed to bow to my lobbying that if I had the *Internet*, I could email him every week, and he could email me back, and it would be much better for keeping in touch since he had decided to move to Derbyshire with his new wife.

But here, *here* was the Internet, free and available for our use, with no one shouting to get off the line because they wanted to talk to their sister or complaining about phone bills or anything! Sarah was not particularly helpful about what exactly we could use it for, looking around her in confusion and finally saying, 'Like . . . research?' before adding the final, most interesting nugget of information.

'Oh yeah. There's like this chatroom intranet thing with loads of other colleges round the country.'

I stiffened. We had been *especially* warned about chatrooms. They were the dominion of perverts and swindlers! In my head, I saw them as actual rooms, with men in stripey jumpers and sacks marked 'swag' and other men with doubtful moustaches and flasher macs, waiting to prey on any young girls foolish enough to venture in with their virtue or their pocket money intact.

According to Sarah we couldn't use public chatrooms because of safety reasons that she seemed vague about, but she told us we could use the college chatrooms to talk to people here or in other colleges about coursework, or stuff we were interested in. Apparently it is an online social network.

'Sort of like a penpal, but with technology?' I piped up helpfully.

Sarah seemed unconvinced, and Rachel snorted in derision, but Tom nudged me and said, 'That's so funny! You're really funny!'

Am I? I wasn't trying to be funny. I decided not to say anything. I was going to try an enigmatic smile, but I was afraid, based on my previous attempts, that he might think I had wind or something.

Luckily, at that moment, a buzzer sounded (I suppose they thought it would be more grown up than a school bell) and Sarah sagged with relief and said it was LUNCHTIME and that she would show us the way to the canteen, before setting off practically at a run, so great was her desire to be rid of us.

To my astonishment, in the canteen, Tom seemed to assume we would just get lunch and sit together. While I was utterly delighted by this, it was also a bit awkward, because I had promised to meet Jas here for lunch, and Rachel was circling ready to swoop in and snatch Tom back for herself. Perhaps, I thought in resignation, it would be easier just to let her? After all, what could someone like Tom possibly see in me, when he had Rachel practically throwing herself at him?

Rachel obviously agreed because she got fed up waiting for me to buzz off and pushed into the queue between me and Tom to say very pointedly, 'Beth, Jasmit is here and looking for you,' then waved towards the door where Jas's tour group had just arrived.

Tom waved too, saying his friend Mark was there and shouting, 'Mark, Mark, mate, over here, yeah?'

Another boy, very nearly as attractive as Tom, came sloping over and Rachel carefully angled herself so she was between me and the boys with her back firmly to me, as they began to talk again about their summer. I sighed, left the queue and went over to where Jas was looking a bit lost and bewildered.

I felt extremely relieved to see her again. Talking to Tom had been very exciting of course, but also very stressful. It was good to be able to just be myself again. I asked how her tour had been and Jas said it had been really cool, before adding that it had also been a lot, 'Like a lot!' She looked slightly tearful. 'I almost wish we'd stayed at school. We've wanted to grow up for so long, and now we are, and it's *scary*, Beth. I mean, Lila, sorry.'

I knew exactly what she meant, but at least, I reminded her, there was food now.

Once we had collected our lunches (despite being called a 'canteen' and not a 'lunch hall', the offerings were still disappointingly school dinnery) we looked round the room for a seat. Every table had someone sitting at it. We were going to have to go and sit with strangers.

For a wild moment, I considered joining Weird Nicky's table where he was sitting with his sad packed lunch, but then a couple of girls sat down and actually started talking to him. I didn't want to interfere. If people were going to be stupid enough to make friends with Nicky, it would save him trailing after us like a wet spaniel. We hopefully surveyed the various tables, looking for people who at least looked like they would be able to talk about *Neighbours* and other normal things.

I suggested two girls chatting over their baked potatoes, neither of whom possessed hair swishy enough or clothes cool enough to suggest they were popular people, but at the same time did not look too outlandish or like they would tarnish us in the same way as Weird Nicky (though the two girls talking to him also looked disturbingly normal).

As we made our way through the tables, I was vaguely aware of someone yelling something behind us. Eventually Jas nudged me and hissed, 'Someone's trying to get your attention, *LILA!*'

Oh God. She was right. I had forgotten I answered to Lila, and Tom was shouting it across the room while I wandered off oblivious.

'Lila! I saved you some seats,' he yelled.

As one, Jas and I abandoned all thoughts of the baked potato girls as we attempted not to sprint across the room to take our places at what was clearly the most popular table in the house that day.

Tom beamed at us as we plonked down at the table, and Rachel shot us death stares, and he introduced me to his friends: the nearly-as-handsome Mark who grinned at us and Kate who was possibly the most gorgeous girl I had ever seen. There were a couple of other boys he said were Luke and Andy, and he asked who my friend was and I stammered, 'Jasmit. Jas. Everyone calls her Jas,' as the beautiful popular people smiled hellos at us with their beautiful popular smiles as we attempted to toss our hair carelessly and look like *obviously* this table was where we belonged. And then it all went wrong.

'We know everyone calls Jasmit "Jas" for short,' said Rachel nastily. 'What I'm wondering, *Beth,* is why Tom is calling *you* "Lila" when your name is Beth?'

I tried a casual chuckle, blinking wildly as I always do when I lie, as I said, 'I don't know what you mean, Rachel! You know my name's Lila. No one's called me Beth since primary school.'

Rachel narrowed her eyes. I had not realised anyone could look quite so spiteful. 'I could have sworn *everyone* at school last term was calling you Beth,' she drawled. 'So where's *Lila* come from, *Beth*? Thought you reinvent yourself as someone as cooler? Call yourself Lila and no one would know you were sad little swotty Beth MacKay?'

My face was burning. I could feel my cheeks throbbing with the hot shame as Rachel smirked at me. I had to say something, or I would look even more stupid. Everyone was staring at me, except Tom, who was looking at Rachel and frowning. I tried to speak, but there was a lump in my throat choking me and I could feel the tears starting in my eyes.

Oh God, please no. Please. The only thing worse than Rachel outing me as a Beth would be being the Girl Who Cried At Lunch on the very first day of college. That would be up there as almost as humiliating, possibly more so, as Weird Nicky wetting his pants at my birthday party. Actually, definitely more so. At least Nicky had the excuse of only being five at the time. And weird. And that was the other thing. Nicky didn't even *care* that he was weird, or what people thought. But I did.

Jas came to my rescue. She laughed heartily, and said, 'God, Rachel. What *are* you on about? I'd totally forgotten about that time when Lila was little and she decided to be called Beth for like a week because she fancied a change. Everyone forgot about it in, like, three days, including Lila.'

'No, she didn't,' Rachel protested. 'That's not what happened at all. Her name is Beth.'

'I'm so confused,' said Kate. 'What *is* your name?'

'Lila' I gulped. 'It's Lila.'

Rachel shook her head furiously, but good old Jas still had my back and grabbed Nicky who had finished his lunch and was passing our table. 'Nicky,' she demanded, 'what's her name?' And she pointed at me.

Nicky looked confused, as well he might, and said, 'Um, Lila?'

Jas was triumphant, as she then asked him how long he had known me.

'Since we were like . . . four? We live next door to each other and –'

Nicky started to explain, but Jas quickly stopped him, saying, 'And has she always been called Lila?'

I tried to telepathically will Nicky to say yes, yes, of course. I promised myself if he would only do this, I would never again mention the pant-wetting, or the weirdness, and I would be *nice* to him. Maybe not friends with him, that was possibly a step too far. But nice. Definitely nice. Like, I wouldn't tell him to piss off anymore when he tried to talk to me.

Oh God, how had it come to this? It was only lunchtime on the first day, and I was relying on Weird Nicky to rescue me. In fairness, Jas was doing most of the heavy lifting, like an emotional Mountain Rescue team.

Nicky got the hint.

'Of course she's always been called Lila,' he said, pretending to look confused. 'What else would she be called? I mean, when she was little her mum would sometimes call her Elizabeth if she'd been naughty. But other than that, I've never heard anyone call her anything except Lila.'

'Why would you say all that, Rach?' Tom wanted to know, as Rachel glared at me. 'That was a pretty crappy thing to say.'

I didn't want to spend the next two years wondering at what moment Rachel would decide to stab me in the back once and for all. It would make it terribly awkward if we ended up doing *Julius Caesar* in English!

'It's just a, like, silly in-joke – from school, ha ha ha. Isn't it, Rachel?' I said, opening my eyes super wide. Come on, Rachel, I'm giving you an out here, I thought. Either you pursue the Beth thing, and yeah, I'll look stupid but you'll look like a mega bitch, or you let it go and you get to keep everyone thinking you're actually a semi nice person and not some kind of sociopath.

Luckily Rachel decided this was not the time or place. I had no doubt that this was not the last I would hear of it, but she nodded, smiled brightly and said, '*God*, obviously it was a joke! I can't believe you thought I meant it, Tom!' Then she playfully punched his arm and beamed up at him, as she tossed her hair yet again. I secretly hoped she'd get neck problems in later life.

Tom grumbled we had strange jokes at our school and then he said something MUCH more exciting. 'Anyway, we were talking about Kate's party on Saturday?'

Everyone began to chatter about the party, about who was going, who to ask, what music to play, what drinks Kate should ask her dad to get. Jas and I concentrated on our tuna baguettes, as we were unsure about the format the party was to take. Kate had said something about it being to 'get to know people', but everyone else at the table, including Rachel, seemed to already know all the people that were coming, or that they were talking about asking.

We had moved on from our baguettes and were opening our low-fat strawberry yoghurts when Kate said, 'Guys, you're so *quiet*. You are coming to my party, aren't you?'

'Yeah,' said Tom, looking directly at me. 'Lila, you're coming, right? And you, Jas?'

He'd asked me first! If I was a bad friend, I'd almost say Jas had been an afterthought, and it was *me* he really wanted to come.

'Yes!' I spluttered, trying not to choke on the bloody yoghurt. 'Yes!'

Jas luckily was a little cooler than me. 'Yeah, sure, we'll try and look in for a bit.'

On the way home that afternoon, Jas and I hugged ourselves with excitement.

'Have we made it?' I asked her. 'Was it that easy? Are we popular people now?'

Jas wasn't sure though, saying that it just seemed *too* easy, because if they were friends with Rachel, were they really that nice? She thought Mark was gorgeous though, and we agreed that Tom and Mark were definitely the best-looking boys in the college as we wondered if there was any hope of them liking them us and felt guilty about being such bad feminists because we shouldn't care about boys' looks or whether they liked us. Eventually we agreed that maybe we could just be good feminists 90% of the time and treat ourselves to a few shallow thoughts about boys instead of smashing the patriarchy.

Even Weird Nicky catching up with us as we got off the bus didn't dampen our spirits over what overall had been a very good first day. And I owed him one, so we let him walk back to my house with us, even if he did try to explain about the colour-coded study timetable he had already created for himself and offered to come in and help us to make our own, when we got to my gate.

I was clear though that there are some lines that cannot be crossed.

EMILY

CHAPTER SEVEN

'How are you today?' Uncle Tom asked anxiously over breakfast. 'Do you feel any better than last night?'

I shrugged. 'I started reading the diary.'

Uncle Tom looked surprised. 'I thought you said it would be too . . . what was it?'

'Cringe,' I said. 'I said it would be cringe, and it is, it is very cringe.'

'What changed your mind?'

'I just didn't want you and Mum to be going on and on at me that things would be different if I read it, so if I've read it, then you can't say anything.'

'Right. So . . . any questions?'

I shrugged again. 'I dunno.' I paused. 'Actually, yeah.'

Uncle Tom visibly braced himself. I thought about teasing him by asking something really awkward about periods maybe, but I still need my phone fixed. I couldn't resist a *tiny* bit of fun though. After all, he was conspiring with Mum to keep me cut off from the outside world, and also forcing me into this incredibly weird diary-reading therapy, so fair's fair.

'She keeps talking about stuff I don't understand,' I said, and gave my best 'embarrassed' look.

A small whimper escaped Uncle Tom. 'Like what?' he asked, giving me a pleading look.

'Something about *My So-Called Life* and Angela or Claire or someone,' I said. 'And *grunge*.'

'You don't know what *grunge* is?' Uncle Tom was so incredulous that he forgot to even be relieved. He explained that grunge was one of *the* music genres of the nineties, the most famous band of which was Nirvana, whose lead singer Kurt Cobain had tragically killed himself in 1994, and that spawned the Foo Fighters. I looked at him blankly.

'You don't know who the Foo Fighters are?'

I shook my head.

'The youth of today!' Uncle Tom gasped. 'You'll be telling me next you don't know who Kylie is!'

'Of *course* I know who Kylie is,' I informed him scornfully. 'Kylie Jenner is like, *mega* famous.'

'Not Kylie *Jenner*, you philistine! Kylie Minogue! The original pop princess! The one true Kylie! "Spinning Around". "I Should Be So Lucky". "LOCOMOTION"!'

Nope. It meant nothing to me. Uncle Tom was aghast.

'What about the *So-Called Life* thing?' I asked.

A look of almost religious zeal came over his face. '*My So-Called Life* was our generation-defining TV programme. As *Dawson's Creek* was to the Millennials –'

'What?'

He sighed. 'As *SpongeBob SquarePants* is to Gen Z then. Or some other programme. Probably with Kylie Jenner in it. Anyway, *My So-Called Life* was this amazing show that made a whole generation of awkward teenagers feel like they weren't alone for the first time ever. It starred Claire Danes – *don't* say 'who?', she was Juliet in *Romeo and Juliet* with Leonardo DiCaprio?'

I clapped my hands with glee. Finally someone I had heard of. I was not a philistine, how rude of Uncle Tom. I told him as much as I said that everyone knew who Leonardo DiCaprio was, he was that weird old guy with the really young girlfriends, and Uncle Tom shook his head again, I don't know why.

'There is one funny thing in the diary though,' I said cheerily. 'Wasn't it weird that Mum fancied a boy called Tom as well as being besties with you? Was Tom just like a super-popular boy's name in the nineties? What happened to Tom from the park with the floppy blond hair and the stormy sea-grey eyes anyway?'

Uncle Tom stared at me for a moment. 'I have absolutely no idea,' he said. 'Come on, if you've finished your breakfast we have about thirty layers of woodchip to start scraping off walls.'

As I scraped the woodchip (horrible stuff, why did anyone thing it was a good idea to have it in their house?) instead of composing SnapChats to Poppy, I treated myself to some of my imagined conversations with Toby. In my head, we chatted at length about everything, our lives, our plans for the future, our parents. I was devastatingly witty and clever, and he found me brilliant and hilarious and obviously was hopelessly smitten with me. The great advantage to these conversations was of course that Toby always said the right thing so I could show off about how clever I was.

I hope if he ever actually speaks to me it will be the same as it is in my head. I could talk to him for hours like this. I wish I had the nerve to talk to him in person, just go up to him and say, 'Hi, how are you, what are you doing?' instead of just gazing at him from afar and hoping against hope he notices me. Poppy says she is sure he likes me, but how can she know? Surely if he liked me, he'd talk to me? But then again, I really like him, and I can't talk to him. Maybe he's just as shy and nervous as I am.

I have such long imaginary chats with him while I'm doing other things that sometimes it's a shock to remember that I have never spoken to him in real life, let alone told him all the things I have told him in my head.

Uncle Tom kept me hard at work all day, which did at least mean I talked to Toby all day, and I was shattered by the time we had dinner. I do think he is taking very unfair advantage of me, and if I knew where to find a telephone box or how to use one, I would be tempted to ring his strange helpline to complain about my treatment.

When I went to bed, I was so tired I didn't think anything could stop me from sleeping. I decided to read a little bit more of the diary though. After all, the sooner I read it all, the sooner it was over with, and the sooner I could point out that it had made no difference at all, and no one had any idea what *my* so-called life was like.

LILA

CHAPTER EIGHT

That was a pretty good first week, if I do say so myself. Every lunchtime, Tom waved us over to sit with him and his cool friends. It would have been rude to say no, really.

Sometimes Rachel sat with us, sometimes she sat with Upper Sixth Sarah and her friends, I think to show how much more mature she was than us. She had been quite chilly towards Tom after the first day. Tom didn't seem to notice though – or if he did, he didn't show it. I feared this would make Rachel even more angry, and I knew of old that Rachel was not someone you wanted as an enemy. Not, of course that she would consider Tom in the wrong. He was too popular and attractive for that. I was the one in her firing line.

We put all thoughts of Rachel out of our minds as we got ready for Kate's party. We had been to the Body Shop and purchased industrial quantities of body sprays, face masks and hair conditioners. Mum choked dramatically when she came into my bedroom, flapping her hands in front of her face as she pretended to feel her way across the room, complaining about how it smelled like a chemical bomb had gone off and how we'd probably doubled the size of the hole in the ozone layer.

I protested that it was all from the Body Shop, and thus it was all *natural*, but Mum sniffed, and said yes, very natural chemicals, and added something about how if any boy showed an interest, we'd probably end up knocking them out with some sort of dewberry-scented chloroform effect. I laughed sarcastically at this and applied another coat of burgundy lipstick and a final slick of eyeliner before informing Mum we were ready to go, as we had persuaded her to give us a lift to Kate's house, so we did not arrive windswept and dishevelled.

Weird Nicky was just going into his house as we came down the path to Mum's car. He stopped and goggled at us.

'Wow,' he said.

'You look great.'

'That's because you're upwind of them, Nicholas,' muttered Mum, locking the front door.

I ran down the path and leaped in the car. Obviously Nicky wasn't asked to Kate's party, and I didn't want to Mum to start guilt-tripping me and saying why didn't we take Nicholas with us, she was sure no one would mind. Wasn't it enough for Mum that I was being pleasant to Weird Nicky now? At least when no one was around to see. It would still be SOCIAL DEATH to be actually seen publicly with him.

Kate's house was massive. Like, twice the size of Rachel's house, and Rachel was always on about how her dad was a lawyer and they were so amazingly rich. I had only known

Kate a week, of course, but she had managed to never mention how rich she was. Rachel had shoehorned it into our English class yesterday, when we were talking about *The Merchant of Venice* and she claimed Portia's argument about the pound of flesh would not stand up in a real court and she knew this because her father was a very successful lawyer. Again, it had only been a week, but Mr Watson our English teacher had sighed and rolled his eyes, and I got the distinct impression the rest of the class were also a little over constantly hearing about how Rachel knew everything there was to know about anything legal because of her father. I mean, my father was a surgeon and my mother was a GP, but that didn't mean I went around trying to whip people's appendixes out, or prescribing cures for my classmates' ailments. (In any case, Mum's cure for most things is 'have a drink of water', 'put some TCP on it' and 'you probably just need some fresh air'. I presume she is more proactive in her suggestions for her actual patients than she is for her only child.)

Tom looked happy to see us, and said we looked brilliant, as Mark handed us cans of warm Budweiser. I attempted a Rachel hair toss, as I said a casual thanks, though I was *glowing* inside. My neck clicked. Seriously, how did she do that all the time?

I was very relieved by Tom's approval of our outfits. After his comments on the first day about girls looking 'individual', Jas and I had nipped back to the Oxfam shop and done a deal with the much less scary lady who works in there on Tuesdays for the rest of the lumberjack shirts, which we had then washed several times until all trace of

Dead People Smell had vanished. I'd been wearing them in one form or another all week. Clearly, they would not do for a party, but we had no idea what sort of a party it was going to be, or what we should wear.

Eventually, since we had already given the impression that we were quirky vintage sort of girls, a raiding of our parents' wardrobes had resulted in Jas wearing a cropped yellow embroidered silk jacket of her mother's as a shirt, while I wore a white pirate-style shirt I had found at the back of Mum's cupboard with an old tweed jacket that Mum thought had been my grandfather's. Jas and I wore them both with denim miniskirts though, to be sexy. We had questioned the juxtaposition of the short skirts with our feminism and had come to the conclusion that it was OK as long as we were wearing them for us, and for fashion, and not for boys. Which we definitely weren't. Well, maybe a tiny bit.

Kate appeared not to have dressed up at all, but I suppose you wouldn't have to if it was your party and you were mega rich and lived in a mansion. She hugged us both and seemed genuinely delighted we had made it.

Outside, there was a swimming pool! I had never met anyone with an actual swimming pool at their house before. I tried to hide how very impressed I was. I also resolved not to get too close to it, because I knew in all the films, the quirky heroine either ends up being pushed in the pool, or pushing her nemesis therein. I did not want to be dunked myself, and tempting as the idea of drowning Rachel was, I feared it would unleash a never-ending torrent of 'MY DAD IS A LAWYER'. Best to just steer clear.

Luke and Andy sat with us for a while, and Upper Sixth Sarah drifted past, unshadowed by Rachel for once. Then Kate staggered out under a huge pile of Domino's pizza boxes. I wasn't quite sure what the deal was with the pizzas, because I hadn't ordered anything and I didn't think I had enough money with me to pay for a pizza, but Tom assured me it was fine, Kate's dad had paid for them and she'd ordered enough for everyone. After some pizza and another beer, I realised that Jas and Mark had not come back to sit with us after we went to get the food. Luke was on the other side of the pool, snogging a girl called Lucy from my French class, and Andy was doing the same with Natalie from Jas's physics class. All around us, people were pairing off.

Tom held out his hand to me. 'Let's go for a walk,' he said.

I suddenly felt shy and slightly anxious as I asked where we were going, and Tom just smiled at me and told me he wanted to show me Kate's garden, as it was amazing.

I didn't know what to do. I had dreamed about Tom or someone like Tom kissing me ever since the first day I saw him in the park, but now it was going to happen, I was terribly nervous. What if I didn't do it right? There had been onions on the pizza I had eaten, I hadn't noticed till I was halfway through, and then it was too late not to eat it without making a scene. Not only onions, but my breath would smell all beery. I wondered if a dab of cherry lip balm would cover it? Or would that make my mouth all greasy when he kissed me? Maybe it was already all greasy with pizza? I licked my lips surreptitiously as I stood up.

Most of all though, I was worried that this scenario had happened so many times in my head and each time it had been perfect and wonderful and amazing and had become an imaginary memory for me to treasure forever and what if the reality just didn't live up to it? I couldn't for a second believe someone like Tom could be a bad kisser, but what if there *weren't* fireworks, or my knees *didn't* tremble? What if it was just incredibly average?

If I couldn't have a perfect kiss with someone like Tom, someone so gorgeous and funny and kind and lovely, then maybe it didn't exist. Maybe love didn't exist. Maybe everything I'd built my hopes around was just a fantasy peddled to us by romance novels. I wasn't ready for that. And how could it be *magical* when I was worrying about pizza and beer breath, and hoping so hard for the magic? A magical kiss should take one unawares, and it was quite obvious what Tom was luring me into the garden for, though I supposed I should be grateful he was being romantic enough to do that, unlike Luke and Andy happily getting on (or should that be getting off) with it in full view of everyone else.

Tom was still standing there expectantly with his hand out, waiting for me.

'Um . . .' I pointed inside, 'I just . . . er . . . need to . . . little girls' room?'

Little girls' room? LITTLE GIRLS' ROOM? What was WRONG with me? Why did I say that? Well, I know why, because I didn't want to make any reference to bodily functions like saying I needed a wee, because it would not help create a mystical, magical romantic moment if Tom was thinking about me going to the toilet. And I didn't want to say something like 'freshen up', thus implying I am stinky! Bathroom! Why didn't I just say bathroom?

Tom gave me directions and then said he'd wait for me. God, he was so nice. I found the loo, gave thanks that no one had thrown up in / over it yet, had a wee (thought I might as well) and washed my hands. Being a downstairs loo, it was obviously devoid of any useful items like toothpaste or mouthwash. I eyed up the rather expensive looking bar of soap. Could I?

I sniffed my breath. It was really beery and oniony. Needs must and all that. I rubbed my finger vigorously on the soap and then over my teeth and then retched. Oh, sweet lord, that was foul. The soap might smell of something deliciously fruity and floral, but it tasted very much of soap. And soap does not taste nice. Worse, I was now foaming at the mouth. I rinsed and rinsed and rinsed, trying not to gag too loudly as I did so, lest people thought I was the first one to puke. At least, when I finally got rid of the suds and sniffed my breath again, all traces of onions had been eradicated.

When I came out, Rachel was hovering outside the door, looking irritatingly chic if somewhat overdressed in a little black number. She smirked and asked if I'd been throwing up, but the smug smile was wiped off her face when I told her I had to go because Tom was waiting for me. She was actually lost for words for a minute, and then to my dismay the smug smile came back and she informed me that she had seen Tom going off with Kate, and didn't

I know that they used to go out together and Tom was still, like, totally in love with her, and in Rachel's opinion they would probably be getting back together tonight.

I made a very childish face at Rachel and stalked off. Outside I found to my chagrin that she had been half right, at least. Tom had not yet disappeared with Kate, but the two of them were sitting and laughing and talking where I'd left him. I hovered beside them, not sure what to do, as Kate talked about some witch hazel bush in the garden that apparently she and Tom used to play hide and seek in. Tom laughed and asked if she remembered the time he hid in there and made scary noises so Kate had hysterics and she punched his arm and called him a beast as Tom insisted she loved him really.

God, this was super awkward. They obviously were far closer than I had realised, and now I was caught in the middle of some weird game between them, or worse, Tom was trying to use me to make Kate jealous. Rachel was right. How could someone like me possibly compete with Kate's beauty and wealth? Even if Tom wasn't shallow enough to care about the money, he could hardly miss how stunning she is.

Kate gave Tom a shove and told him to go and show me the garden because she had a party to host. Tom jumped up and grabbed my hand and towed me past the pool and down a gravel path edged with shrubs. Kate called, 'Tom, remember what I said,' but he didn't seem to hear her. We fled on down another path, until we found ourselves in a little clearing surrounded by flowering bushes, with another larger tree in the middle that Tom flopped down under. Behind us we could hear the shrieks and whoops of the party, and what sounded like a splash as someone fell or was pushed in the pool, just like I had predicted.

Tom patted the lawn beside him. 'Sit down. The stars are coming out. We can watch them.'

Oh, this was possibly the most romantic thing that had ever happened to anyone ever in the history of romance. It was perfect. Or at least, it should've been perfect, but I couldn't get Rachel's digs about Kate and Tom out of my head. I wanted nothing more than for him to kiss me, but how could it be the magical moment I had dreamed of if I was wondering if he'd rather be kissing Kate?

I couldn't stop myself.

'So you and Kate seem really close,' I blurted out.

Then he told me he'd known Kate since nursery school, and she was one of his best friends, and how they'd even had an ill-lived, brief period when they tried dating. 'That was just *weird*. She's more like a sister, you know? We both agreed very quickly we were better just being friends.'

Oh yay, most yayest of yays that could ever be yayed! Just friends. More like a sister. Ha, Rachel, you don't know everything! In fact, for all you're pretending to be *such* good mates with Tom and Kate and the others, you in fact know *nothing*! I, Lila MacKay, Uncool Girl, know more than you. And who, may I ask, is out here in the garden, alone with Tom? NOT YOU, RACHEL!

I hoped the splash I had heard had been Rachel falling in the pool and that everyone had seen her pants. And that she was wearing her very worst pants. Then I checked myself for being so childish. How could I project an air of sophisticated mystique if inside I was busy wishing underwear mishaps on my worst enemies?

'Anyway,' Tom went on. 'Tell me about yourself, Lila MacKay. What is your family like? What do you want to do with your life? Start with that?'

Wow. 'Start' with that?

I didn't know what to say. I wanted to sound fascinating and bohemian but I found myself telling him about my very ordinary family. About how my parents were divorced, and I mostly lived with my mum, and Dad lived in Derbyshire with my stepmother and she breeds Border terriers (which is about her only redeeming feature). That Mum and Dad were both doctors, and I thought that they were hoping I'd become a doctor too, or at least go into something science-based. I admitted that they weren't very thrilled with my choice of A-levels and that I think that's partly why they agreed to me leaving school and going to the college for A-levels, because then they didn't have to pay school fees for me to do subjects they didn't really approve of.

'I know what you mean.' Tom nodded wisely as he pulled a couple more cans of beer out of his jacket pocket and handed me one.

I didn't know how to decline without saying, 'Look, I have just literally gargled with *actual soap* so I don't have beer breath in the event of you kissing me, because frankly at this stage how can you *not* kiss me, when we're alone in this beautiful garden having a deep and meaningful conversation under the stars. It's practically the *law* that you have to kiss me, and I don't want to be all beery.'

On the other hand, Tom had opened his own beer and didn't seem to be worrying about whether *he* was beery when he kissed me. Of course, he would have kissed dozens of girls before, I reminded myself. This wasn't such a big deal for him, like it was for me, waiting in breathless anticipation for my first, and hopefully magical, kiss.

It was so ridiculous that I had made it to the ancient and decrepit age of sixteen without ever being kissed. It probably hadn't even crossed his mind this was going to be my *first* kiss. He probably assumed I snogged boys without a thought every single weekend. Well, maybe I would be doing that soon. Or maybe Tom would turn out to be my one true love and he would kiss me, and we would be together forever and get married and there would never be anyone else.

I had put this romantic theory to Jas earlier, and she had been quite squashing about it, saying, 'The thing is, Lila, what if Tom's *rubbish* at kissing, and he's terrible at sex too, but you won't realise?' She had reminded me that it was 1996 and that we read *Cosmopolitan* and *More!* magazines, and were confident, sexually liberated, modern women who were not afraid to ask for what we wanted. But, she had gone on sternly, if I'd never even *kissed* more than one boy, how would I know what I needed or wanted if I'd nothing to compare him to?

It was a valid point, but I still thought that if by some miracle, Tom *was* The One, then surely the universe would not be so cruel as to make my One a horrible kisser who was bad at sex? None of this solved my breath dilemma though, so I just took the beer and had a swig. We could be beery together. At least I'd got rid of the onion whiff.

Tom lay back under the tree and gazed up at the stars and started talking about how he understood about disappointing my dad, because he'd done the same. Tom's dad works away all week for a big international bank in the City of London, and had just assumed Tom would also go into something financial, and keeps asking Tom if it's too late to change his A-level courses as in his father's opinion 'English, French and Philosophy aren't quite the A-levels banks are hoping for, old chap.'

Tom sighed that he didn't want become another pinstriped City boy though, and I asked him what he *did* want to do, even though I was fairly sure the conversation was supposed to be about what *I* wanted to do.

Tom sat up, his eyes shining with passion, and announced that he wanted to be a writer, to be remembered, to leave his mark on the world, to write poetry that people would still read in a hundred years and find it still meant something to them, something important.

I didn't know what to say to this, so I just said, 'Wow,' as I thought well, bang goes any chance of me ever plucking up the courage to tell Tom that *I* wanted to be a writer too. I'd just seem like a copycat now. Tom had just come out with it, so confidently, as if he knew everyone would just accept that of *course* clever handsome Tom wanted to be a writer, that he would obviously be an excellent writer and very successful, because that's what happened to people like Tom.

If you are attractive and popular, things just fall into place for you. And I don't know if it's because people like that have so much confidence that they just expect things to be how they wanted them to be, or if they have so much confidence because things *have* always gone their way. Because they've never spent hours staring in the mirror, mired in self-doubt, wondering if anyone would ever love them, if they would ever be brave enough to stand up and be themselves, or if they would ever be good enough. That was the sort of thing that ordinary people like me had to do. The people who did not blaze through the world like a comet, but rather plodded along, like a medieval peasant behind a cart of turnips.

That was, I reflected, quite a good analogy for Tom and me. For now, he had chosen to shine his light on me, the mud-smeared turnip peasant, but soon he'd soar over the horizon and away, leaving me in darkness more unfathomable than ever, having once basked in his glorious light, and probably chewing on a cabbage stalk, or something equally disgusting. Or maybe he wouldn't.

In all the romantic novels I had ever read, the heroine was always rather ordinary and not conventionally beautiful, and the dashing and devastatingly handsome hero always fell for her anyway. I'd just finished reading Jilly's Cooper's book *The Man Who Made Husbands Jealous*, and the unimaginably gorgeous Lysander Hawkley ends up with the incredibly plain Kitty because he loves her kind and generous nature. I could have a kind and generous nature! Even in *Pride and Prejudice* grumpy rich Mr Darcy falls for Elizabeth precisely because she is *not* like all the other girls. So Tom could definitely fall in love with me and rescue me from the turnip cart!

I flew into wilder flights of fancy. We could be like the Shelleys, and he could tit about writing his heartbreaking works of deathless poetry while I'd just casually produce one of the greatest gothic novels ever written. Oooh, we could have a *salon*! I wasn't sure what a *salon* was though, apart from a French sitting room, nor if the Shelleys had had one.

Actually, what poems had Shelley written? Was he *La Belle Dame Sans Merci*? No, that was Keats. *Ozymandias*! That one was of Shelley's. I've never been totally sure what it was about, but it made more sense than Samuel Taylor Coleridge, though of course he was off his face on laudanum or something the whole time. Had Shelley been a Victorian Drug Fiend? Or had he died of the consumption? A lot of those poetic types died of the consumption. I should not like Tom to die of the consumption, though I would nurse him most tenderly in a dilapidated Venetian palazzo if he did. Well, from a distance. I don't really like sick people, which is another flaw in Dad's brilliant plan for me to become a doctor.

'Did Shelley die of the consumption?' I burst out, rather interrupting Tom's description of how he planned to travel for a year before university, to 'work on his poetry'.

Tom said he thought Shelley had drowned, as he looked at me oddly and asked if I was all right.

I assured him that I was fine, and it was just that him talking about travelling and poetry had made me think of Shelley, because he was a poet who travelled a lot. I fervently hoped that Shelley was indeed a well-travelled poetic sort. All those Romantic poets were, weren't they? They were always getting run out of England for something and having to go to Italy till the scandal passed.

Tom leaned forward and took my hand, gazing into my eyes and looking very serious.

Ooooh, I thought deliriously. Here we are! It's finally going to happen. Someone is going to kiss me. Tom. Tom is going to kiss me. And how perfect it is. This balmy late summer night. The stars. The music playing faintly in the distance. Perhaps he will write a poem about it!

Tom continued to stare into my eyes. God, he was really building up to this. It had better be worth it. I closed my eyes in anticipation, to hurry him up. Mum had said Jas and I had to be home by midnight.

'Do you think . . .' Tom breathed.

'Yes,' I sighed. 'Oh yes.'

'Do you really think I could be another Shelley?' he whispered intensely.

I opened my eyes. He was still talking about his wretched poetry! How was he ever going to write a heartbreaking love poem if he couldn't even recognise the optimal moment for a tender yet passionate kiss?

'I don't know,' I said peevishly. Then, as his face fell, I added more gently, 'Maybe. I've not read any of your poetry yet. You *might* be another Shelley. But you might be the new Keats, or another Byron. Or Tennyson.'

Tom made a cross noise. 'Not Tennyson. Tennyson was so mainstream. I don't want to write jingoistic nonsense like *The Charge of the Light Brigade* or mawkish sentimentality like *The Lady of Shalott*.'

I made a noncommittal noise, wondering whether to mention that I rather loved *The Charge of the Light Brigade*, which always made me cry, and that I also found *The Lady of Shalott* rather affecting.

'Shelley's rather a hero of mine,' Tom informed me. 'I've written some poems in tribute to his *Stanzas Written in Dejection*. Would you like me to show you them on Monday?'

I made another noncommittal noise about this.

Tom let go of my hand. 'You're cold,' he said, stripping off his jacket. 'Here, put this on.'

I *was* cold, and I snuggled gratefully into Tom's jacket which smelled deliciously of him, but I did rather wish he had thought to warm me up by pulling me into a loving embrace. Then, with his arms wrapped manfully around me, *surely* something would happen?

But no. He was pulling me to my feet, and it seemed we were to return to the party. So much for him finding me so interesting and wanting to know all about me. I'd told him about myself for about twenty seconds before he had started on about himself. There was so much more I could have told him, so many more interesting things, than just about my stepmother's Border terriers, if I'd had a chance.

We found Jas looking for me, and many glances and nudges being exchanged between people as Tom and I emerged from the shrubbery, with me wearing his jacket.

Jas also indulged in a sly nudge and wink at me, and I realised her eyes were shining, and all her carefully applied lipstick had vanished, leaving her mouth looking slightly puffy. It looked like she had had a more successful time with Mark than I had had with Tom, and apparently Mark had offered to walk us home.

Nothing like being a BIG FAT GOOSEBERRY on a balmy moonlit night, is there? Luckily Tom came to my rescue, and said he would walk us home too, so it wasn't just me three's-a-crowding Mark and Jas.

Jas and Mark clutched each other's hands all the way back to my house. Periodically they stopped to try and eat each other's faces off. It was very sweet in a gross and sort of slurpy way. Each time this happened, Tom and I discreetly walked on and continued our civilised and adult discussion of poetry. He referenced several other poems he would like to show me. It seemed there was no escape. At least Shelley probably had the decency to seduce Mary first before he made her look on his works and despair.

Mark and Jas stopped just before my house for one last tonsil hockey session. I had always cringed when I heard Mum use this phrase to refer disapprovingly to such public displays of affections, but now I seemed destined to be a love-starved spinster forever, I might as well embrace such expressions.

Not that Mum was a love starved spinster, of course. Even *she* had persuaded someone to fall in love with her and marry her and have a child with her. And I had seen the photos of Mum in the seventies and at her wedding. She was pretty, but her clothes were terrible. If Mum could get a husband wearing some sort of Laura Ashley *Little House On The Prairie* dress, why, why could I not even get a kiss?

Was it so much to ask for someone to fall in love with me? Love is the most important thing in the world. It's why people *write* poems and songs and fight wars.

How long did the Greeks besiege Troy for the love of Helen? It was years and *years* and I don't care what Mum says about the Trojan war not being about love at all, but about power and strength and how foolishly men behave when they think those things are threatened and they feel their pride has been insulted.

I don't want Tom to start a war for me. I don't even mind if he doesn't write me a poem – though given how much I've listened to him talk about his poems tonight, I think it would be rude if he didn't. I deserve a limerick, at least. I just want him to fall in love with me.

I think I am falling in love with him. I think I have been a little bit in love with him ever since I saw him in the park that day, and now I'm getting to know him, I'm sure I'm falling in love with him. What will I do if he does not love me back? Will I pine away, and become reclusive, and die for the love of him? Growing pale and wan, gazing longingly out the window from whence I last saw him go?

That seems quite a stupid idea, to be honest. I don't think I'll do that.

Unless it would make him feel *really* bad once I had died and he realised he had loved me all along and then he would write amazing poems about me, and in a hundred years, *My Lovely Lila* would be a byword for the most romantic poem EVER WRITTEN, and my name would be immortal. I'd prefer the immortal name without the dying of misery bit though. I fear, to pine away properly, one would have to give up HobNobs, which really would be enough to make one die of misery. I am not giving up HobNobs for any man. Not even Tom.

While Jas and Mark attempted to suck each other's faces off outside number 72, Tom and I walked on and up my front path. Weird Nicky's bedroom light was still on next door, but at least he didn't appear to be adding Voyeur to Frog Dissector on his list of Weirdnesses.

'I really enjoyed tonight,' Tom said. 'Talking to you is amazing. I don't think I've ever felt able to tell someone so much about my writing.'

Oh my God. Talking to me is amazing. I forgave him for talking about himself all night and barely letting me get a word in edgeways, because talking to ME is AMAZING!

'Anyway, I can't wait to show you some of my stuff on Monday,' Tom said softly, looking right into my eyes.

I tried not to blink and break the moment. Why is it that as soon as you start thinking about not blinking – or scratching your nose, or moving the hair tickling your neck – it immediately becomes the only thing you need to do, right now, and you can think of nothing else?

I was scarcely able to breathe, let alone speak, as Tom leaned in even closer. I could smell the apple shampoo on his hair, and the faint traces of his aftershave – Ralph Lauren Polo, I thought, from our afternoons sniffing tester bottles in Debenhams, pretending we were thinking about buying them for our (imaginary) boyfriends' birthdays and wondering what they would smell like on actual boys. Marvellous, as it turned out. I took another heavenly, heady, surreptitious sniff.

I must remember every detail about this moment forever, I reminded myself. The light shining through Tom's hair. The smell of Tom mixed with the drifting scent of the fading honeysuckle climbing over the porch. The sound of Jas and Mark laughing softly as they made their way up the street. These things were all to be treasured and kept, and maybe if I am a writer one day, I can describe this moment, of love's young kiss, so perfectly, so tenderly. I closed my eyes in anticipation, the better to heighten my other senses, and also because after much discussion and watching of film kissing on rewind and freeze frame, Jas and I had decided eyes closed was definitely the way to kiss. I felt Tom's breath against my cheek, and his lips on . . . also my cheek?

What? Had he missed my lips? MY CHEEK? What was he doing?

I opened my eyes as he cheerfully said, 'See you Monday' as Mark yelled from the gate, 'MATE, c'mon, we need to go!' and Jas tottered up the path, looking weak with either love or lager.

Tom turned with a wave and trotted off with Mark, as I rummaged in my bag for my keys, and Mum opened the door before I could find them, thanks to Mark's bellowings, and demanded to know what was going on and did we know what time it was, and didn't we have any consideration for the neighbours?

'Sorry, Mrs M.' Jas breezed into the hall. 'Thanks for letting me stay over, sorry about the noise, a couple of the boys from college walked us home, we didn't mean them to be so loud.'

Mum raised her eyebrows. 'Walked you home, did they? That was very *nice* of them.'

Jas was too befuddled with love to recognise Mum's sceptical tone.

'Well, I'm sure you can tell me *all* about these "nice" boys in the morning, but for now, I think it's time for bed, don't you?'

Mum was clearly not taking no for an answer to this after we had doubtless 'woken up every neighbour in the street'. Jas and I meekly shuffled up the stairs, to undo all our hard work earlier with a few seconds of warm water and cucumber cleanser.

Later, when we were in bed, Jas said, 'I can't stop smiling. Isn't it *wonderful*? Falling in love? Are you in love with Tom? I'm sure I'm falling in love with Mark. He's just *amazing*. Do you think he'll fall in love with me? He's so cool. And GOD, when he kisses me! Did Tom kiss you?'

I made vaguely affirmative noises. I wasn't really lying to Jas. He *had* kissed me. Just on the cheek: a nice, friendly kiss goodnight. Maybe he respected me too much to snog me in the shrubbery? Maybe he knew I was The One and he just wanted to take it slowly and make it really special when something happened between us? Or maybe he just wanted someone to talk to about his poetry and I had seemed desperate enough to listen? Either way, white lie or huge lie, I had never lied to Jas before about *anything*. We were always totally honest with each other. If I ever plucked up the courage to tell anyone about my dream of being a writer, it was going to be Jas I told first. But now I had basically lied to her about Tom kissing me.

Is this what love makes you do? Lie to the people closest to you? Maybe love isn't the wonderful thing I have always thought it would be.

EMILY

CHAPTER NINE

I jumped out of my skin as Uncle Tom tapped on my door, and suggested I should really put my light off and get some sleep. I had been miles away, with poor Lila, holding my breath, willing Park Boy Tom to kiss her, feeling almost as if I was about to be kissed myself. Is that what it will be like when Toby is about to kiss me? The anxiety and worry about it being perfect, about me being perfect? Surely though he won't turn out to be as selfish and self-centred as Park Boy Tom and his poetry.

Oh Lila. Does he kiss you? I was so tired when I went to bed, and now I'm awake and really want to read on, but I don't want to risk Uncle Tom coming back to tell me to go to sleep again and that we have a lot to do tomorrow. I suppose I have to listen to him, because I do still very much want him to get my phone fixed at the weekend if I can't persuade him to do it sooner. I wonder if he was at Kate's party? Mum hasn't mentioned him yet, but I know they met at college. Maybe it was later on? Maybe he didn't come until they were in Upper Sixth? I'll have to ask him tomorrow. And find out more about Park Boy Tom, who doesn't seem to be the catch that Lila thinks he is.

It was so weird reading all that, because now I've got a bit further into the diary, it's really hard to think of Lila as my mum. She's a whole separate other person, just out there living her life in 1996 in her weird flannel shirts and her grandad's tweed jacket, hoping and longing for someone to kiss her and to fall in love with her. I suppose if I remember that Lila is my mother, I know at least awful Park Boy Tom didn't turn out to be the one true love of her life forever more, and that she did get her wish for someone to fall in love with her, because Dad must have been in love with her at some point if they got married and had me. But then that didn't end very well either, did it?

I wonder if Mum still hopes she'll find her one true love one day? Ew. Gross. That is my mother. She has no need of love, or anything else (double gross). She is a *mother*. That should be enough for her.

And that is why I am never going to have children. I don't want to have to give up my life for them. I want to be an artist, I love drawing and painting. I wonder if I will ever have the nerve to say that to Toby. If I told him, would he listen, or understand? Or would he also just launch off into talking about himself, and not bother to pay any attention to what I had said. Could talking to the real Toby ever live up to the version of him I chatted to in my head all the time? Mum had thought Park Boy Tom's floppy hair and sexy eyes was enough to fall in love with, but so far he was proving a terrible disappointment. What if Toby was the same? What if no one was ever as good in real life as they were in your dreams?

When we had finished working today, I decided I would do some drawing. I hadn't done anything since I got here. I had been so cross about my phone and being sent away that I hadn't even brought my sketch pad or anything, but I was sure I could find some scrap paper and a pencil to doodle with. Maybe if I drew Toby, it would remind me of why I loved him and stop my worries that I didn't actually know anything about him, and what if he turned out to be shallow and annoying?

Uncle Tom came into the kitchen while I was drawing. To my surprise, he didn't say, 'Who is that?' when he saw the picture of Toby, but just said, 'Wow, Emily, that's really good!'

I blushed and then threw caution to the winds and said, 'I think maybe I'd like to be an artist when I grow up.'

Uncle Tom didn't laugh, or say, 'Who do you think you are, going around thinking someone like *you* could be an artist?' He just nodded and said, 'It's important to have dreams. It's important to have a plan as well. Are you thinking of art school?'

I hadn't really thought about how I was going to become an artist, beyond vague thoughts of *being* one, so I just said, 'I don't know. I haven't really thought about it much yet.' Uncle Tom then said, 'Well, you're still young. Plenty of time to think about these things. Can you draw me, do you think?'

I'd never drawn anybody in real life before. But Uncle Tom insisted I tried, and it came out all right. It's a lot harder to draw someone in front of you than someone you are imagining though. You have to make them look like they really are, not how you want them to look.

I attempted to sell Uncle Tom his drawing for the price of getting my phone fixed, so I didn't have to scrape any more woodchip off walls or paint off doors. I pointed out that this was a very reasonable offer I was making him, and one day, if I become a rich and famous artist, it would be worth a fortune and he could sell it to keep him in luxury in his old age. I even was generous enough to remind him I wasn't even asking the price of a *new* phone, just the repairs to my existing one, so he was getting a bargain, especially when you took into account all the work I have already done on the house for him, that I was willing not to charge him for.

Uncle Tom was having none of it, and said he would consider my drawing of him a kind gift that would warm the cockles of his heart in his dotage. I don't even know what that means, except that maybe he doesn't believe I can be an artist, if he won't even buy one little drawing from me.

I carried on drawing for a bit when I went up to bed though. Uncle Tom insisted that his refusal to buy my drawing was not a sign of his lack of faith, but rather that he did not think one could put a price on such things. I suspected he was talking rubbish, but he also gave me a pep talk about the importance of practising something as much as possible if you ever wanted to turn a passion into a career. And I had realised how much I had missed scribbling and sketching over the last few days. I drew Toby again, and Poppy, and I even drew Mum. Then I tried to draw Mum as Lila, but I couldn't make it come out right. I drew until I was too tired to read anything before bed, and decided to wake up early and read a bit more of Lila's – Mum's – diary before I had to get up.

I slept in though, because I had strange dreams all night, about Toby almost kissing me and then something terrible would happen, like him turning into Frankenstein's Monster at the last moment and or he'd lean in to kiss me and cough and then it would turn out he was lying on his deathbed and dying and I had to nurse him.

The worse dream though was when his lips were just about to touch mine, and then at the last minute he laughed and turned around and kissed Poppy. How could she! I was furious with her, and wished I could tell her so, for being such a bad friend!

Maybe it's best I don't have my phone, so I can't give her a piece of my mind about her behaviour. And Toby. Not that I could message him anyway, because I don't even have his Snapchat and anyway, then he might guess that I like him, and that would be the very worst thing that could possibly happen.

Would it? Would it be worse than him and Poppy?

I did wish I could message *someone*, like Evie or Alice, to make sure nothing was going on with Poppy and Toby. Poppy wouldn't, would she? She's my best friend, that's got to count for something? But I'm so far away, and what if Toby asks her out?

I hate this, I hate being away from everyone with no idea of what's going on.

By the time I had spent the whole day sugar-soaping walls (I have no idea what sugar soap is, or why I had to wash walls with it, I'm starting to think Uncle Tom is just making up jobs for me to do for his own amusement, to torment me, but according to him it was very important),

I had worked myself into such a state of anxiety about Poppy and Toby that I had forgotten all about the diary.

Uncle Tom hadn't though. He said he'd found *My So-Called Life* online and downloaded it, and would I like to watch it with him? We watched three episodes before I excused myself. Uncle Tom seemed to enjoy it, but I didn't really get it. Maybe you had to be there in the nineties?

I finally went upstairs and did that thing where you scroll through every platform and there is literally nothing to watch, because all I actually wanted to do was to chat to my friends. I threw the remote across the room, and then saw the diary again on my bedside table. I decided I might as well read a bit more. What else was there to do? I didn't want to draw tonight, not if it was going to give me such horrible dreams again.

LILA

CHAPTER TEN

MONDAY 9TH SEPTEMBER 1996

Today, I think, was a really good day.

Tom automatically sat with me in French and English, and at lunch, instead of giving me a casual wave, suggesting there is a spare seat, but he's not that bothered about where I sit, we queued up and then found a seat together, *just us*, not Kate, Luke, Mark or Jas etc (Mark and Jas were also sitting together, making goo goo eyes at each other, which made me glad that Tom and I clearly have a far more mature relationship).

We talked a bit about what we'd done yesterday. He'd been out to his grandmother's birthday dinner, and I tried to make it sound like I'd had a more exciting day than being dragged to the garden centre with Mum and then helping her to plant up her 'autumn hanging baskets'. Like, why? Why are grown-ups so obsessed with hanging baskets? I am never going to be that sad and boring.

After we'd eaten, Tom got out a notebook full of his poems for me to read. I was terrified he was going to make me sit there and read them in front of him, which would have been awful, but instead he told me to take them away and read them and let me know what I thought. He really seemed bothered about my opinion.

Surely he wouldn't care what I thought if he didn't like me?

I read Tom's poems in my free period after lunch. I didn't really know what to say to him about them. How do you know if something is good? I didn't really like them, but what is the mark of a 'good' poem? The bit at the beginning of *Dead Poets Society* when they are ordered to rip out the pages explaining what defines a poem's worth was no use at all. I had hoped that some of the college teachers this year might turn out to be the sort of inspirational 'oh Captain, my Captain'-type figures, but so far they mostly seem dispirited and underwhelmed by another year of shaping impressionable young minds. This is not much use in my quest to find out the right way to talk to Tom about his notebook.

It strikes me that it would be much more useful if passing exams was about being taught *to* think, not being taught *what* to think. When we answer questions about Keats' *Ode to Autumn,* if we can justify it, and back up our arguments, we should be able to say that it's all well and good, but he does *go on* a bit. Instead, we just have to trot out the lines we've had drummed into us, about his richness of language.

It's the same with *Wuthering Heights*. We are not allowed to say that Cathy is a bit annoying and Heathcliff is clearly a psycho and if Cathy had written to the *Just17* problem page they would have defo told her to steer clear of Heathcliff and stick with nice Edgar Linton (or better yet, speak to a 'trusted adult' about her problems, which, to be fair, Cathy didn't really have), and maybe it might be interesting to reflect on what that said about Emily Brontë and her state of mind, that she thought Cathy and Heathcliff were the perfect couple, but no, we just have to talk about the *imagery* and what that means. And what use is that when we are grown up, and out in the big wide world, and we can absolutely tell you that the wild landscape of the Yorkshire moors as evoked by mad old Emily is representative of the tumultuous and passionate relationship between Heathcliff and Cathy, but we can offer no opinions of our own on whether something is good or bad? Maybe that is what you learn at university, though it seems a waste of time to go to all the trouble to teach us to regurgitate other people's thoughts before we are shown how to form our own.

It occurs to me that discussing this could be a very cunning way of not having to actually tell Tom my thoughts on his poems. After all, he is doing a Philosophy A-level, so I will present it as a philosophical question and then no doubt he will do all the talking and I won't have to say anything and I can just nod.

That is a total cop-out, of course, but I don't know what else I can do. If I say, 'Oh yes, these are brilliant, you are so clever,' firstly, it will seem very sycophantic, even though I know it's what he wants to hear, and secondly, what if I am right and they are awful and he shows them to other people and they laugh at him and it's all my fault?

I feel like any criticism I offer him about the poems, however mild, will hurt him, for all he said he wanted my 'honest opinion'. He's obviously so very proud of them, and it must have taken a lot for him to show them to me, when we have only known each other a short time. But he must feel we have a connection. It's surely another Sign that we are meant to be together. After all, what would I rather, that he trusts me enough to let me see this very personal and important notebook, or that he just wants to stick his tongue down my throat and try and grope my boobs? No, this is far better than what Jas and Mark seem to have found. Tom and I have a real, deep connection.

I am sure that is what the *Just Seventeen* agony aunt would say too. Love is not about sex. It's about your minds being in the same place.

Now I just have to pluck up the courage to show Tom some of the things I've written. Not this diary though. Never this. This is where I put all the things I can never tell another soul.

Anyway, I had double French after my free period, and now that we are into the second week of term, we are starting to get homework, so I decided to go to the computer lab after we finished for the day to make a start on my English essay, because the computer is in the sitting room at home and it's hard to concentrate with Mum wandering in and out and talking to me all the time.

After hours, the college computer lab has always looked pretty empty, so I thought it would be easier to get some work done. Sure enough, the only other person in there was Weird Nicky. I gave him a cursory nod when he said hi, and then made 'busy and important' gestures at the computer on the very furthest side of the lab from him.

After about half an hour of Brontëan imagery, I had lost the will to live and decided to investigate the Internet. It was terribly exciting. I wondered what I could find out and look at? Not a lot, it turned out. The college's Internet access was only to websites that the college considered to be 'educational'. BORING!

I decided to have a look at these 'chatrooms' and 'message boards' we had been told about.

There were dozens of chatrooms on all sorts of topics, which was hardly surprising since this network connected about two dozen colleges across the country. With that many people, I was sure to find some like-minded souls to chat to about something. I scrolled through the lists, looking for something to catch my interest. There were lots of literary sounding chats, about novels and poetry and even, terrifyingly, some in French about French literature. I didn't think either my French or my literariness was up to that. Maybe next year, when I had achieved the terrifying sophistication of Upper Sixth Sarah?

I moved on to the history-based chatrooms. Wow. There were discussions about every period and famous figure who had ever lived. But would my favourite have made it? I anxiously clicked down the page. Bad King John had a chat. If *he* was up for debate, then surely . . .

Yes! There he was. My poor dear Richard III. The most uncool monarch in history, toppled by horrible Henry Tudor, the Welsh upstart, vilified by William Shakespeare as part of his massive suck-up campaign to Elizabeth I and generally a much maligned and misunderstood king. I had always taken Richard's side, despite all the accusations about the Princes in the Tower and his usurping the throne. I wondered if I would find anyone else who agreed with me in the chatroom, or if everyone would be there to slag him off. I pressed the join button and waited to be see what happened.

Nothing. There was no one else on there right now. I contented myself with reading back over the previously posted messages and found that, as I suspected, my poor Richard had very few supporters. Well, two, if you counted me. There was me and someone called TSNO80. This was not as cryptic as it sounded, as we all had to use the college chatrooms under the usernames we had been issued which was a random selection of letters from our first and surnames and the year we were born. I was MKLB80.

TSNO80 had been putting up a spirited defence of Richard, but he only appeared to have been in the group for the last week, so I assumed he was in my year. Most of the other posters had 79 in their usernames, so I assumed they were from the year above. There were only a smattering of 80 usernames, which gave me hope that maybe others might join and TSNO80 and I would be less of a minority.

I read a few more anti Richard posts, and then decided to make my own post. I didn't want to be too controversial, so I just suggested that a lot of the negativity about Richard was Tudor propaganda. I waited nervously, to see what reception I got.

Oooh. Someone had replied. It was LNVR79. LNVR79 said that I was . . . oh. Rude! I was a lickspittle Plantagenet lackey, and there were undeniable facts about Richard in the contemporary Tudor accounts which I could not argue with, such as he usurped the throne, and if he had not, his nephews would never have disappeared, so directly or indirectly he was responsible for their murder and what did I have to say about THAT?

I didn't know. I didn't want to be a lickspittle Plantagenet lackey. I had been looking forward to some gentle historical debate, not medieval mudslinging. I felt a bit like I wanted to cry. I wasn't sure of the etiquette of these chatrooms either. Did one return the insult and call LNVR79 some suitably Tudor slandering name, or did I remonstrate and say that wasn't a very nice way to welcome me to the group, even if my views did not agree with them, and after all, wasn't that why we were here? To discuss differing viewpoints? To learn things, to see things from a different perspective? How were we supposed to do that, if you said anyone who thought old Henry Tudor's claim to the throne was a bit dodgy was a lickspittle Plantagenet lackey?

I was still wondering what to do, when horrible, horrible LNVR79 popped up again.

Nothing to say, MKLB80? No defence to be made of the 'Tudor propaganda' about how R3 stole the throne? Come on, you basically accused Henry Tudor of lying, you must have something to back it up.

OK, now I really wanted to cry. I wouldn't be surprised if LNVR79 turned out to be the reincarnation of Henry Tudor himself, and now you couldn't rampage round the country starting wars at will, he (or she, who knows?) was having to content themselves with stirring up trouble in Internet chatrooms. Oh, Henry, how the mighty have fallen.

Someone else was posting.

There is a strong argument that R3 took the throne not for personal power and advancement, but to try and prevent England sliding back into civil war, which the boy king Edward V could not have done.

Oh yay of yays! It was lovely *lovely* TSNO80, riding to the defence of 'R3', as they seemed to call Richard III here.

Yeah LNVR79. What TSNO80 said. IN YOUR FACE. I typed this, then deleted it before I sent it, as I suspected it did not carry enough historical gravitas, regardless of the name-calling by LNVR79.

I sat there for over an hour, fascinated by the chat, not contributing a great deal, but gratified nonetheless to have TSNO80 post a welcome message to me, saying it was 'nice to see another R3 supporter in here.' It was strange to be 'talking' to all these people and have no idea who they were or what they looked like. I didn't even know if they were boys or girls.

We had been warned, despite these chatrooms only being accessible by college students, that it would still be prudent not to give away personal information about ourselves. Mum had also been very clear that when it came to the Internet, there be dragons, and I wasn't to tell ANYONE anything about myself. It was liberating in a way, because if everyone I was talking to was faceless and anonymous, well, so was I. It was very freeing to be able to say what I really thought, without the fear of anyone saying, 'Oh my God, did you hear how dumb Lila

LILA MACKAY IS VERY MISUNDERSTOOD

sounded just there?' It was one of the reasons I always hated speaking up in class, even when I *knew* I was right. Just in case I wasn't or in case I said it wrong, or even just in case people thought I was too full of myself for venturing my opinion. Here, I didn't have to worry about it. I could pretend I was like Rachel who never had any qualms about holding forth, and even when she was proved utterly wrong, was still convinced of her own rightness.

All good things must come to an end though, and at five o'clock I was thrown out the computer lab because the college was closing for the night. I was relieved to see Nicky had already left at some point so I didn't have to get the bus home with him.

FRIDAY 13TH SEPTEMBER

Friday 13th is indeed the unluckiest day. Fate has struck me a cruel blow. Well, I say Fate, but really it's Weird Nicky's fault. I take back all my resolutions about being nice to him. There is literally no part of my life that he will not ruin.

All week everything had gone so amazingly with Tom and me. Everyone now seemed to accept that we sat together in class and at lunch. Even Rachel had stopped trying to barge in and sit beside him in English, and yesterday when I was a bit late for lunch because I'd stayed behind to ask Mrs Lavery the history teacher about something, and there were no seats beside Tom, Kate said, 'Hey, have my seat, Lila, I'm nearly done anyway,' so I could sit beside him.

If his best friend approves of me, well, that must mean nething, right?

It is a bit strange to think that he has a girl for his best friend. I can't imagine a boy being in Jas's place, telling them everything, knowing they would understand without having to explain. Maybe Kate and Tom *do* have to explain things to each other. After all, how could he get what Kate meant if she was talking about period pains or something?

Kate probably doesn't get period pains. She's too perfect. It's so unfair that she is also so nice. I guess if I had to pick a female best friend for Tom, I'd want someone like Kate rather than Rachel. And maybe once Tom and I are officially going out, Kate will also be my best friend – well, second best friend after Jas – and she will show me how to make my hair all shiny and swishy like hers, instead of it managing the unusual trick of being both quite limp and quite frizzy.

I hope Tom asks me out soon, so we can be Official. Jas and Mark are Official already. I asked her if she wanted to do something with me tonight, but she can't because she's going to the cinema with Mark – their first proper date. Jas is so excited, I can't really be annoyed about her ditching me for a boy, but all yesterday and even all morning today I hoped that Tom might say, 'Oh, I don't suppose you're free tonight and want to come out with me?' and then we could go on a double date and we could tell the story of our first date together at our double wedding in a few years' time.

When it got to lunchtime, I was desperately crossing my fingers for Tom to ask me out. There was still plenty of time. I was sitting talking to Kate in the canteen when he appeared with his tray and collapsed beside me. I was feeling quite positive. Kate had just told me how much she liked my T-shirt and that it really suited me. I felt that was a good omen.

Tom groaned as he stabbed at his baked potato with his fork and complained he had had a terrible morning. Then he brightened up and started waving at someone.

I went cold. Tom waved at *me*. Had he found someone else already? Had he gone off me before he had even asked me out, or even kissed me? Did I . . . did I repel boys? Please God, I prayed. Don't let it be Rachel he's waving at. I could not bear the nuclear-level smugness if he has decided he does like Rachel after all.

It was worse than Rachel. It was Weird Nicky he was waving at. And Nicky, being Nicky, was wandering off in the opposite direction, oblivious, so Tom yelled, 'YO! The Nickster! Over here, mate! Over here!' And Nicky turned around and grinned at Tom and came over.

What was Tom doing? We were running out of time for him to ask me out tonight. And if he asked Nicky to sit here, then he'd have to stay and talk to Nicky and we couldn't go off by ourselves and talk about books or poetry (more precisely, Tom's poetry, but still, poetry was *romantic* and might remind him of something he meant to say!) and then there would only be a brief window left after school and I needed to think about what to wear and what to say to Mum, and what his film suggestion might mean and if I even wanted him to kiss me in the cinema, or if it would be better if we just watched the film and then he kissed me outside afterwards, and oh, so many things I needed to consider that I definitely hadn't spent all week dreaming about and imagining the exact right scenarios for it all to play out. And none of those scenarios had featured Nicky hanging round. Why was Tom even talking to him?

As Nicky plonked himself down on Tom's other side, Tom punched him on the arm and cried once again, 'The Nickster! Hero of the bloody hour, mate! I don't know what I'd've done without you.'

Nicky grinned bashfully and mumbled something about it was nothing, anyone could've done it.

Tom then breathlessly related the fascinating tale of how he had been in the computer lab just before lunch finishing his philosophy essay, which he insisted was bloody good, when he accidentally pressed a button and 'BOOM! Whole wretched thing was just GONE!' and he snapped his fingers for dramatic effect.

Tom had been saved from his existential despair (including shouting hopelessly at the computer, as he envisaged spending all weekend rewriting his essay and lamenting that it wouldn't be as good as the Lost Work) by Weird Nicky, who had also been in the computer lab and hearing Tom's anguished bellows had come over to see if he could help, whereupon apparently he had pressed another couple of buttons and 'BAM! It was back! The whole thing! I couldn't believe it!' And now according to Tom, he and Nicky are sworn blood brothers, and 'the Nickster' as Tom seems to insist on referring to him, has Tom's undying gratitude and devotion, 'because MATE, you totally saved the day!' Tom punched Nicky again and Nicky tried not to wince. God, he was so wet.

Tom was now happily shovelling in his chilli potato, with baked beans on top, I noticed. Yuck. Could I really love a man who ate double beans for lunch? I was sitting next to him in English this afternoon too. What if he decided to ask me out then, and then ruined the moment by farting? Literally the only thing that would be worse is if *I* farted.

Tom was still busy chatting away to Nicky as he ate, and Nicky was starting to smile and answer back instead of mumbling. He was even sitting up straighter. Tom just had that effect on people, when he turned his attention on you. It was like the sun was shining on you, and you could feel the warmth of his personality lighting up everything. Also, what was this 'the Nickster' business? This was Weird Nicky. 'The Nickster' made him sound like a completely different person.

Tom was now insisting that everyone must befriend Nicky as he was a computer genius who could rescue them from the dreadful danger that lurked in the vicious jaws of Microsoft. He was asking Nicky about himself, and what courses he was doing, and even I was stunned when it turned out Nicky was taking not three, not four, but FIVE A-levels, including all three sciences, maths and history.

'Wow,' said Kate, impressed, 'Are you, like, an *actual* genius then? Nobody does FIVE A-levels!'

Nicky demurred, blushing and shy again now he was the centre of everyone's attention and mumbled that the history one was just for fun really, to make a change from all the science stuff and he was super lucky the college had been really helpful with his timetable to fit it all in.

Poor Nicky was almost cringing in embarrassment now at everyone staring at him, and Tom tactfully changed the subject and asked him where he lived.

I regretted thinking 'Poor Nicky' when of all the answers he could have given, like 'Near Manor Park' or 'On Church Road' or 'beside the number 63 bus route', instead he simply said, 'Next door to Lila.'

'Wow,' said Tom in wonder. 'You and the Nickster are neighbours, Lila? Why didn't you say? And why am I only meeting him now, two weeks into the term?'

'I didn't realise you lived next door to each other,' chimed in Kate. 'I'm so sorry, Nickster, I'd've asked you to my party last week. You'll definitely have to come to the next one.'

Luke wanted to know when the next party would be, but Kate said she didn't know. Her father had been unimpressed with the fallout from the last one, as Adam Trent had been watching *Free Willy* and he threw a packet of fish fingers in the koi carp pond, shouting, ' Go free!', trying to return them to the wild, and since koi carp aren't really meant to eat fish fingers, Kate thought she'd have to leave it for a bit until he forgot about that before she could have another party.

Tom was undaunted by the fate of the koi carp and had a splendid idea for this weekend, as he announced that the new film of *Emma* was out today, and he suggested we should all go tonight. He slung an arm round my shoulder, and I tried not to visibly glow as he said, 'Lila? Are you up for that?'

I nodded blissfully. Maybe it hadn't been how I had envisioned, but he'd asked me out!

Then he asked Kate too. But he'd asked me first. I hoped Kate would say no? But Kate was keen. And oh good, so was Weird Nicky. *Emma* was totally the perfect first date film, but not with Kate and Nicky along. And *then* he asked Luke and Andy and Mark and Jas, and I thought why not just stand on your chair and shout to the whole damn canteen, Tom, see if anyone else wants to come on MY DATE with you!

To my relief Luke and Andy declined as they had football practice, and Mark and Jas were going to see the new John Grisham film, which I felt was distinctly less romantic than *Emma*. On the other hand, they weren't double dating with Kate and Nicky, so maybe we were even.

Why did it have to be *Nicky* coming on my date though? Of all people. Kate and *anyone* else would be fine, we could still tell the amusing story at our wedding, even if it wasn't a double wedding (I didn't really want a double wedding with anyone but Jas anyway), but not when Nicky was a part of it. Also, even though I didn't think the back row of the cinema was the *perfect* venue for a first kiss, at this point I would take pretty much anywhere that wasn't an alleyway by the bins. But how could anything possibly happen with Kate and Nicky sitting there staring at us? Well, staring at the screen hopefully, but still just *being* there. I wouldn't put it past Nicky to stare if Tom kissed me. It's the closest Nicky will ever get to kissing a girl.

In English after lunch, Tom sat and whispered to me almost the whole time, making me laugh so much I almost *did* fart, at which point I obviously would have had to simply stand up, leave the college, change my name (again) and move to Australia out of mortification, but he was so sweet it was almost impossible to stay angry at him over the Kate/ Nicky double date situation, even when we were leaving at the end of the day and he said, 'So I'll just see you and the Nickster at the cinema at seven, yeah?'

I reminded myself yet again that I was a strong, independent feminist woman and I didn't need a man to collect me and escort me to places, I was perfectly capable of making my own way there, and it would have been rather insulting if Tom had thought otherwise, and he was right, it made sense for Nicky and me to go together.

By the time Nicky and I got home, he had lost all the glamour he'd briefly worn in Tom's presence at lunch and was just as weird as ever. Outside our houses he asked if I wanted to walk or get the bus to the cinema, adding he had all the bus timetables memorised so could plan us a route. Who even has all the bus timetables, let alone memorises them? I suggested we walked, as it was a nice evening and there was less chance of being seen with him if we took the back streets.

Mum was incredulous and ecstatic to hear that I was going to the cinema with Nicky. I had hoped not to tell her, to just say I was going with 'friends', but Nicky came round about ten minutes before we needed to leave, instead of just meeting me outside like I'd told him to, and said we were off to the 'picture house' together. The 'picture house'? Was it 1896, not 1996? Would we go by horse-drawn charabanc?

Mum did not seem to notice anything strange about this expression though, and simply said, 'Oh how nice! I'm so glad you two are finally friends, it was always such a *waste*, living next door to each other and not making more of it.'

We at least achieved the walk to the cinema without Nicky growing an extra head or speaking in tongues or any of the other things I was quite sure he was capable of. Kate and Tom were waiting for us when we got there and Kate held up four tickets, saying her dad had insisted on buying them for us all. Which was very nice of him, but now I would never know if Tom would have chivalrously paid for my ticket. He had given Kate popcorn and drinks money too. He was excited she was making new friends at college, apparently, and was worried that if she just hung out with the same people as she had at school, then she would struggle to make friends on her own when she got to university.

Kate grinned. 'He was especially thrilled when he heard about your five A-levels, Nickster.'

What about me? Wasn't he excited about me? And is this new nickname of 'Nickster' here to stay? It is a ridiculous name. 'Nickster'. His name is Weird Nicky. Everyone knows that. Well, I do. And Jas. (Her and Mark's film had started before ours, so I didn't see Jas at the cinema.)

We didn't sit in the back row in the auditorium. It would have been awkward for Kate and Nicky. They might have thought they were expected to snog each other. Poor Kate! The film was lovely though. Gwyneth Paltrow is so beautiful, and Ewan MacGregor is possibly the sexiest man alive, though the actor who was Mr Knightly was also gorgeous. I snuck a look at Tom when Mr Knightly declared his love for Emma to see if he was going to look at me, but he seemed to be concentrating on his popcorn. We did have a *lot* of popcorn, thanks to Kate's dad. I don't think I've ever had such munificence in the cinema. Usually Jas and I shared a small popcorn and snuck in cans of Coke.

When we came out afterwards, Kate ran across to a huge Mercedes, explaining that her dad was picking her up and she'd see if he'd give us all a lift because it was starting to rain.

I have never been in such a swanky car. Mum says cars don't matter, as long as they are reliable enough to get you from A to B, so she drives the same Volvo estate car she has had for the last ten years. Dad likes nice cars, but his cars are very boring compared to Kate's dad's, which was red and shiny and had all sorts of buttons I longed to press but didn't dare.

Kate's dad, who told us to call him Kevin, was not at all what I had expected. Kate was so posh, and elegant, and so very rich, I had assumed her father would also be incredibly posh. But Kevin was anything but posh, having a very strong cockney accent, and wearing a suit I knew my grandmother would describe as 'loud'. I had a feeling he was the sort of person my grandmother had in mind when she spoke in disapproving tones of the 'nouveau riche'. I always assumed she looked down on people who she deemed to be 'new money' because she was jealous they had so much more of it than us, which would definitely also apply to Kevin. I liked him very much though, as he was almost as loud as his suit, but very kind and jolly with it.

Kate sat in the front and I was in the back, sandwiched between Tom and Nicky, who was suddenly talking very knowledgeably to Kevin about the car's specifications.

'You'll be the genius boy Katie was telling me about then?' boomed Kevin. 'Five A levels? I'm impressed. I'm always telling Katie that education is the most important thing in the world.'

'Dad!' groaned Kate, seemingly unbothered by her father's interrogation of her friends.

'Well, it is, sweetheart,' insisted Kevin. 'I should know, I didn't I have any. I left school at fourteen and started work down the market.'

'I *know*,' Kate sighed. 'And so does Tom, you're always telling us about it.'

'Because I want better for you. I want you to have all the things I never did.'

Kate shook her head, but she smiled fondly at her father.

Later, in bed, I found myself thinking about Kate and Kevin again. I wished I had that sort of relationship with my father. I wondered what the difference was between Kevin's ambitions for Kate, and Dad's for me?

After thinking about it for a while, I realised that Kevin had told me exactly what the difference was. He wanted all the things he'd never had for Kate, for her to do the things he'd never had a chance to, and to give her the opportunities no one had given him. Dad just wanted me to do the same things as he'd done, to follow the path he had and to become another safe Dr MacKay, like him, and his father and his grandfather. It was what the MacKays *did*, he had insisted when he heard about my subject choices.

I wondered though, if in her own way, Kate carried as heavy a burden of expectation from Kevin?

EMILY

CHAPTER ELEVEN

Uncle Tom took me to the pub for dinner after we'd finished the day's work (*more* sugar-soaping of more walls but today, yay, he let me start painting. Painting is *way* more fun than sugar-soaping).

I felt very grown up going out for dinner with him, especially when he let me have a sip of his beer when no one was looking. It was disgusting. It wasn't the first time I had tried alcohol of course, Mum has let me taste her wine and gin and tonics and stuff before too, but it is always so horrible. I really don't understand what adults see in it. Uncle Tom just shrugged when I said this, and said that your palate changes as you get older, and did I want pudding, which made me feel about five again, but actually, yes, I did want pudding, please.

This is the trouble with being a teenager. One minute you feel like you are totally doing what the millennials would call 'adulting' (ugh. How are they so cringe too? Nearly as cringe as the old boomers!), and the next you are reduced to being a child again. Why does no one understand how hard this is for us? On the one hand we are constantly told we are not old enough to do this, or to understand about

GILL SIMS

that, and on the other hand, people are pushing us to make decisions about things like our GCSE subjects – decisions that will affect our A-level choices and in turn probably will have some effect on what we will end up doing with the rest of our lives. But at the same time as we are told to basically decide what we want to do FOREVER, people are laughing at our emotions, and saying things like we are far too young to possibly understand what love is.

If we are too young to understand about love, or to think we've met someone we want to spend the rest of our lives with, firstly, why are we old enough to know what job we want to do for the rest of our lives, and secondly, why do schools insist on teaching us so many books that are about people falling in true passionate, life-or-death love at ridiculous ages? Yes, I am looking at you *Romeo and Juliet*, since apparently Juliet was only supposed to be thirteen, which is *not even legal*, and even Emily Brontë and Cathy and Heathcliff who supposedly discovered they were twin souls and fell in love when they were basically *children* (I had been terribly shocked by Lila's revelations that she was not a fan of Emily Brontë or *Wuthering Heights*. What was wrong with her? Did she have no soul? Still, I assume that means that I am definitely *not* named after Emily Brontë, which is a shame)! Even *Pride and Prejudice* which is a bit more sensible about things has Lydia running off and getting married at fifteen (though I suppose at least Jane Austen made it clear this was a Very Bad Life Choice and no one approved or declared Lydia and Wickham the greatest love story ever written).

Anyway, it is very confusing for us. And judging from Lila's diary, a couple of years more maturity doesn't make it any less confusing. Do I love Toby? Is he my Park Boy Tom? What will I do if he shows me bad poetry he has written? I hope he doesn't. Park Boy Tom must've been really hot for Lila to keep fancying him despite the bad poetry.

I keep forgetting Lila is my mum. I suppose I can take heart that she must have seen the light eventually, because obviously he is not my dad! I asked Uncle Tom if he was *sure* he didn't remember Park Boy Tom, explaining again that apparently he had been really gorgeous, at which Uncle Tom looked thoughtful, but also that Mum said he had written really awful poetry. I don't think Uncle Tom had been listening to me properly though, because he choked on his fish and chips at that point, and by the time he'd recovered, all he said was that Park Boy Tom sounded ghastly, quite frankly.

I did like the things Lila said about why weren't we taught to think for ourselves, and only taught to repeat other people's opinions on things. I think I need to work on this. I am always too scared to say what I really think about things, and always wait until someone else goes first and says they love or hate a song or a film and then, whatever I really thought, I just agree, because I am too scared of looking stupid. I have overheard talking Toby talking about things, and he always has an opinion though. I wonder what he would do if I just walked up to him one day, and said he was wrong? Maybe I should wait for him to ask me out first before I do that. Or at least, you know, talk to me. Is that bad?

I wonder if anything I learn at school will ever be of any use? I have to choose my subjects *next term* and beyond my vague 'artist' aspirations, I have no idea what I want to do, or even what sort of artist I want to be, or what I would *do* at art school, assuming I could even get in. I look at all the adults around me, and none of them seem to love their jobs. Even when it looks glamorous, like Dad on his archaeology dig in the desert, he spent months complaining and huffing over the endless grant applications he had to fill in, and the hoops he had to jump through to get any money from people to be able to do it.

I always thought Uncle Tom's job as a property developer was pretty cool. Buying old houses and making them look nice and then selling them sounded like an amazing way to make a living. But I've seen this week it actually involves a lot of back-breaking labour, and also Uncle Tom seems to sit up quite late swearing at his laptop, 'balancing the books', as he calls it, so it seems to involve a lot of dull admin stuff too.

Mum, well, *technically* she fulfilled Lila's dream of being a writer, but somehow I don't think it's quite what she envisaged back when she was Lila MacKay, full of hope and ambition. She certainly doesn't *look* like a woman who finds writing *Daily Mail* clickbait articles and 'Your 100 best storage solutions' to be nurturing her soul. And maybe now she *is* following her dream, but look how long it's taken to make it happen. Nearly thirty years. I don't want to wait thirty years to have my dream job. I'll be so *old* by then. Almost dead. I'll have wasted my life. Kids will be saying, 'OK, boomer,' to me. Or whatever the kids say in thirty years. Probably, 'Why aren't you dead yet, Grandma?' Not my kids, obviously, because I am never tying myself down like that.

At least Mum (and Dad) never tried to push me into being what they want. They've always gone with the 'you can be anything you want to be' line – which is great and all, but not *actually* that helpful. I never realised Mum was under so much pressure to be a doctor. That must have been pretty tough for her to stand up to Granddad, he can still be quite scary. I think it's just as well she did though, I can't think of anyone being a worse doctor than Mum. She'd get distracted in the middle of someone's operation or something and wander off and they'd find her googling the life cycle of fairy penguins or something, like when she burnt my dinner because she'd had this idea for a penguin metaphor in her novel.

The end of my cruel isolation is in sight though, and I need to work really *really* hard tomorrow, because after that it is ONE MORE DAY till phone fixing! Uncle Tom has made me an appointment with the Apple Store, and in less than forty-eight hours I will be back in the 21st century, and Poppy can fill me on how much Toby is pining for me (oh please, please, let him be having just a bijou pinette at least). I was very wrong to think Poppy might steal him for herself, she is too good a friend to do that. We are going to be best friends forever, like Mum and Aunty Jas.

It's so funny to read about Aunty Jas with a boyfriend, because as long as I have known her, she has said men are more trouble than they are worth and ranted at me about feminism. I do agree with lots of her points about feminism, of course. But I also would quite like a boyfriend. I might just read a little bit more of the diary and see if there's any more information about how Jas went from boy obsessed to Man Hater!

LILA

CHAPTER TWELVE

I have neglected this diary most sadly. How will I become an actual writer if I can't even keep a diary? Still, I suppose even Cassandra Mortmain in *I Capture the Castle* left big gaps in her notebooks when real life got in the way. Not that Cassandra is *real*, but although she was obviously very busy with being poor and noble and trying to find her sister a rich husband and then accidently getting off with her future brother-in-law, I think she would have had even bigger gaps in her notebooks had she been a modern teenager. A-levels and college have turned out to be a *lot* of work, and that's without all the extracurricular things we are supposed to do to make us into well-rounded people who are functioning members of society, and also will look good on our UCAS forms when we start applying for university.

University. God, that's a scary thought. I thought starting college was scary enough, and in a year's time, I will have to think about applying to *university*.

I remember when I was about six or seven, it felt like school, junior school, would be *forever*. I would never grow up. Even in first and second year at senior school, the years still felt endless. I thought I would be twelve or thirteen for the rest of my life. And then suddenly, time started to move. I was fourteen, then I was fifteen before I knew it, and now I am sixteen, and the years seem to be *flying* past at this terrifying speed, and I am getting older and older and I still haven't *done* anything with my life. Mary Shelley was seduced and ran off to France with Shelley when she was my age. And I – I still have never been kissed. Not by a tortured poet in a graveyard, nor even by my sister's dodgy bearded fiancé *à* la Cassandra Mortmain.

It is not for want of trying. I have given Tom every possible opportunity to kiss me. We see each other almost every weekend, usually at his suggestion. He plans trips to the cinema and ice skating, or just hanging out at someone's house, and watching films or playing on the Nintendo or Sega.

He usually involves Kate and Weird Nicky in these plans too though. Tom seems to have formed some bizarre attachment to Nicky, who he still insists on referring to as 'the Nickster'. I had hoped the novelty of Nicky's weirdness would have worn off by now, but Tom got quite cross with me when I suggested that we ditched Nicky, telling me that 'the Nickster' was a really nice guy and he was surprised at how shallow I was, just because Nicky was a bit 'different'.

A bit different! I'll say.

Different though he is, Nicky is not as weird as he used to be. As part of the drive to flesh out those UCAS forms and impress the universities of Great Britain (or even further afield if you are horrid Rachel, who has taken to wittering about Harvard or the Sorbonne, because according to her, 'Cambridge is letting in all sorts these days'), we've all joined the student newspaper.

I was quite excited about this. I had a Vision of myself in a black polo neck, and maybe some sort of sexy glasses (I'd have to buy them off-the-peg in Boots, Mum refused to take me back to the opticians on the grounds I had gone last year and my eyes were fine), and my hair in a severe (in a hot way) bun, investigating . . . oooh, maybe a story about government corruption? And then one night, Tom and I would be working late on our scoop, and I would take down my hair and remove my glasses and he would gasp at how unexpectedly beautiful I was and then finally he would make his move, and also we would save the world!

This Vision was immediately crushed when we went to the first meeting for anyone interested in getting involved and found Rachel holding forth importantly. She looked disgusted to see Nicky and me, but couldn't say anything because we were with Kate and Tom, who she is still desperate to suck up to. The Upper Sixth students in charge did not seem to understand there was government corruption to be exposed and the world to save though, and instead were boring on about a story on more vegetarian options in the canteen.

That was what not what I had hoped for. I was clutching a proper reporter's style notebook (as was Rachel) and had been poised to set the world alight with my cutting-edge journalism. In my head, it was only a matter of time before the *Telegraph* or *The Sunday Times* called and I was offered a groundbreaking and award-winning column. Or maybe

I would become a war reporter, I had seen a film about them, and they mostly seemed to sit in hotel bars wearing combat trousers and drinking whisky and looking terribly intense before having it off with each other. I could do that. Jas had gently suggested that there might be a bit more to it than that, like the *wars* that would be going on around me. But none of that was going to happen if all the world's cutting-edge media knew about me was an article complaining that macaroni cheese was a boring option for vegetarians and couldn't the dinner ladies see fit to spice things up a bit, both literally and metaphorically.

Still, I thought bravely, one had to start somewhere. And maybe Jas was right, and being a war reporter would be quite scary and unpleasant. And I don't think I would like whisky. So this could be my start of being . . . a top restaurant critic! I rather liked that idea. I would look mysterious and wear elegant black dresses and perch on barstools sipping cocktails and live in a high-ceilinged, book-cluttered apartment in London or Paris or New York, where I would write my articles, bashing away rapidly on a vintage typewriter, a glass of whisky at my elbow.

Was whisky *really* necessary to be a journalist or writer? Or had I just been overly influenced by a photograph I once saw of Ernest Hemingway?

I nobly put up my hand to volunteer for the canteen story, but Rachel intervened, turning to me with her little laugh.

'Oh "Lila",' she sneered, 'I don't think writing anything will be *your* forte. Your talents are surely more as a backroom girl.' Making tea, I fear, is what Rachel has in mind for me.

The editor of the paper though, an intense-looking Upper Sixth boy called Ian, who I suspect is rather affecting his John Lennon spectacles to give him an intellectual air (which definitely had not been my plan if I got some glasses from Boots), murmured something placatory about how everyone would get a chance to write something if they wanted to, and was there anyone though who wanted to do anything else?

To my astonishment, Nicky put his hand up and muttered up he'd quite like to be involved on the photography side. He produced a sheaf of pictures and handed them to Ian, who glanced at them and then said, 'Wow. Mate, these are *really* good! Where did you get them developed?' And he handed them round for everyone to look at.

Nicky said he had developed them himself, his mum had let make a darkroom in the airing cupboard. An unkind part of me thought that I shouldn't be surprised that Nicky had found a hobby that legitimised him sitting in a dark cupboard, but then Kate handed me his photos, and they *were* really good. For a moment, I felt like I was seeing Nicky for the first time, seeing past the *weirdness* and the party pant-wetting, and the cutting up frogs, which now I thought about it, I might have made up. Tom was right. I was shallow. And looking at Nicky's photos, I could glimpse what Tom saw in him.

Then I handed the pictures back to Nicky and he dropped them all over the floor and started scrabbling around to try and pick them up and he was just Weird Nicky again.

Maybe if I was less shallow, more like Tom, a nicer person, then Tom would finally make his move? I resolved once again to become a new and better person. Such a good person that surely Tom could not resist me. But no one really falls in love with the VERY good girls, do they? They usually just end up dying of the consumption or nursing their ailing fathers to the end and then living a noble life of impoverished spinsterhood. It was very hard to strike the perfect balance between being good and kind enough to make Tom love me, but also saucy enough for him to not see me as some sort of untouchable Florence Nightingale figure. Boys in general were very difficult to get right. Too slutty and they won't respect you, too virtuous and they'll say you're frigid. You just had to hope you hit the happy medium for whichever boy it was you fancied.

Now we've all joined the student newspaper, Tom and me and Kate and Nicky seem to be regarded as a foursome at college. Luke and Andy hang out with us sometimes, as do Jas and Mark, but I've never seen so little of Jas in our lives because she is always 'busy' with Mark. I'm happy for her, I really am, but part of me is also jealous.

Jas stayed over last night for the first time in ages, and given things with Mark seem to be getting very serious, I gave her the approved *Just Seventeen* Sex Talk, about not doing anything she didn't feel ready for, and not being pressured into it by Mark and also *precautions*.

Jas was unconcerned by my lecture, and said they weren't even close to that stage, and I was worrying about nothing.

I insisted that you could never be too careful when it came to boys and sex, I had read the problem pages, and then I squeaked in horror as Mum picked that very moment to walk into my bedroom with a pile of clean laundry. How does she *do* that? She has an uncanny ability to appear every single time we are talking about something like that, or if we're watching a film and a rudey bit comes on, sure enough Mum will pop her head in ask if we want a cup of tea. Even when it's just kissing, it's still mortifying to have your mother standing there, and if you pause it, it looks even worse, people freeze framed in all sorts of compromising positions.

Luckily, she didn't appear to have heard what Jas and I were talking about, or she would probably have gone into full GP mode and had a 'doctorly chat' with her about it all and put Jas off for life. I could never forgive myself if Mum ruined Jas's relationship and she was forced to join me in what looks like will be my perpetual spinsterhood. I suppose perhaps if I am destined to spend my life unloved and alone, I could pour all my unrequited passion into a book, like Emily Brontë. But with less of the wretched *imagery* and my characters would definitely make better decisions than Cathy and Heathcliff. I wonder how Cathy's life would have turned out if she *had* been able to consult the *Cosmopolitan* problem page?

Since Jas seems to have totally nailed the whole 'how to have a boyfriend' thing, I asked her for advice on what I should do about Tom. When we're together, he treats me like more than a friend, he puts his arm round my shoulders, he hugs me, even when we're out with Nicky and Kate, or in bigger groups, he'll make excuses to sit next to me, or to be alone with me. I have read *a lot* of his poetry now and I have been exceptionally nice about it. He doesn't seem to be interested in any other girls, Kate is the only other girl we really hang out with, and I know there's nothing but friendship between them. So *why* doesn't he take things any further? I confessed that even after Kate's party, his much-vaunted kiss had been nothing more than a peck on the cheek, and I had perhaps exaggerated the romance of the situation to her just a tiny bit.

Jas was slightly impatient with my pathetic pleas for dating advice, and pointed out that is 1996, and I could take matters into my own hands. I was not, she reminded me, some damsel in distress, waiting for a dashing knight to come and rescue me, and *maybe*, she suggested stoutly, Tom was in fact, a New Man or a metrosexual and he didn't want to be a sexist pig or take liberties. Maybe, Jas insisted, he just really respects me.

I still was unconvinced this meant he liked me, as in *liked* me, but Jas was confident that he wouldn't always be wanting to hang out with me if that was the case, and he was probably worried about making the first move in case I thought he was just After One Thing, and that it was a Good Sign that Tom had not tried to snog me at the first opportunity and had got to know me first. It meant he was sensitive, Jas declared.

Sensitive. He does write all that poetry, I suppose.

I asked Jas what that said about Mark though, as he had made his feelings clear with a week.

'Mark's Mark and Tom is Tom,' said Jas in a very wise and knowing way, which despite the confidence with which she imparted this wisdom, was not really much help. She was insistent, though, that clearly I had to make the first move.

'Me?' I said in horror. 'What, you mean, ME kiss HIM? I couldn't possibly.'

'Of course you can,' Jas said firmly. 'Why *should* he always have to make the first move? Maybe he's talking to Mark or Kate right now saying the exact same thing, and wondering why you've never taken any of the opportunities he's given *you*? After all, who's the one always asking you to go for walks on your own and trying to get you by yourself? You can do this. Go on. For the sisterhood.'

I am unconvinced by Jas's insistence I should kiss Tom. Apart from anything else, that is not how I had ever envisioned my first kiss. Somehow I had always imagined it would take place in an orchard, surrounded by apple blossom. He, whoever he was, would gaze into my eyes, with his own gorgeous (sea-green) eyes, and breathlessly compare my flawless skin (look, it's a PERFECT FANTASY, OK) to the apple blossom, then lean towards me and gently, so very gently, brush my lips with his own, before being overcome with passion and kissing me harder and harder until . . .

Well, I'd never thought beyond that point, other than he would then declare his love for me and we would go off into the sunset and live happily ever after.

There are no orchards where we live though. And even if there were, if I want apple blossom, I'll have to wait till next spring and I'm damned if I'm hanging around for that long, I will basically be a dried-up has-been if I still haven't kissed anyone by then. If my Perfect Dream Kiss is never going to happen, maybe I should just go for it. Get it over with.

No, not 'get it over with'. This is my first kiss, it needs to be a moment to be cherished and treasured, not 'got over with'.

But why *shouldn't* I instigate it? We *are* modern women; *I* do not need to wander the moors lamenting my lost love and catching fevers. I can go out and get what I want. And what I want is Tom.

I have a week to think about it, because I am staying with Dad for the half-term holiday. My stepmother Anita is away visiting her own mother (and sadly has taken her dogs with her, which is a pity, I like her dogs) so it's just Dad and me here. An exciting thing has happened though, as Dad has succumbed and got THE INTERNET. So I have had a very good idea about someone else to talk to about what to do about Tom!

I had been a bit disappointed in the Richard III chatroom on the college computers. Apart from TSNO80, there were no other fans of poor old R3, and a lot of the other posters (OK, there were only about a dozen of them, 'R3' was unsurprisingly not the hot topic of the day) were very snipey about our attempts to defend him from their accusations of murder, tyranny and even impropriety with his niece Elizabeth of York. After a few days of being shouted down, I saw a message in my inbox from TSNO80, ruefully saying that he didn't think there was much more point trying to change the other group members' minds, but we could always talk about R3 here on the private messaging facility, if I wanted, since we both seemed to feel he was rather misunderstood.

So that is what we did. And then our chats drifted away from doomed Plantagenet monarchs on to other things. Like our ambitions, and our hopes for the future. It was strange telling this to someone called TSNO80 so I suggested we call each other something more . . . friendly, though still being mindful of the college's instructions not to reveal identifying details.

TSNO80 said I should call him (for he had indeed turned out to be a him) 'Al', after his favourite Paul Simon song. I didn't really know what to make of that. My *dad* listens to Paul Simon. Was TSNO80 (or 'Al') being a fan a sign he was a loser who liked Dad Music, or that he was in fact very sophisticated in his musical tastes?

But what should I say for a name? In a panic, my mind blank, I suggested Elise, which for some reason was the only name that I could think of. Too late I realised that Elise was in fact, a French version of my own name, Elizabeth, which was probably why it came into my head. Hopefully it would be such a cunning double bluff that Al would be confounded and never realise.

I wondered what his real name was. Perhaps he had also gone for a play on his own name and was in fact called Alan, or Alastair or Alexander or Algernon. Not, I prayed, Algernon. How could you take a boy called Algernon seriously? More to the point, what sort of strange parents would he have, to name a child Algernon in this day and age? Even the Victorian parents who had favoured such names could not have much liked their offspring, to saddle it with the hideous name of Algernon.

Algernon or not, I enjoyed 'chatting' to Al. He was funny and wry, and he teased me and I teased him back in a way

I never felt comfortable doing with Tom. I suppose it was because with Al, I could just be myself. I had nothing to prove and no one to impress. To Al, I was just an anonymous person with a fascination for R3. I didn't have to be the cool girl or pretend to like strange poetry or music that I didn't understand.

I felt like I could tell Al anything. I never been able to be so honest or open with anyone, not even Jas. I had even told him about my dream to be a writer, and when I told him about the elaborate scenarios I imagined for my life, such as War Reporter Whisky Drinker or Restaurant Critic Vintage Typewriter, he laughed but in a nice way and didn't say I was mental or sad or delusional. He told me that it was important to exercise my imagination if I wanted to be a writer. I had never thought about it like that before, when I spent hours daydreaming about the mythical day when I will Grow Up and all my problems will be solved, because like a butterfly emerging from its chrysalis, I would no longer be boring ordinary Lila MacKay, but someone else. Someone better. Al made me feel like all the dreaming wasn't a waste of time, despite what my teachers always said when they caught me gazing out the window in a reverie yet again. Al made it seem like a valid thing to be doing.

In turn, Al told me things about himself. His interests and passions. He loved science, and said if my goal was to be a famous writer languishing on the Left Bank in Paris (just languishing in an elegant way on a velvet chaise longue, not in a starving-to-death-in-a-garret sort of way) then his was to win the Nobel Prize. For what, I had asked, and he had replied:

:-D :-D :-D For everything.

Everything? What, like everything?

Why not? OK, not literature. I'll let you have that one ;-)

Thanks. That's very kind of you. Are you even going to win the Peace Prize?

Yes, obviously. Because once I've won the physics, chemistry and physiology prizes, I'll be the greatest scientist the world has ever seen, and I'll invent something to end all wars. You'll see. You'll probably win your literature prize for the amazing book you write about me.

What makes you think I'll want to write a book about you?

Durrr. Why wouldn't you want to write a book about me? I'm going to bring about world peace, end famine and disease and YOU KNEW ABOUT IT FIRST! I'm giving you a SCOOP here. It would be RUDE of you not to write a book about me.

OK. WHEN you bring about world peace, end disease etc etc, I promise I'll write a book about you.

Thank you, Elise. That wasn't so hard, was it? I'm not asking for much after all. Given I'm going to totally save the world!

Hahahaha.

The one thing Al and I hadn't discussed though was romance, and love. I spent so much time thinking about Tom and worrying about what he thought about me, and whether he liked me or not, that it had been nice to have a romance-free space, a *Tom*-free place to talk about anything other than him. I am now quite firmly convinced I must be in love with him. Why else would he occupy so much of my time and my energy?

I still wasn't quite sure of the etiquette of this 'place' though, and I wondered if talking about other people here would be odd. I wasn't sure how I would feel if Al started talking about girls he liked. This was our safe place. But, odd or not, Al was the only boy I knew, even if I'd never actually met him, who I could possibly talk to about this. I hoped he'd understand, and be able to give me advice from a male point of view. Jas meant very well, I know, but she's not a boy, and despite her insistence that she is now some sort of Relationship Guru based on five weeks of going out with Mark, I am unconvinced she is as knowledgeable as she thinks she is. And I have no intentions of taking her up on her offer to ask Mark what I should do.

I went downstairs to the sitting room and told Dad I needed to use the computer for college work, and also I would need to go on the Internet, to 'look some things up'.

He huffed and he puffed a bit about how it would cost the same as a telephone call to use the Internet, and did I *really* need to use it, and couldn't I just consult an encyclopaedia or a dictionary for any pertinent information I was lacking.

I insisted I could not.

He had one last try at offering me an atlas in lieu of spending a few pence on the wonders of the online world, but I held firm. College, I said. Their website. Stuff. Needed to look up. He eventually sighed and capitulated, with a stern reminder NOT to spend any more time on the Internet than was strictly necessary, Elizabeth, and to think of the cost! I nodded and gave him my solemn promise I would indeed connect the computer for no longer than I absolutely HAD to. Which was true. I wouldn't. But I did have to talk to Al. My whole life might depend on it.

Dad stumped out to his shed, still muttering of expensiveness. I got the impression he was regretting both getting the Internet and telling me about it. But it was too late now, for knowledge is power.

I logged on and messaged Al. I was hopeful of a reply even at the weekend because he had previously told me he had his own computer in his bedroom with Internet access, and sure enough, he binged me straight back.

Hey Elise, what's up? Didn't think I'd hear from you this week, everything OK?

Yeah, everything's fine. I'm at my dad's today, using his computer. Do you have time to chat?

Always time to chat to you. What do you want to talk about? I was reading this article I found on a website about how Henry Tudor could have broken into the Tower of London and murdered the Princes in the

Tower to frame Richard and discredit him. Will I send it to you? It's a bit far-fetched but it might give you a laugh.

Sure. Though actually, I was wanting to talk to you about something else. A bit more personal.

We're not really meant to talk about personal stuff on here, Elise.

I know. But . . . it's more like general advice? Like, from a male point of view?

Oh OK, sure, I'll try to help if I can. Maybe don't apply the WWRD rule though.

WWRD?

It stands for What Would Richard Do. I ask myself that sometimes, when I don't know what to do. Usually the answer is not to do what Richard would.

But I thought you were an R3 supporter, Al?

I am, but he wasn't the luckiest of people, was he? Anyway, what can I help you with?

I attempted to explain about Tom. About how close we had become, about the way he would ask to meet up after college or at weekends, the way he always walked me home, put his arm round me, lent me his jacket, had deep and serious and intense and meaningful conversations with me. How we talked about all sorts of things. But that nothing else had happened and I didn't know what to do, if he liked me, or what exactly was going on with him. I admitted I didn't really have much experience with boys, and I was finding it all very confusing, and told him my best friend had said she thought I should make the first move, and what did Al think about that?

I must admit that I don't have much experience with girls either. So I don't really know what to say?

Do you think he likes me though? Would you do all those things with a girl if you didn't like her?

I don't know. Probably not. Not the pulling her away to be on my own with her, or the jacket or the arm around her things, no. Those are all things you do for a girl you like, I think.

So you think he does like me? But what should I do? What would you do if you liked a girl? What would you do if a girl kissed you first?

You're asking the wrong guy there, Elise.

What do you mean?

I don't know if we should be talking about things like this?

Please, Al. I just really need some advice, and there's no one else I can ask. Every other boy I know is a friend of the guy I'm hopelessly in love with, so I can't say anything to him.

You're in LOVE with this guy?

I think so, yes. So, do you think I should make the first move?

Oh Elise, like I said, how would I know?

Well, what happened with your first kiss with your girlfriend?

I don't have a girlfriend. Why would you think I have a girlfriend?

I just . . . assumed. Someone as cool and funny and NICE as you must have a girlfriend.

Well, I don't. Bye Elise.

And with that, Al logged off abruptly.

What had I said? Was it so terrible that I had thought he must have a girlfriend? I had been trying to be nice. I stared hopefully at the screen for a while, hoping he would come back so I could apologise, ask him why he had left, but he didn't, and then Dad came in and started chuntering wildly about wasting money, and I must surely have been on for long enough, and for heaven's sake, what if someone was trying to phone him, they wouldn't be able to get through, and it might be *important*, or Anita might need to get hold of him.

I don't believe Dad ever gets important phone calls apart from when he is on call, which is fair enough that no one is allowed to tie up the phone line then in case someone needs their spleen urgently removed or something. Anita, if she was trying to ring, wouldn't be phoning for anything desperate either, she would just be wanting to check that Dad wasn't having too much fun with me, or spending money on me that could be better spent on her. I did intend to extract a promise for driving lessons when I finally turn seventeen, while Anita wasn't here to explain at length why it simply wouldn't be possible for my father to make such a financial contribution to his only child. At least if I could wring the promise from him while she was away, it would be harder for him to renege once Anita was back.

It is my greatest fear that one day I will get the call from Dad to tell me that Anita was With Child. It obviously would be bad enough that I would have to face the fact that they had Definitely Done It, but also, I would almost certainly be cut off entirely in favour of the Spawn of Anita. My only hope is that she is far too selfish to have a baby and too involved with her Border terriers, who hopefully fulfil her feeble maternal feelings.

Despite my disbelief that Dad was waiting like a coiled spring to hear from Roger Patterson about next Sunday's game of golf, I dutifully got off the computer. After all, what was the point, if Al wasn't there?

MONDAY 21ST OCTOBER

I sneaked back on to the computer a few times yesterday when Dad was busy, to see if Al had logged on. I'd sent one short message just saying that I was very sorry if I'd said anything to upset him, but there was no response.

This morning, Dad had suggested he took me shopping and out for lunch. Normally I'd have been thrilled about this, but I just wanted to keep checking to see if Al had replied. I could hardly say that though, and it was very nice of Dad to want to make the effort with me.

For a brief, wild moment, I considered asking Dad what I should do about both Tom and Al, which is clearly a sign of my desperation. I could already hear his reply about Tom, that if Tom was acting like a gentleman, there was no need to go throwing myself at him like a harlot, and anyway, I shouldn't be wasting my time mooning over boys, when I had important things to be doing, like working for my exams, and had I decided what on earth I was going to *do* with my life with these French, English and History A-levels and was I *quite* sure it was too late to change courses to do subjects that would get me into medical school?

And that would just be the response to telling him about Tom. I couldn't even *fathom* how I would explain Al. 'Well, there's this boy I've never met, but I talk to him through the computer because we have a lot in common, for example we both really like Richard III, and maybe I'll become an archaeologist and find where Richard is really buried, and surely that's a respectable and practically scientific career, isn't it, Daddy, but anyway, so I've upset this boy I've never met by saying I thought he had a girlfriend and he doesn't but now he's not talking to me because of it, but if he doesn't ever read my message, I don't even know who he is or his real name, or where he is or how to find him and make it up to him, but I find myself really missing talking to him, which is ridiculous when I've never even seen his face.' Dad would be baffled, confused, convinced Al was some kind of dubious human trafficker out to debauch and ruin me, and end by giving me the same lecture as he would over Tom about wasting my time on boys, career prospects etc.

Nonetheless, as I trailed round the shops, Dad spluttering behind me about 'HOW much for a T-shirt? It's not even all there. It's half a T-shirt. How are they charging double the money for half the T-shirt? And that's not a skirt, Elizabeth, that is a . . . a . . . PELMET!' I kept thinking about what I could possibly do to make amends to Al.

If this was a film, I would be a cool computer person, with an edgy haircut, who could hack into the college systems and track him down and also hack into the Pentagon and prevent a missile crisis at the same time. But I barely know how to use a computer. I only found out how to copy and paste things last week.

At the very least in a film, I'd have a friend, probably a dark and handsomely brooding friend who was secretly in love with me but who would never tell me, but anyway, he could do the hacking / missile foiling / Al-finding for me. And then once he'd found Al, we'd get on Broodingly Handsome Friend's motorbike – no, not a motorbike, think what the helmet would do my hair, OK, some kind of cool vintage American car – and Mr Brooding would drive me to Al's and I'd leap out the car and explain everything and Al would understand immediately and everything would be all right and then he would kiss me and

OH!

I let out an audible gasp in TopShop beside the earring rack, which caused Dad to say, 'Elizabeth? Did lunch give you indigestion too? Do you need one of my Rennies? I'm not surprised, that soup is repeating dreadfully on me! Too much garlic, in my opinion.'

It wasn't the soup though (which had been very garlicky, but I had eaten and enjoyed regardless, because what did it matter if I stank of garlic, it wasn't like anyone was ever going to get close enough to me to be bothered by it). It was the sudden realisation that . . . it seemed like I fancied *Al,* as well as Tom.

How? How could I be so in love with Tom, and also thinking about Al like that? And how could I feel like that about someone I hadn't even met? I didn't even know what he looked like.

It didn't matter anyway, because the only person I knew who was clever enough with computers to find out who Al really was was Weird Nicky, and there was no way I was undergoing the humiliation of explaining to *him* what had happened. How could Nicky possibly understand? What did he know about love? Or sex? I could more see my old teddy falling in love or being moved by uncontrollable passion than I could see Nicky comprehending such things.

I had to admit, my eternal spinsterhood was looking more and more likely, now it turned out I could make men shun me without them even *meeting* me. That was it. There was no hope for me.

'Are there any moors near here?' I asked Dad, who looked nonplussed to have such an enquiry in the middle of Top Shop. He said he thought so, and enquired why. He looked even more nonplussed when I said it was because I wanted to go for a walk, and then I had to make up excuses that it was for a college project, when really, I just wanted to shout

Don't QUESTION me, Father, if I need to bestride the moors contemplating writing a great work of thwarted passion and love eternal to make up for the shrivelled apricot that is my loveless and rejected heart! Did Parson Brontë question Emily? I bet he didn't, I bet he just said, 'Carry on, love, and try not to die of the consumption before you have finished.'

Obviously, I just sort of shrugged about the whole walk thing, and Dad sighed and said, 'You really want to go for a walk on the moors now? Instead of shopping?'

I nodded my head, and Dad shrugged and turned to leave the shop.

'Wait!' I cried. 'Can I just get this top and these jeans first?'

Later that evening, post walk, which had not had the romance or drama that I had hoped for, and had mainly just ruined my Adidas trainers and made Dad and me fall out, as he shouted at me to look out and not fall in a bog and I had fallen in a bog and then he had grumbled all the way the home about how much mud I was getting over his car, Dad suddenly remembered he had a Rotary meeting that he said he couldn't miss, and would I be OK on my own for a couple of hours?

I looked up from my crouch on the kitchen floor, where I was dejectedly scrubbing at my trainers, trying to remove the bog stench and filth and made brave 'I'll be fine' noises. I might as well get used to being alone. After all, this was my fate now. Alone forever.

After Dad had gone out, and I'd put my poor shoes on the radiator to dry, and got the boggy jeans I was wearing earlier out of the washing machine and hung them up, as Dad had insisted they went straight in the wash, and I'd had a shower, I was at a bit of a loose end. There was nothing on the TV. I cheered up a bit when I remembered the new top and jeans and went and tried them on and was pleased with the effect. I hoped Tom would like them, and then I remembered it probably didn't matter now I was officially a Man Repeller.

Finally, out of boredom, I decided to log on to the computer. If nothing else I could judge the idiots in the old R3 group for their slavish adherence to Henry Tudor. And possibly plan my latest career idea to be an archaeologist. Not an Indiana Jones type archaeologist, that would be silly. I had no desire to be chased down tunnels or dive under crushing rocks, or even to defeat the Nazis. No, I would dig in Egypt, and wear a white shirt despite the digging, because it would only be sandy, and floaty trousers and tie my hair back with a silk scarf.

Maybe not the scarf round my hair. I had tried tying it back with a bandana a couple of weeks ago, and Mum had enquired why I was dressed as a Soviet housewife going to queue for beetroot, and I had to admit she had a point. A *silk* scarf would probably give a *totally* different effect though. And then there would a French archaeologist, who would see me discovering the amazing lost treasures of the Pharaohs, and he would be charmed by my English rose complexion, and be unable to resist kissing me by the Nile in the moonlight, and then . . .

Oh, WHY did everything, *everything* have to come back to awful old love?

All right, no. I would reject him, the French archaeologist, there by the water, as the warm breeze ruffled my hair, my soft, sexily tousled hair, from which he had gently tugged the scarf, so he could inhale its intoxicating perfume.

'Non, Jean Pierre,' I would whisper tenderly. 'Non.'

Ha, Father dearest, 'What use is French?' you said. Well, it will probably be quite useful when I have to turn down amorous Frenchmen in order to explain to them that my work is my first, my only love, and that I am devoted, nay *married* to it, and thus, I cannot return his feelings, nor his kisses, and now I must go, 'Au revoir, Jean Pierre,' and I would turn and run so lightly up the riverbank that Jean Pierre would wonder if I had been there at all, or if I had just been a river sprite or a ghost. I would return to the dig site, and throw myself into my labours, and become feted and adored by the British Museum and travel the world archaeologising, and one day, when I was an old lady, and the veritable Grande Dame of Archaeology, I would be in a Parisian bookshop, signing my latest book, a seminal work on how I discovered what *really* happened with Cleopatra and Mark Anthony and Julius Caesar, and an old, but still dashing, man would come in, and lay something on the table in front of me, and say softly, '*Chérie*, I think you have forgotten something,' and it would be the silk scarf he had taken from my hair all those years ago and treasured ever since. 'I have never forgotten you, *chérie*,' he would tell me.

'I see now, you were greater than anything I could have offered you. But I will always love you . . .'

Oh bloody hellfire! What was wrong with me?

I was *trying* to give up on Love and concentrate on a Career and Being An Independent Feminist Modern Woman as Jas was always telling me I must be, and again I just end up daydreaming about imaginary men falling in love with me!

Sullenly I turned on the computer. I might as well make the most of it, I thought, before Dad came home wailing about his precious phone bill.

There was a message in my inbox.

I nearly didn't even look, convincing myself it would only be from the college about coursework credits or something equally tedious, but I decided how much worse if I waited an hour to look, telling myself it would be nothing, but hoping all the while it was from Al, and *then* it wasn't. I might as well just get it over with now. But it *was*. It was from Al.

I hardly dared open it, in case all he had come on to say was, 'Go away, you horrible beast and never darken my inbox again.' But I closed my eyes and clicked, and then opened them again nervously.

Ooooh, it was a long message. Surely it wouldn't take that many paragraphs to tell me he never wanted to hear from me again? Unless he had decided to send me an essay about what a terrible person I was, and surely, he didn't know enough about me yet to write *that* much about how awful I am? I took a deep breath and began to read.

Dear Elise,

God, this is harder to write than I thought it would be. I'm sorry I went off on Saturday when you asked about a girlfriend and said you just assumed I would have one. That was nice of you to think that. I wish you were right. The truth is, there is someone. I've been in love with her for a long time. I think she's amazing and I would do anything for her, but I don't think she even knows I exist. Wow, that sounds a bit creepy when I write it down. Obviously, she knows I exist. I'm not secretly hiding in her garden at night spying on her through the window. That sounds even creepier. I'm definitely not doing that. Please keep reading while I try to explain.

It's just that she's this funny, cool, beautiful girl. She's so far out of my league that I know she would never think of me as boyfriend material. She's kind of going out with the sort of guy that girls like that go out with – the cool guy, the good-looking guy, the guy who doesn't have a weird obsession with R3! I don't know if it's serious between them, but it doesn't matter. If it wasn't him, it would be some other good-looking popular boy. If she notices me at all, it's as a friend. I know there is no way someone like that could ever like me. Which makes it hard, because I love her so much. I do stupid things, just to be near her, to see her or to speak to her for a moment. And it makes me sad sometimes, because the guy she's seeing, he's a really nice bloke and all that, but I know, I just know, he doesn't love her like I do. I'd do anything for her. Literally <u>anything</u>. But it doesn't matter what I do, and it never will.

So, I guess you touched a nerve, asking what you should do about this boy you say you are in love with. I don't know what you should do. I've never had a relationship. I've never even kissed a girl. There, I've said it. I've never wanted to kiss anyone but her. But I'm going to have to get over her one day and move on, and I don't know how I'm supposed to do that. In books and films, when someone is unrequitedly in love with a girl who doesn't care about them, either the girl turns out to be a total bitch and the scales fall from their eyes and they meet someone else, someone nicer, or she sees the light and falls in love back with him. Neither of those things are going to happen for me. I don't think she's a bitch. Even when she sometimes is unkind, she's still funny and I don't think she really means it. And she'll never fall in love with me. So how can I advise you on what to do about this boy, when I don't even know how to get over this girl?

Part of me wants to tell you to go for it. Maybe this boy really likes you and doesn't know how much you like him and is afraid of saying anything and making a fool of himself, and if you make the first move, he'll be delighted and over the moon. That's because that is the thing I would love most in the world to happen for me. But I have no idea about this boy or your situation, and it's hardly fair to use you as a guinea pig for my own disastrous love life. Or lack of.

So, I don't know what to suggest you do. What I want the girl I love to do, isn't necessarily what you should do. And I am the last person you should listen to about love. What can a loser like me tell anyone?

The only real, unselfish advice I can give you is – I know you like this boy, but are you sure you're in love with him? From what you've told me about him, sure he sounds great, but you don't sound like you can really be yourself around him. How can you be in love with someone if you have to hide who you really are to make them like you? But again, what do I know? Maybe my girl (not that she's 'my girl', but I hope you know what I mean?) would like me better if I could be someone else when I'm with her. But I don't know how to be anyone but myself, and also I don't want to be someone else for her. I want her to love me for ME, not for some fictional person I have invented to please. And you should want that too. At the very least, that is what love should be – loving the person for who they really are, don't you think?

I'm sorry I can't be more help to you. I hope you aren't too horrified by how pathetic I am. I love talking to you, and I value our friendship, and really appreciate that you felt able to confide in me. I hope me doing the same hasn't freaked you out too much.

Your friend,

Al.

Wow. I was stunned. And also – I hated this girl. Al might say she was not a bitch, but she certainly sounded like it, leading poor Al on while going out with her popular cool boyfriend who was probably incredibly pretentious and boring and just had nicer hair than Al. How *shallow* was this girl that she couldn't see how amazing and kind and sensitive and lovely Al was? What was she thinking? OK, there was a chance this boyfriend was *actually* Mr Perfect and also kind, sensitive etc, but what were the chances?

Poor Al. *I* wouldn't treat him like that. I'd see him for what he really was. And now, as well as fancying a boy I knew nothing tangible about, I was also jealous of a girl I knew nothing about, except that in my head she was called something like Marisa and I would put money on her having shiny swishy hair, like Kate's. Or maybe Marisa's not horrible at all. Al's description of her is very like Kate, and Kate is lovely. I suppose it *could* be Kate, and Al is someone at our college?

Wait, no, Kate doesn't have a boyfriend. Unless someone has mistaken Tom or Weird Nicky for her boyfriend because we've all been hanging out together. Ha ha ha. If anything could have cheered me up tonight it's thought of *Kate* going out with Weird Nicky.

OK, so it's not Kate. That rules out any last hope of Al being someone at our college and me being able to make him fall for me instead, because there is no one else that would fit the description. Rachel would like to think she did, but there is no way anyone as smart as Al would fall for Rachel who really *is* a Grade A bitch.

I could see Al had logged on. He would have seen I had read the message. I needed to reply.

Hi Al,

I'm sorry if I hurt you or made things difficult by asking for your advice, that was never my intention. And I don't think you're a loser or sad or pathetic. You seem like one of the nicest people I've ever met. Well, not 'met', but you know what I mean. I feel like I've met you. I wish I had met you. Do you think one day, like at uni or something we'll actually meet each and have no idea that we are 'Al' and 'Elise'? How freaky would that be? Would we work out who we are? Now I'm going to have to start uni asking every clever guy I meet what he thinks about R3! Unless by then you've decided I am a total loser too and deny knowing anything about him when a mad girl comes up to you in Fresher's Week demanding to know your opinions on him! Ha ha, just joking, obviously.

Seriously though, thank you for being so honest with me. If it makes you feel any better, well, I've never kissed a boy either. So there we are. We're both as bad as each other, I guess. Marisa must be mad if she doesn't see how great you are though. Any girl would be lucky to have you in love with her. If she doesn't realise that, then it's her loss. I think you're amazing, and she should chuck her stupid boyfriend and go out with you straight away.

I don't know if I'm in love with this boy. I don't know what it feels like. I feel like I spend most of my life daydreaming about <u>being</u> in love but I don't know how it really feels with a real flesh-and-blood person who is there right in front of me. Maybe that's why I find Heathcliff and Cathy's love story so unconvincing in *Wuthering Heights*, because Emily Brontë never had a relationship and so had to imagine what a passionate love affair would be like. Maybe I just want to be in love so much I am convincing myself that I am.

I think if I could just be sure he liked me, then I would feel freer to be myself with him. But then, you're right. Even if I was sure he liked me, if I've never been myself with him, then it's not me he likes. So how can I then let him see the real me, when he likes the girl I have created for him? Just like I can't really love the romantic heroes I create in my head (who are much MUCH nicer than Heathcliff – I do judge Emily a bit for that, if she was going to invent the ultimate doomed romantic couple, she could have made both of them far better people, instead of a spoilt brat and a psychopath! God, I keep going on about *Wuthering Heights*, and I don't even know if you've read it!)?

This is so HARD, isn't it? Do you think I'm mad, falling in love with imaginary men, and pretending to be someone I'm not to make a boy fall in love with me?

Elise x

I had never written Al such a long message. It felt cathartic, to finally have someone I could confess so many things to. Just telling him I wanted to be a writer had made that feel so much more real, and now, talking to him about Tom, but honestly – more honestly than I could even to Jas – was helping to sort out all my tangled and confused feelings. Even if they weren't helping with the confused feelings I now had about *Al*. Feelings that seemed to be increasing with every message he sent.

Oooh, he'd replied.

I'm confused. Who is Marisa?

I had to explain that Marisa was the name I had given the girl he was in love with and enquired what he envisaged my own beloved to be called.

Nigel. And yes, I have read *Wuthering Heights*. I saw 'Marisa' reading it, and thought it might give us something to discuss. It didn't work, as she seemed to love it, and just kept talking about the 'imagery' and I wasn't that keen on it myself.

NIGEL!!!!!????? What? I gave you Marisa, a cool, sexy American sort of a name, and I get NIGEL? Nigels are not sexy! Nigels are not hot! No one breathes 'Niiiiigel' in a throaty, husky voice in the throes of passion! NIGEL! Nigel IS a feeble loser, who breathes through his mouth and has a permanently dripping nose and clammy palms.

Nigel is someone who is not good enough for you. You deserve better than a Nigel. You deserve someone who makes you feel like you can be yourself with them. That's why I've called him Nigel.

I don't know if that person exists. The only person I've ever been able to be myself with in real life is my best friend. I'll call her Susan, because Susans are kind and trustworthy and steady and reliable, and she's always been all those things for me. The only other person I've ever been able to really be myself with is you.

I've always found Susans to be psycho bitches myself. But if you want a Susan for your best friend go ahead. You're lucky to have someone in real life you can talk to like that though. I wish I did.

Oh Al! I wish you did too! I've got to go now, my dad's just come home, and he'll be yelling at me to get off the computer. Talk soon.

Elise xx

EMILY

CHAPTER THIRTEEN

I was stunned by the latest revelations in Lila's diary. There is a *lot* to unpack there!

Firstly, Lila / Elise and Al. I was wondering how you can fall for someone you don't even know, but I was sure I was hopelessly in love with Toby just from seeing his smile across the lunch hall the day he started at our school. I suppose this is the other way round. Lila knows loads about Al, just not what he looks like.

There seem to be so many different ways to be in love though. With Toby, I feel all butterflies and silly and awkward, even more so the times I've seen him looking over at me, and I thought I would die of joy when he smiled at me one day and more than anything in the world, I want him to kiss me. For months I have felt that if he would just kiss me and ask me to be his girlfriend, then everything would be OK with the world, nothing else would matter.

But then, Lila seemed to feel like that about Tom. And now she thinks she is in love with Al as well. And I know she doesn't end up with either of them, so maybe despite all those strong feelings, she wasn't in love with them at all. She seemed almost as in love with the imaginary characters in her head and perhaps her romantic dream of an archaeologist on the banks of the Nile was how she ended up marrying Dad instead?

I think it's much easier to imagine what love is when all you really know of it is films and books when they kiss and the credits roll and that's it. But now I'm wondering happens after that? Love in real life seems to be so much more complicated than in the fairy stories, where all you need is the handsome prince to sweep you off your feet and you live happily ever after.

I am also starting to see where my obsession with running away to the moors and people dying of the consumption comes from. Poppy says that is weird, she says she's never even heard of anyone dying of the consumption, which makes me suspect Mum has been sending me subliminal messages about it my whole life, given how obsessed *she* also seems to be with it, despite how incredibly rude she is about Emily Brontë.

Lila's diary has given me so much to think about. Uncle Tom had said this was to make me see that Mum *did* understand what it was like to be a teenager, and to make me realise she also understands what I'm going through, but actually this is just making me more confused. And also, all the talk about how Lila shouldn't wait for Tom to make the first move is making me consider if I should ask Toby out? Not hang around? Maybe that's what he's waiting for?

I really want to read on and find out what happens next, to give me an idea of what I should do about Toby, but I have to go to sleep, and anyway, I can't do anything till Saturday, so there's plenty of time. Maybe I'll just read one more entry. Maybe two. Sleep is for the weak, after all. I don't even know what that means, Mum says it sometimes, usually when she's not had enough sleep, so I think she might be being sarcastic. I should definitely read a bit more though, so I've time to think about what I should do about Toby when I get my phone back.

LILA

CHAPTER FOURTEEN

MONDAY 28ᵀᴴ OCTOBER 1996

Al and I continued to message all week, every time Dad was busy. He will go ballistic when he sees the phone bill, but I'm back at Mum's now, so there's not a lot he or Anita can do about the phone bill.

It won't be that bad anyway. Dad just has the same mentality of everyone who grew up with the last of the rationing from the Second World War, that everything has be eked out and scrimped on. Unless it's to do with golf or Border terriers, in which case he and Anita seem happy to throw money at it. I do understand in the case of the Border terriers, I sometimes harbour hopes of Anita giving me a puppy, in which case I would take back everything I have ever said about wicked stepmothers, but Mum always vetoes it when I mention how nice it would be if we had one of Anita's puppies, and points out that with her at work and me at college all day, there is no one to look after a puppy and we couldn't leave a dog all day on its own, that would be cruel.

I found it hard to concentrate in college today, because all I could think about was chatting to Al after classes when I could get to the computer lab. Admittedly, sitting with Tom again at lunchtime after a week of not seeing him distracted me somewhat, as did the huge hug he gave me, and how genuinely pleased he seemed to be to see me.

And then at lunch he had insisted on sitting next to me so we could talk about our holidays. His trip to his family's holiday cottage in Cornwall did sound a little more exciting than my week at Dad's but I styled it out as best I could, though I could almost hear Al raising his eyebrows and saying 'Why not just be yourself?' as I tossed my hair and laughed and embellished the rather prosaic activities Dad and I had partaken of to sound far more exciting, as I tried not to be jealous of Kate's Lanzarote tan.

At the end of the day, I dashed out of my last class, waved to Jas who was coming along the corridor with Mark (of course), and said I wasn't getting the bus home with her, because I needed to 'finish an essay'.

Jas complained I seemed to have more essays than anyone else she knew, and I always seemed to be in the computer lab working on an essay.

'Well, you know me, I'm a perfectionist,' I said breezily, and Jas burst out laughing and told me I was funny.

Then Weird Nicky, appeared from behind me in that disconcerting way he had and made me jump, and he said he'd walk up to the computers with me, because he wanted to talk to me

Nicky was looking quite normal for once, so I agreed, and I even found myself remarking that I liked his T-shirt.

He blushed, and admitted Kate had picked it out for him.

'Kate and you went *shopping?*' I was incredulous. 'When? HOW?'

Nicky blushed even harder and mumbled he had mentioned to Kate that he always bought the same things because he never knew what to buy and how did she always look so nice, and apparently Kate had taken pity on him and offered to take him shopping.

'Kate is so lovely' Nicky breathed, his eyes gleaming fervently behind his glasses. Oh dear. Poor Nicky had obviously developed a thumping great crush on Kate. I couldn't help but feel this was going to be terribly awkward for them both. Then I had an awful thought – he had wanted to talk to me. Oh please, Nicky – don't ask me to set up some sort of date scenario with Kate!

It was OK though, because it turned out Nicky just wanted to invite me to his birthday party on Saturday. I made vague noises about how nice of him that was while I grasped for a plausible excuse.

But then Nicky said that Jas and Mark were coming. 'And Kate, and Luke and Andy. And Tom,' he added. 'So will you come too?'

So I didn't really have any option but to agree to go, since all my friends were already going. Why had I been the last to be asked? Was I an *afterthought?* Ugh.

I was still smarting from the idea of being Weird Nicky's B list, but I cheered up when I saw there was a message from Al that he'd sent at lunchtime, checking in with me and how it was going with 'Nigel'. I hit reply.

Actually I have a plan. I'm going to a party this weekend, and I think I'm just going to tell him how I feel. You keep telling me I should be honest, and to be myself with him. Well, surely telling him how much I like him should be part of that?

How's 'Marisa'?

The green dot appeared next to Al's name. I waited for his reply.

Go for it then with old Nige, if you think it's the right thing to do. He's a fool if he doesn't immediately declare his undying love for you, any guy would be mad not to.

Marisa is more loved up than ever with Him. I had vaguely hoped she might have had a holiday romance and come back and dumped him, but it doesn't look like it. She was really nice to me too. Every time I think maybe I'm getting over her and could think about someone else, she seems to give me hope. Do you think I'm mad to keep hoping? I know it's shallow of me, but she had a new outfit on too, and looked so gorgeous.

I felt yet another pang of envy. I had worn the new top and jeans Dad had bought me and Tom hadn't even noticed. Maybe he didn't like what I was wearing? I'd been phasing out the lumberjack shirts and charity-shop jeans and replacing them with more mainstream clothes, trying to make it look like I was just gradually changing my style from the grungy look I'd accidentally started college with. But once again, I supposed I still wasn't being honest with Tom.

Yet, I reminded myself. I wasn't being honest with him *yet*.

I was starting to wonder though, if I really cared as much about Tom as I did about Al now.

When I was with Tom, and looking at that floppy blond hair, and the smile that could light up the whole canteen, and he gazed at me through those stupidly long lashes and gave me a grin just for me that sent shivers down my spine, yes, I was sure I was madly in love with him. How could I not be? Just *look* at him! But when I wasn't with him . . .

Well, I found myself thinking less and less about Tom, about clever and witty things to say to him, and more and more about Al, and the clever and witty things *he'd* said, and coming up with funny ways to relate the mundane happenings of the day in a way to make him laugh.

I had half hoped that when Al said he sometimes thought he was getting over Marisa, that it would be for *me*. That one day, he'd send me a message saying, 'To hell with that stupid creature, I adore you, tell me your real name, and let's meet up, because I see now that Marisa is not worthy of my love, unlike you.' But that was unlikely to happen. And Tom – well, Tom was lovely, and handsome, and *here*. And also did not appear to be in love with a snarky cow like Marisa.

Tom suddenly appeared in the computer lab looking worried because Jas had said I was here working on an essay and he thought he had forgotten an English assignment. I hastily invented a history essay instead and he sighed with relief and asked if I wanted to grab a coffee because he had something he wanted to show me.

Oh, please don't be another poem, I found myself thinking, even as I nodded enthusiastically, and started gathering up my bag and coat, hoping he wouldn't notice

Nicky hunched in the far corner and issue the invitation to 'the Nickster' as well. To my joy, although he did see Nicky and wave as he ushered us out the door, he said nothing about Nicky joining us.

I only realised halfway down the stairs that I hadn't replied to Al's message, and had just logged off without saying anything.

We went to a coffee shop on the High Street, where it turned out it was not a poem Tom wanted to show me, but his holiday photos, which he'd had developed in the one-hour service in Boots.

He wanted my opinion on the photos, because he was thinking of taking up photography as a hobby. His face was so earnest as he said this, his eyes so sincere as he pushed the hair out them in a way that did quite peculiar things to me. He carried on talking about his wretched photographs, about how it would look good on his UCAS form and then telling me he was planning on entering the college's photography competition because 'it would be amazing for the uni applications if I won, wouldn't it?''

There it was again. That sheer *confidence* that he was in with a chance of winning, with these . . . well, they seemed perfectly pleasant photos, but they looked to me as though they fell firmly into the category of 'decent holiday snaps'. They certainly weren't a patch on the photos Nicky had shown us.

That gave me an idea, which got me off the hook of having to issue an opinion.

'These look lovely,' I said. 'But to be perfectly honest, I don't know *anything* about photography. Why don't you ask Nicky? Tomorrow,' I added hastily, in case he suddenly went haring off in search of Nicky right now.

Tom grabbed me a huge hug, and declared 'The Nickster' to be a brilliant suggestion, as he told me that he didn't know what he would do without me and my good ideas!

SUNDAY 3RD NOVEMBER

It was Weird Nicky's party last night. The night I had finally decided to push things with Tom and try and make something happen.

I had apologised to Al for running off without replying on Monday, and told him my plan to simply come out and tell Tom how I felt, like a brazen hussy. I did think his only comment about this – 'Well, at least then you'll know one way or the other, won't you?' – was quite lukewarm. He was right though. If Tom had his own Marisa, or if he was just being gentlemanly, at least I would *know*.

Once again, Jas and I spent ages getting ready, and Jas assured me that I was doing the right thing with Tom, telling me how important it was that your first kiss was with someone special, as hers had been with Mark.

Before we left, Jas hoicked up the straps of my Wonderbra, the better to adjust my cleavage. I reminded her she was against Wonderbras and objectifying ourselves for men, and she laughed and reminded me that I was being a feisty feminist taking my needs and desires into my own hands, so it's OK to wear a Wonderbra and flash a bit of flesh if it's about what *I* want, not what *he* wants.

I just nodded wisely, as if I understood. Feminism was confusing. I wasn't entirely sure I saw the difference between wearing a Wonderbra to attract Tom's attention and wearing a Wonderbra because *I* wanted to . . . attract Tom's attention, but there was no time to debate this, we had to go.

We went down to the road and back up Nicky's front path (we had debated scrabbling over the wall but risking laddering our tights and falling in a flowerbed after all the effort we had gone to was not really worth it for the thirty seconds we would save), where Mark joined us.

I thought this really was the perfect night for Tom and me. It was cold, but crisp, the stars were shining, and if there was not an orchard full of apple blossoms, at least Nicky had an apple tree in his garden, which would have to do. I knew about the apple tree because Nicky brought us quantities of apples every autumn, until Mum and I were thoroughly sick of apples, pies and crumbles. This year I had begged Mum, when he appeared with his laden baskets, to tell him we didn't need any, that we'd gone allergic, that we had discovered a forgotten Great Aunt Mabel who was supplying all our apple needs, but Mum just said, 'Don't be silly, darling. It's terribly kind of Nicholas.' We were still eating the wretched apples, so I thought the least the tree could do was provide me with a romantic backdrop.

The only thing that could have made the night more perfect was if the moon had been a full one, not a half one, but there *was* a moon, and one can't have everything.

Nicky flung open his front door, beaming with excitement. It turned out we were the first to arrive. Oh God. I had wanted to be 'fashionably late' but Jas had refused, saying she had arranged to meet Mark outside Nicky's at 8pm sharp and she didn't want him to think she had stood him up. I had suggested she could have just WAVED at him out my window, or better yet, waylaid him to come into my house for half an hour, but Jas was having none of it.

In Nicky's kitchen, which was pretty much as I remembered it from when we used to play together (before the birthday party incident), Nicky handed out beers to everyone, and Jas and Mark started giggling together in the corner. I smiled at Nicky and wished him a happy birthday.

'Cheers.' Nicky clanked his can against mine. He really was being almost normal. Then he cleared his throat awkwardly and said, 'Um, Lila, can I ask you something?'

'No,' I said jokingly, hoping desperately he wasn't going to ask me for something awful, like a birthday kiss, or even worse – a date. Knowing Nicky, he was perfectly capable of asking me to help him cut up a frog to celebrate his birthday.

So I was astonished when he asked me if I knew about the photography competition at college, and said he was thinking of entering in the portrait section, and wondered if I would sit for him.

'Me?' I said disbelievingly. 'What, like model for you?'

Nicky wittered at me for several minutes about how portraits weren't like modelling at all, because it wasn't about the subject's *looks* but about the composition of the photo and he was looking for someone with *interesting* features rather than classical beauty. I felt that was a little rude, he was basically saying, 'It's OK that you're a minger, because you've got an "interesting" face.'

He went on to explain he was hoping to take a few photographs now, before everyone else arrived, and then he'd had an idea for some pictures where I wasn't aware of him, with the party in the background.

'I won't get in the way, I promise, Lila, or cramp your style, I only need one or two, I'll not be hovering over you with a camera all the time or jumping out of bushes at you when you least expect it.'

I flushed. Did Nicky suspect I had designs on his apple tree? But it sounded fun. Something different. And I could already see the story I could turn this into for Al – the time my weird neighbour had me sit for portrait photos. Maybe he would make me hold a cut-up frog though?

'There won't be any strange props, or anything?' I asked suspiciously.

Nicky assured me there would not be. Just me, him and his camera.

'And you won't be expecting me to take my clothes off?' I checked, equally suspiciously.

Nicky's horrified look and recoil was answer enough. Again. Rude.

'OK then. Let's do it.'

Nicky looked thrilled (maybe because I was going to keep my clothes on), and explained he had set things up already in his dining room in the hope I would say yes, and ushered me through. I wondered if it was disloyal to Tom to be helping Nicky with the competition. But there had been something slightly annoying about the way Tom had just been so sure that he could win. Anyway, it wasn't like Tom couldn't also ask me to sit for a portrait if he wanted to.

Perhaps as well as being a writer, capturing perfectly the essence of human existence, I would end up being a famous artist's muse. I could lie on a chaise longue in a Parisian studio, a wolfishly handsome paint-splattered man staring intensely at me from behind his easel. Impossible though it seemed now, maybe even Weird Nicky would grow up to be a famous photographer, and he would tell everyone of how it was really all down to me. 'If Lila MacKay hadn't agreed to pose for me, I would never have managed those iconic shots, without her grace and beauty. I owe her everything.' Not beauty, I suppose. He had been quite clear that I was not beautiful. Maybe bone structure. 'Her exquisite bone structure is a visual poem. It's impossible to take a bad photo of Lila'? Sadly, I knew from my school class photos that this most certainly was not true. Hopefully Nicky could do better than the school photographers.

As he arranged me in a chair, and pointed various lights at me, I looked at him properly under the bright lamps and asked if he'd done something different to his hair. He put his hand up to his head self-consciously and said that Kate had taken him to her hairdressers. It wasn't that though, his hair was a different colour. It used to be really gingery and now it's a sort of dark red. I asked Nicky if he had dyed it.

Nicky laughed. 'Dyed it basically the same colour in a slightly different shade? No, if I was going to dye my hair, I'd have a bit more imagination and dye it pink or blue or purple. It just got darker as I got older. It's been like this for a while now.'

Either way, it looked nice.

He told me to look over towards the window and started fiddling with his camera. Ten minutes later we were done, and everyone else was starting to arrive, having gone for the fashionably late option Jas and Mark had denied me. Tom and Kate appeared, shortly followed by Luke and Andy, and some other people from Nicky's classes that I vaguely knew. The only class Nicky and I had in common was history, so I was surprised by how many people he seemed to know and who had turned up.

A couple of hours later, I put my head on Tom's shoulder and murmured the line I had rehearsed to myself a dozen times, 'I think I need some air. Will you come outside with me?'

Tom jumped up, asking if I was OK and did I want water, and I said I was fine and that it was just very hot in here. We went through the kitchen, where Kate was sitting on the counter attempting to throw peanuts into the mouths of six boys lined up in front of her like performing seals, and Jas and Mark were kissing in a corner, and out the back door. I was relieved to see that my eyes had not deceived me when I had peered out Mum's bedroom window, and there *was* a bench under the apple tree at the bottom of Nicky's garden.

I pointed to it and suggested it would be a good place to sit.

Tom led me over and we sat down. He gave me his jumper and put his arm around me and tipped his head back to look at the stars. 'What a beautiful night. I'd love to go somewhere really remote, with no light pollution and spend the night just lying there watching the stars moving above me.'

I was confused. Did stars move? Surely they stayed still, that was how people navigated by them.

'I suppose they don't move, the Earth moves and gives the illusion of the stars moving,' Tom explained. 'Wouldn't that be amazing, to just be lying on a beach somewhere, watching the stars?'

Well, I thought, this was about as romantic a conversation as anyone could hope for. Surely Tom must be thinking the same as me. Why sit here with his arm around me, talking about watching stars on our own if he didn't want this as much as me?

I turned my face up to his.

He looked down at me.

I took a deep breath. If something was still holding Tom back, then I was going to have to take the plunge. I leaned in towards him and attempted to press my lips to his. Tom leaned towards me for the briefest moment and then jerked his head back.

'I can't,' he blurted. 'I can't do it. I want to, I want to be able to do it, but I can't, I thought I would be able to, I'm so sorry, I'm so sorry, Lila.'

And he leapt up and almost ran back into the house, leaving me sitting alone on the bench in the starlight, still wearing his jumper, trying not to cry and wondering what the hell had just happened?

It's hard to sit outside in November without a coat, and Tom's jumper was very thin. Without the warmth of his body pressed beside me, my teeth were chattering in less than a minute, and I was forced to go inside before I died of hypothermia and they found my poor little frozen body huddled beneath the apple tree, like the Little Match Girl.

By the time I got in the house, I could see Tom in the hallway, shrugging on his jacket and almost *shoving* Kate into her coat, as he had apparently agreed to walk her home, but had suddenly remembered 'Just this thing, I completely forgot, I need to get back, come on Katie, I promised your dad I'd make sure you got home safely' as Luke and Andy protested they could easily walk Kate home if Tom had to go, and dragged Kate, who looked nearly as confused as I was, out the door.

As the door slammed behind them, and everyone looked at each other in surprise, Jas looked over at me, standing inside the back door, watching Tom exiting in haste, and hurried over.

'What happened?' she hissed. 'Did it work? Why did he leave?'

I couldn't speak, only shake my head as the tears threatened to brim over. I sniffed and blinked hard.

Jas asked if I wanted to go home too, and when I nodded, she said if I went out the back and through the side gate, she would get our coats and bags and meet me at the front so I didn't have to talk to anyone.

I nodded again, so grateful that Jas understood without even having to be told, and stumbled out the door again, the door I had skipped out of with such hope less than fifteen minutes before.

Jas found my keys, hustled me in my own front door, yelled, 'Hi Dr MacKay, really boring party, so we're home early' and got me into the safety of my own room before Mum could come into our hall and see my face.

As soon as Jas slammed the door behind us, I collapsed on the bed face down and cried bitterly for what felt like an eternity, while Jas lay next to me and hugged me. Eventually, the racking sobs faded into hiccups and gulps, and then into sniffles. I lay there for a moment, feeling utterly wrung out, and Jas finally asked me what had happened. And then I poured it all out. The apple tree. The stars. Tom's face frozen in fear and then jerking away and fleeing from me into the house.

I just kept repeating how I felt so humiliated and asking Jas what was wrong with me? It had been so bad. Why come outside with me at all if he didn't fancy me? Why spend all that time with me if he didn't fancy me? And if he didn't fancy me, why not just *say*? I mean it would have been *awful*, but the full on running away and leaving was worse. And leaving with *Kate*.

If he was so in love with Kate, why not just *be* with her? Why lead me on all this time? Have they been laughing at me all along, has everyone else known about Kate and Tom and it's all been some sort of sick joke, watching me make a total fool of myself?

Jas was firm that none of our friends would do that. Especially not Kate and Tom, she insisted they were not cruel or spiteful, though Jas didn't know what *was* going on either.

Eventually, after going round and round in circles, and a lot more crying, we fell asleep. I had been sure I wouldn't be able to sleep a wink, but strangely, the emotional stress seemed to have had an exhausting effect and I slept soundly for ten hours and was astonished to wake up with Mum knocking at my door, and saying it was really time to get up now, girls.

I prised my eyes apart, reflecting that at least all the crying had removed my eyeliner and mascara last night, as by the time I fell asleep I was too shattered to think about washing my face, and Jas, loyal friend that she is, had not left my side.

'Ugh,' said Jas, looking in the mirror on my dressing table across the room from the bed. She had a point. This is why we don't sleep in our makeup. Jas wanted to stay with me, but she was very apologetic she had a family lunch thing that she couldn't miss.

After Jas had gone, I shuffled into the shower and stood under the hot water for twenty minutes until it ran out. I had been running over possible scenarios in my mind about where to go from here. Could I leave college and get a job? I couldn't see Mum and Dad allowing that. Maybe I could transfer colleges and go somewhere else, where I'd never have to see any of them again. I could go and live with Dad and Anita and go to college there. Anita would hate it, but I was Dad's daughter, what could she really do?

Maybe, I thought, with a brief glimmer of hope, it would turn out that *Al's* college was in Derbyshire as well, and we would meet in real life and he would be captivated and won over by my beauty (not beauty, I could hear Nicky again explaining he didn't want to photograph me because I was *beautiful* but because I had an *interesting* face, which was practically the same as telling me I was ugly as sin). Maybe just my wit and repartee then. Because that had worked so well for Tom, hadn't it?

As I sat on my bed, in my oldest jeans, and baggiest T-shirt, my wet hair scraped up, because even drying it seemed like too much effort, I realised that even if I could get my parents to agree to any of these plans, there was no way they could be implemented by tomorrow, and come what may, I was going to have to go back into college and face everyone in the morning.

I had just lain down to wallow in the pits of despair again, when Mum knocked on my door to tell me that she was on call for the surgery today and had to go out, she didn't know when she'd be back, but there was stuff in the fridge for dinner. I heard her go back downstairs, and then yell, 'LILA! You've a visitor, I need to go NOW, can you come down?'

Oh God. I didn't want to see anyone. Who on earth could it be? But Mum had to dash off, she was a doctor on call, this could be a life-or-death situation she was going to and I didn't want someone dying on my conscience on top of all my other misery, so I heaved myself off the bed and down to the hall, where Mum was standing impatiently beside the door with Kate.

Kate was looking as radiant as ever, and I was horribly aware of the difference between my red, swollen eyes, scruffy jeans and messy bun and Kate's immaculate appearance, her perfect skin glowing, and her hair, if possible, shinier than ever. As Mum dashed off, I felt a surge of rage that Tom had sent Kate on her own to talk to me and hadn't even had the courage to come himself.

'What do you want?' I asked, trying to sound cold and dignified.

'I wanted to talk to you. About last night.'

'You and Tom left early, that's about it.' I shrugged casually and clenched my fist to drive my nails into my palm to stop myself from crying. Just give the impression you don't care. That however much of a fool you made of yourself, that it doesn't matter. The only thing that could make this situation any worse was to make a scene in front of Kate or Tom, so they knew how *much* I cared, how they had humiliated and hurt me. I would not, could not let that happen. Jas was the only one who would ever know how painful this had been for me. Because the only way I could possibly front this out at college was to pretend it had never happened. And hope that that at least would spoil whatever horrible prank this was.

Kate looked awkward and said her and Tom wasn't what I thought.

'I honestly couldn't care less about you and Tom,' I interrupted her. 'Now if you'll excuse me, I've an essay to be getting on with, so bye, Kate.'

I gestured angrily towards the door, but Kate begged me to come for a walk with her, to give her five minutes of my time. There were things I didn't know, she said, things I *should* know.

This sounded mysterious enough to pique my interest. Perhaps Tom was terribly ill. I could nurse him back to health and he would love me again. Not *again* – he hadn't loved me in the first place. Or maybe Kate and Tom were some sort of international teenage secret agents and wanted to recruit me to their spy ring. That would be more exciting than playing journalists with Ian and Rachel and the ongoing saga of the canteen drama. I could see Kate as a Bond girl. Where would I fit in? Probably some sort of Miss Moneypenny figure, reliable and loyal. Not *quite* as exciting. But I wondered if you could put 'MI5 Agent' on the UCAS form.

And there definitely would be someone at MI5 who could find out who Al really was for me. They could probably have Marisa discreetly 'removed' from the picture as well.

'All right,' I said grudgingly, and shoved my trainers on.

Kate suggested the park, and promised that she would explain everything once we were there. I gave a non-committal grunt. The park was fine, but if MI5 were trying to recruit me, surely the least they could do was pay for a coffee first!

When we got to the park, Kate steered me to an isolated bench on the other side of the duck pond. Oh God. She thought I was a Russian spy, and she was going to murder me with a poisoned umbrella. Or maybe *she* was the Russian spy! I could push her in the pond and foil the Soviets' dastardly plot. They weren't Soviets any more though, were they? The Cold War was over, and we were all supposed to be friends now. Still, best not to trust them. I tensed, ready to fling Kate amidst the mallards if need be. Before I could do that though, a familiar figure came loping down another path and made for the bench.

'What are you doing here?' I asked Tom furiously, before turning to Kate. 'You brought me here under false pretences.'

Kate insisted she had not, but the things she had said I needed to know were Tom's things to tell me, not hers.

Tom, I was gratified to see, looked nearly as awful as me. His sexy hair was lank and greasy instead of artfully tousled and he looked like he hadn't slept a wink. He asked me to sit down and I collapsed sullenly onto the bench beside him. Then he reached over and took my hand as he said, 'I need to explain about last night.'

I snatched my hand back, staring ahead and refusing to look at him. Why make this easy for him by letting him charm his way out of it, like he no doubt always did?

'It wasn't you,' he said. 'It was me.'

'Ha!'

I was quite pleased with that. I have never quite managed to pull off a sardonic laugh, but I think I pretty much nailed it that time.

'No, really,' Tom pleaded. 'When you went to kiss me, I wanted to kiss you back. Or rather, I *wanted* to want to. I wanted to *so* badly. But in the end, I couldn't. I just couldn't.'

'Is this supposed to be making me feel better?' I demanded.

'I don't know if it will make you feel better or not,' Tom admitted. 'But you deserve to know the truth, because I haven't treated you very fairly.'

I sniffed, to indicate that there would be no argument from me about that. It was supposed to be a cold, sneering, dismissive sniff, to put him in his place, but I just sounded like I needed a tissue.

'Please believe me.' Tom tried to take my hand again. 'You are so beautiful, and so funny. If I could be with any girl, it would be you. But . . .' He stopped and swallowed hard and looked at Kate.

'Go on, Tom,' she said, putting her hand on his shoulder. 'You can do this. You said yourself, Lila deserves to know.'

Tom nodded, then let go of my hand and just stared at the ground. I frowned. This was not how this was supposed to be going. I was supposed to scornful and angry, and Tom was supposed to grovel before my righteous fury. But it was increasingly hard to keep my rage burning, Tom looked so . . . broken, and Kate looked so anxious, and then he finally muttered, still looking at the gravel path, 'I'm gay, Lila.'

'What?'

Tom just gave a sob, and Kate sat down on his other side and wrapped her arms round him. 'Tom's gay, Lila,' she said gently. 'No one knows except me. And now you. And please don't tell anyone else, Tom doesn't want that yet.'

'I'm sorry,' Tom gulped. 'I'm sorry I let you think something could happen between us.'

I was too stunned to really know what to say. Tom being gay was the last thing I had expected. Of all the scenarios I had run through as being the explanation for last night, I honestly would have listed the MI5 agent one as more likely.

'I don't understand,' I said. 'Why didn't you just tell me that in the first place? It's not the sixties, it's OK to be gay now. Why can't you just say that's who you are?'

'It's not OK if you're me,' said Tom bitterly 'Not in my family. My dad is disappointed enough in me writing poetry, not wanting to go into finance like him, liking art and music, instead of rugby and cricket and other good, wholesome MANLY pursuits.'

'I mean, being gay is quite a manly pursuit.' I couldn't help joking to try and cheer Tom up. Five minutes before I had been so angry with him, but I had never seen him like this, and it was horrible.

Tom made a noise that I wasn't sure was a laugh or another sob and wiped his eyes. I could've kicked myself, thinking for God's sake, Lila, why can't you just be *normal*? Why can't you just say . . . whatever it is you are supposed to say in these situations? Kate had clearly said the right things when he told *her*, why did I have to make bad jokes?

Tom gave a sniff though, and then made a noise that was definitely a laugh, and said that my awful black sense of humour was why he liked me. Then he stopped laughing, and asked if he could try to explain how the three of us had found ourselves here, and I just nodded.

He told me he was the only son of an ambitious, old-fashioned, overbearing father who believed the purpose of sons was to follow in their father's footsteps, and make them proud by doing exactly what their father had done before them, and then marrying a nice girl and making them a grandfather, so that *their* sons could follow in their footsteps etc etc. But Tom had always known he was different, ever since he was small. Different from his father in so many ways. And in his early teens, he knew for sure that he was different in more ways than his father knew.

'So Katie and me, we tried going out for a bit, but it was stupid. We know each other too well. We really are like brother and sister. Even if I wasn't gay, it would still have felt wrong. Kissing her . . .' Tom screwed up his face in mock horror.

'Thanks,' said Kate, pretending to hit him.

'You're the one who said it was gross and I quote, "icky",' Tom protested.

Despite the failure of the relationship with Kate, Tom knew though, that the one thing his father could never, would never accept, was a gay son. And so, he thought, perhaps he could find another girl. Someone he liked, someone he felt comfortable with, but wasn't as close to as Kate, then maybe he could make it work. Suppress who he was, squash his real feelings and be more like the son his father expected him to be. And in me, he thought he had found that.

'But I kept putting off taking it any further,' Tom admitted. 'I kept thinking, "Another time. Next week. The next party. Then I'll kiss her, and it will all be OK." But I never could, because I think I knew that it wouldn't be OK.'

Kate had told him it was a bad idea. That this wasn't fair on me. And that was another reason for Tom to keep putting it off. Because as long as nothing had actually happened, he could tell himself he hadn't really done anything wrong to me. We were just friends. Good friends. And the more he got to know me and like me, the harder it got, and then last night, in the garden, he knew he couldn't go through with it.

'Not that I couldn't kiss you.' Tom said sadly, 'I could've. But I knew that it wouldn't make any difference to who I was. And then, well, then I panicked and I ran away and grabbed Katie because she's the only person I could talk to, and I'd realised that no matter what I did, I couldn't *make* myself straight, and that what I was doing would only hurt both of us and that you didn't deserve that.'

He didn't deserve any of this either. I thought I understood about his father, but I didn't understand why he couldn't tell people at college. 'In the rest of your life, can't you just be *you*?'

Tom laughed. At least I think it was a laugh, it was a bitter sound. Mark was one of the reasons why. Tom's father plays golf every week with Mark's dad and Mark is incapable of keeping a secret. He wouldn't *mean* to say anything, but invariably he would let something slip to his dad.

It wasn't just his dad and Mark though. He just wasn't ready for everyone to know. He was still, in many ways, working out who he was, and he didn't want people's preconceptions affecting that.

'Being gay is only part of who I am,' he said. But he was worried that if everyone knew, some people wouldn't see beyond it and he didn't want to be asked to go shopping as someone's gay best friend or be roped into the annual theatre production *just* because he was gay. He just wanted a chance to be *Tom* first.

I knew how hard it was it try and work out who you are at sixteen, even without any further complications. I had just never realised Tom was also as unsure and uncertain about himself, and the place he wanted to occupy in the world. It seemed impossible that Tom could have any insecurities or doubts, yet I only had to look at his face to know it was true.

I promised I wouldn't tell anyone, but then I had to ask what we were going to tell people about last night? Tom said he was going to tell people he left early because I knocked him back. I told him he didn't have to do that, but he said he wanted to. It would make people less likely to guess the truth, which worked for him too.

'Are we all still friends?' asked Kate, who had stayed silent until now. 'I hope so. I want us to be friends.'

'Me too,' said Tom.

I said yes, and also that I was glad I knew now. 'It was . . . confusing before.'

Tom gave me a hug. I hugged him back, and thought – actually, what have I lost here? Nothing. Tom and I will hopefully go on like before, just without me constantly trying to impress him. And maybe I won't have to keep reading his poetry. That can only be a plus point.

Tom said he owed both me and Kate a coffee. It was not quite the same as MI5 buying me a coffee, but it would do.

As we walked to the café, Kate asked Tom if there wasn't anything else he wanted to tell me, like how he fancied Giles Atkinson. I was gobsmacked. Giles Atkinson? The rugby captain?

'Is he gay?' I managed.

Tom just smirked and winked and said his gaydar was rarely wrong.

EMILY

CHAPTER FIFTEEN

I am so tired today. I stayed up FAR too late reading Lila's diary, but I couldn't put it down. As well as being tired though, I am mortified, because I couldn't believe I had been so stupid as not to realise that Park Boy Tom was in fact *Uncle Tom*.

In my defence, Lila had talked so much about being in love with Park Boy Tom that it never even crossed my mind that it might be Uncle Tom, because as far as I was concerned, of course it couldn't be Uncle Tom, because Uncle Tom was gay – something I'd known for as long as I could remember. I was also thrown off the scent by Lila's many mentions of Park Boy Tom's amazing hair, because Uncle Tom had never had *any* hair in all the time I'd known him, which was my entire life.

But I was so embarrassed. How could I have asked him what happened to sexy Tom with the good hair and the stormy sea-grey eyes, when it was *him* all along? And why hadn't he said something? And I had told him that Lila thought his poetry was rubbish! Why had I said that? Did he know? Both that his poetry was terrible and that Lila had thought so?

I was also terribly sad for the teenage Tom. I knew, of course, that it had once been very difficult to be gay – almost impossible, in fact. But I thought that had been like a hundred years ago. I didn't realise it was so recent that people I knew and loved had experienced it. That shocked and appalled me.

I was so glad he'd had Kate and Lila. Aunty Kate was one of the most wonderful people I knew, and I was starting to see Mum in a different light too. Not just for standing by Uncle Tom, I wouldn't have expected anything less of her, but for being so accepting of his truth, and forgiving him for hurting her when he explained his reasons.

I realised perhaps I had been unfair to Uncle Tom too, when I told him he had no idea how confusing it was being a teenager. He must have experienced more confusion than most teenagers. So must Lila, between Tom coming out to her and her feelings for Al. I am glad things are different now, and no one really cares if you are gay or straight or bi or non-binary or anything else.

I wish Tom and Lila could find their happy endings though. Uncle Tom and his husband got divorced two years ago, and I've overheard Mum and Kate and Jas trying to persuade him to go on the odd date since then, but he's always refused. I don't know what he wants or hopes for from life now. And as for Lila – Mum – well. What would her happy ending be? Maybe getting her novel published. Maybe Tom's happy ending would be getting his poetry published. It might not have been as bad as Lila said it was. And he seemed to enjoy writing it.

Perhaps I could make it happen. I will encourage Uncle Tom to start writing poetry again, and I'll secretly send it to a publisher, and surprise him when it comes out in a book? Or I could start an Instagram account and publish it on there, the sort of old people that would read his poetry love Instagram, and then he would go viral and get published and famous like that, and then maybe he could give up the filthy capitalism for that Parisian bookshop. Mum seemed quite keen on the idea of a Parisian bookshop too. Perhaps they could both make their fortunes publishing their novels and poetry and move to Paris to run a bookshop together as best friends and live happily ever after like that?

Either way, I was starting to see why Mum was so keen on telling me that I was too young to be in love, that it was complicated, that love wasn't what I thought it was. If I'd had Lila's complicated love life, I'd be saying the same, and urging me to concentrate on friendships and my schoolwork too!

I brought up the subject of Uncle Tom being Park Boy Tom over breakfast and asked him why he hadn't told me.

Uncle Tom looked down into his coffee cup. 'I suppose, at first, I thought it was funny that you didn't recognise me. And then you asked me what happened to that boy and when I opened my mouth to reply, I realised I didn't know. I didn't know what had happened to him. I thought he was still me, but when you asked me that, I suddenly knew I hadn't seen that boy in a long time.

'In some ways,' Uncle Tom paused and took a gulp of coffee and a deep breath, then went on, 'in some ways I don't miss him, that poor kid. He was so confused and so scared, and he put on such a show of bravado and confidence for everyone that he really didn't feel. And so for a long time, I tried *not* think about him, and now, when I do think about him, I feel sorry for him. For growing up when he did, and not now. Nowadays, everyone is so much more open and relaxed. I'm so glad, and I hope no one ever feels like I did again.

'But at the same time, without that boy, I wouldn't have friends like Lila. And Kate, and Jasmit. I can't imagine life without them. And sometimes, I wish I could be young again, without the angst and the fear, just with the joy, and the excitement of having your whole life ahead of you.'

'You're not that old,' I lied, to try and make him feel better.

Uncle Tom laughed. 'Oh, you wicked child. You call me a boomer! Don't fib to me now. But Emily, this is why your mum and me – we try and tell you not to grow up too fast. You will never have these days again, so try and enjoy them. Enjoy your friends. Enjoy not worrying about bills and responsibilities. Enjoy not having the stress of relationships. There is plenty of time for all that.'

'I'll try,' I promised. 'I'm sorry though, that you couldn't enjoy it properly when you were young. I'm sorry people were like that.'

'So am I,' said Uncle Tom quietly. 'But you can't change the past, Emily, only the future. Things are better now, for me, for young people. I hope there is no one at your school who would be afraid to come out now. I know the world is still not perfect, but it's hopefully improving. So I am just going to try and remember the good times. The fun I had with people like Lila. I don't know what I would have done without friends like her.'

He smiled. 'Talking to you about all this, it's made me want to remember who you call Park Boy Tom with more joy, because there was a lot of happiness in those years at college too that I think I've forgotten about. Come on,' he drained his coffee, 'let's clear this away and get on with it! We have floors to sand.'

We stacked the dishwasher and wiped the counters and tidied away the cereal and bread and juice and milk. I washed up the cafetière, and then I realised there were two things I still needed to ask him.

'What happened with your dad in the end? In the diary, Lila said one of the things you were most scared of was your dad finding out you were gay. Was he all right when you finally told him?'

Uncle Tom shook his head. 'I never told him. He never knew. He died, very suddenly, in my first year at university. It's one of the biggest regrets of my life, that I never was honest with him. Because maybe I judged him too harshly. Maybe all he was doing was reflecting the expectations of his generation, and it wasn't how he really felt. But I never gave him the chance to accept me as I really was, and I wish I had. I think . . . I think this is why it's important to me that you and Lila don't waste precious time at loggerheads. Because you never know how much time you have left with the people you love. A small step to stopping a repeat of past mistakes.'

I had tears in my eyes. 'I'm sorry. About your dad. And . . . I'm sorry I told you Lila said your poetry was rubbish. I'm sure it was really good and she didn't know what she was talking about. I've had this idea for a poetry

Instagram account for you, and then it could go viral and everyone would think it was amazing!'

Uncle Tom laughed, to my relief. 'No, my poetry was awful. Lila MacKay was not the only one to think so. I gave up on the idea of poetry a *long* time ago. Why do you think that among all those essays and papers, and even Lila's diary, you didn't find any of my poetry? I burned it all, bar one small notebook I keep as a guilty pleasure to remind myself how bad it was. I don't think Instagram needs my poetry, thank you. If it went viral it would be for ALL the wrong reasons. You've been drying that coffee pot for the last ten minutes, young lady, come on. Those phone repairs won't earn themselves!'

Later, Uncle Tom having taken pity on me and let me go on painting duty instead of floor sanding, I found I had quite a lot of time to think about Lila and Al, and about Toby, as I slapped magnolia on the walls. I had realised I missed Poppy, talking to her, messing about with her, being silly with her, far more than I missed Toby.

But I was in love with him, wasn't I? Although I had never felt the way about Toby that Lila seemed to feel about Al. I hadn't even really felt the way Lila felt about *Tom* about Toby. What did I even know about Toby?

He was very good looking, of course, and had great hair – but as Lila and Tom had proved, good hair was no basis for love. There *were* those butterflies in my tummy when I thought about him. Well, if I thought about him *enough*. Specifically if I thought about him kissing me. But also when I imagined him kissing me . . . if I was totally honest, I wasn't really sure whose face I saw. It was just a sort of generic boy face, that I had attached the name 'Toby' to. When I looked at the drawing I did of him the other night, I don't even know if it *is* Toby, or if it is just my idea of what an attractive boy looks like.

I wished I could talk to Poppy about this, but then I had made such a *fuss* about being in love with Toby, I could hardly say, 'Oh, maybe I made a mistake.'

If only I could ask Lila for advice. The more I read about her, the more I found myself thinking of her as a friend. I kept forgetting she was my mother, and that if I wanted to, I *could* pick up the phone and ask her. Lila and Mum seemed a million years apart, and I felt like the advice that Lila would give me would be quite different to the advice Mum would give.

I don't think I could ever make Mum understand how Toby was the sort of boy the popular girls went out with, and if I went out with him — well, I'd be a bit closer to being a popular girl myself, to fitting in. Mum would tell me I was being silly, that I didn't need a boy to help me fit in, that why did I want to fit in anyway, why not be an individual. Why can't she see how important it is to be just like your friends when you're a teenager? How has she forgotten what a bear pit the popularity stakes are?

Lila would've understood, in a way I don't think Mum ever can.

Sometimes I think Lila is a figment of my imagination and nothing to do with Mum at all.

LILA

CHAPTER SIXTEEN

It was quite extraordinary how everything seemed perfectly normal when I walked into college today. No one seemed any different – not Tom, not Kate, nor anyone else who had been at Nicky's party on Saturday. Well, Nicky himself seemed rather more animated than usual, because he was quite excited about the photography competition, the exhibits for which will be put on display this week. He refused to show me my photographs though, claiming he wanted me to see them for the first time when they were properly mounted and hung on the wall in the main atrium, as part of the competition is the 'people's choice' where we all vote for our favourite picture, as well as the other categories which are judged by the art department and some local photographers.

I hadn't realised the photos were going to be up in the atrium when I agreed to this. I'm not sure I relish the thought of seeing my own face every time I change class. Still, at least they're not in the canteen. Imagine staring at myself over a tuna jacket potato every day for a week?

Also, I'm mildly concerned about Nicky's refusal to let me see them, and his desire for them to cause a 'maximum impact'. Has he made me look like a freak?

Jas was the only person who looked at me with concern. I assured her I was fine, that Tom and I had talked, and how we had both decided we weren't ready for a relationship, and we were just going to be friends for now.

I wish I could've told Jas the truth. I *was* fine, but also, my feelings were quite confused. I needed someone to talk to about it, because although I had been stunned by Tom's revelation on Sunday, I was not as hurt as I think I would have been if Al hadn't been occupying my thoughts so much.

If I was really honest with myself, it was more the *idea* of being Tom's girlfriend that I had enjoyed, because of how popular Tom was, how much Rachel was annoyed by the whole thing, and how associating with Tom vastly increased my own social standing. In a strange way, I was sort of relieved that I wouldn't actually have to be his girlfriend, because the person I really wanted to talk to, be with, hang out with, be kissed by, was Al.

But that was never going to happen.

Al was no more real that the French painters or archaeologists I peopled my imagination with. I had about as much chance of actually going out with one of Take That as I did with Al. He was just another figment of my imagination, really, albeit a more interactive one.

But who could I tell about this? I had spent weeks thinking of Al as the person I could tell anything, but how could I tell him I was starting to think of him as more than a friend? And how could I explain to Jas that I seemed to be falling in love with a boy I'd never met, and really knew nothing concrete about? Oh, and who was in love with someone else? But it was OK, because at least my feelings for Al had cushioned the blow of Tom's rejection and subsequent confession?

I could barely explain it to myself, let alone anyone else. I couldn't even talk to Al because all the college servers were down for maintenance so no one could log on to anything.

Tuesday 5ᵀᴴ November 1996

The photos went up today for the competition. Tom was waiting for me outside college when I arrived this morning and dragged me inside, saying, 'You will not believe this.'

There were crowds of people standing in front of Nicky's photos of me, exclaiming at them. I don't think anyone has ever exclaimed with pleasure at a photo of me before. I have a tendency to close my eyes at the wrong moment, or pull a face. Even Mum generally sighs when she gets the photos back from Boots and says, 'Darling, it's not that you're unattractive, it's just something very unfortunate seems to happen when someone points a camera at you. Couldn't you just *try* to keep your eyes open, or not to sneeze?'

Nicky's photos of me were incredible. I barely recognised myself. I looked like the girl I longed to be.

He had entered one of me in the dining room where I look like I'm floating against a black backdrop, just this pale sort of ethereal fairy queen. And there was another that I recognised as being just inside his back door. Nicky must have taken it while I was standing there on the verge of tears, watching Tom tow Kate out the door. I hadn't even noticed him taking it, and I was slightly cross that he had taken advantage of my emotional distress for his competition, but on the other hand, it was another glorious photo. I didn't look distraught, I looked distant, pensive, calm, while the party raged in the background behind me. Nicky had called it 'The Eye of the Storm' which was a bit pretentious, but also, I could see what he meant. He had made me look like the epicentre of the chaos around me, a weather goddess thoughtfully considering the carnage she could wreak with one twitch of her nose. The other one, the fairy queen in the dining room, he had simply titled 'Lila'.

'Can't believe I ever thought I was in with a chance of winning!' Tom laughed ruefully and waved to his own portrait entries, which were perfectly nice photos of Kate on a beach somewhere. Kate looked beautiful, but then Kate always looks beautiful, and the photos were golden and sun-drenched and joyful, but they lacked the magic of Nicky's photos. 'The Nickster has it nailed, I think.'

Nicky walked through the doors at that moment, having some sort of complicated struggle with his backpack, and Tom hailed him, and threw his arm around him. 'Nickster! Man, you are like a serious *genius*!'

Nicky glowed with pride and gave a shy smile, as I asked him how he had made me look like that.

'Like what?' Nicky pushed his glasses up his nose and looked confused.

'Like *that*?' I pointed to the photographs again.

Nicky went red. 'I dunno. That's just how you look, isn't it?' And he stumped off, still entangled in the straps of his rucksack.

I asked Tom if I really looked like that and he assured me I did, though he then spoiled it by adding that I looked a *bit* like that, which isn't the same thing at all. He claimed Nicky had managed to 'bring something out'.

FRIDAY 8TH NOVEMBER 1996

FINALLY the college computer servers were working again. Apparently the 'routine maintenance' had been more difficult than the IT departments had expected, and I headed to the computer lab after college to find a super-excited, if now somewhat out-of-date, message from Al, sent on Sunday before we were so cruelly cut off from the 20th century.

Elise! How did it go for you at the weekend? I think things are finally changing for me and Marisa. She is being really nice to me! And I think she had a row with her boyfriend last night. I don't know if they've actually broken up, but if they have, maybe once she gets over him, she'll finally realise how I feel about her. God, I'm so happy. It's stupid, how one little thing, a glimmer of hope, can just change everything, isn't it? Is that awful of me? I don't want her to be hurt by him of course. I don't even want <u>him</u> to be hurt, I actually like him. Anyway, how was your weekend? Did things work out with Nigel?

I didn't know what to reply to Al. But at least I could talk to him about Tom.

I couldn't stop thinking about how unfair it was that Tom had to keep who he really was a secret. Kate had confided in me, during the week, that he was often desperately unhappy. I felt bad about all the times I had been irritated by his casual confidence in his poetry and his photography, when underneath he was even less certain about himself than I was. Kate also thought it would be good for him to have another confidante, someone else he could be open and honest with. It would help him feel less alone. I suspect she was also relieved that the whole burden of Tom's secret no longer fell solely on her. But I had no idea how to help.

Al often seemed much older than me, in his outlook of the world, although I knew we were the same age. He had the detachment of distance and anonymity that might be able to give me some ideas. I had promised Tom that I wouldn't tell anyone about him, but Al didn't count. Hell, for all I knew, Al was in the same position and 'Marisa' was a boy with a girlfriend, hence his hopeless unrequited love for her, and he would be relieved to be able to tell me the truth too (though probably not, as it seemed like there was hope on the horizon for Al and STUPID Marisa, which I wasn't jealous about AT ALL).

So I replied to Al's exuberant message, feeling a bit bad about raining on his parade.

That's brilliant. I'm glad things are looking up for you and Marisa. I hope things work out for you both soon, and you get your happy ever after. What happened this weekend to turn it all around?

Things didn't go so well for Nigel and me. Turns out that he is gay. So I guess we're just going to stay as friends.

I decided that was enough for now, until I knew how Al would react.

A small, selfish part of me hoped he would be horrible. If Al revealed himself to be a terrible person in some way, that would make it far easier to put all thoughts of him out of my head, and move on, instead of entertaining increasingly wild fantasies about him binning off Marisa and using those potential Nobel Prize winning skills to do the hacking thing and find me and turn up on my doorstep declaring his undying love.

That would take some explaining to Mum.

If he would just do something dreadful though, then everything would be sorted. But since at the moment, his main flaw was his chivalrous love for foolish Marisa, he was the perfect man, in an online sort of a way.

I knew it was terrible of me to want him to be awful about Tom, of course, but I could really do with Al having a few more faults and flaws. Maybe he wasn't homophobic, but kicked a kitten once. That would do. As long as the kitten wasn't actually hurt and just mildly disgruntled.

Al's kitten-kicking status was still unknown, but to my relief he did not appear to be a raging homophobe (for Tom's sake I was also relieved to find I *was* relieved about this, so I'm not a totally terrible selfish person). He replied almost immediately.

Shit. Really? I take it no one else knows? Poor guy, that must be tough for him.

Yes. It's also not ideal for me though.

Please give me some sympathy, Al. Because I am starting to despair if anything will ever happen between me and anyone. All I want is one nice guy to love me. God, even if Al would say something to indicate he thought of me as more than a friend that would be nice, Marisa or no Marisa. After all, Mary Shelley had to put up with old Percy having it off with his first wife, *and* Mary's sister at the same time as Mary, so I could overlook the passion for another woman if Al would just give me some hint that he thought I might be lovable –

It can't have been easy for him telling you.

I guess so. I'm just a bit stunned. It explains a lot though. And we're still going to be friends.
I just don't know if I'll ever meet anyone . . .

Seriously Al, give a girl a bit of validation here, I'm practically begging you!
But no.

I know what you mean. I wonder the same. If I can't have Marisa, will I ever meet anyone? Will I ever get over her? Will I ever feel this way about anyone else? But something else amazing has happened this week . . . is your college having a photography competition too?

Oh, for crying out loud! I'm TRYING TO HAVE AN EXISTENTIAL CRISIS HERE, ALGERNON! Please, for the love of all that is holy, I want to be soothed and told I am pretty and lovable and that men will fall swooning at my feet and launch battleships in my name and write

sonnets that will endure for a thousand years. I DON'T
WANT TO TALK ABOUT SODDING MARISA!

I was so cross I couldn't stop myself from typing a
furious reply. After all, Al was being very selfish here. And
I had had quite a difficult weekend, *actually*, while he had
been mooning over that psycho bitch and dancing like her
little puppet and going on about photography competitions.
Well, yes, we *were* having our own competition actually and
lots of people were noticing me after seeing the photos of
me, so IT'S NOT ALL ABOUT YOU AL, I fumed to myself,
and then typed:

Are you really in love with her? Or are you just in love with the *idea*
of being in love with her? What do you even know about her? How can
you love someone who barely knows you exist? Is 'being in love with
Marisa' just a habit? Or a way to make yourself seem more interesting?
Does she even exist, Marisa? I don't mean she's not a real girl, but are
you projecting this girl you're 'in love with' on to Marisa? Maybe there's
a dozen better people for you out there and you can't see them because
you're so hung up on some imaginary 'perfect girl'?

I'm having a really difficult time here, and I feel like you are the only
person I have to talk to, because I can't tell anyone what happened last
weekend, not even my best friend, and I had hoped for maybe a bit of
understanding. A bit of sympathy. And all I get is you banging on and on and
BLOODY ON about photography competitions and Marisa, and even Nigel.

I KNOW it's hard for him, I'm trying to be supportive of him. And I'm
trying to be supportive of you and Marisa. Even though the more I talk to
you, the more I like you, like LIKE you like you, and wish you weren't so
hung up on Marisa, because I think you're amazing. And despite all the
stuff that happened this weekend I'm not as upset as I thought I would be

because it's YOU I really like, not him. And despite that, I still am trying to be there for you about HER! And you can't even be bothered to take a bit of time out of your bloody navel-gazing to say, 'How are you though, Lila, are you OK?' Oh well, thanks yes, I've been better, ACTUALLY, but YOU CAN ONLY TALK ABOUT YOURSELF!!!!!

I hit send in a blind rage, and then sat back to breathe for a moment.

Maybe I should've waited a few minutes before I sent it. Cooled off a bit. I read it over to see how bad it was.

Oh no! I had called myself Lila!

Still, it wasn't that big a deal, was it? It wasn't like I'd sent him my full name, address, date of birth, star sign, favourite colour, and preferred flavour of ice cream and hired the Red Arrows to fly over my house and skywrite 'Please stalk me now'. I didn't really get why the colleges made such a thing about us not revealing any personal details about ourselves in the chatrooms anyway. But I had been a bit harsh to poor Al. Perhaps I should send an apology.

I was just thinking how to word it, when I heard a gasp from a corner of the computer lab, and someone said '*Lila?*' in incredulous tones. I peered round my monitor and saw Nicky in the far corner looking round his screen at me. I hadn't seen him when I came in.

'*Lila?*' he said again. 'It's you, isn't it?'

'What?' *Obviously* it was me. Who else did he think it was?

'You're Elise, aren't you?' Nicky said.

I went very very cold. 'What?' I said again, without much conviction this time.

'You're Elise,' he repeated. 'Elise that's been talking to Al. Aren't you?'

'How do you know?' I gasped. 'Unless you're . . .'

'Al!' Nicky beamed. 'I'm Al! And you're Elise!'

He came across the computer lab to me. Thankfully at that time on a Friday afternoon we were the only ones still there.

I stared at him. I couldn't quite process what was going on.

'We've been talking to *each other* all along! Who knew?' He still had a stupid grin on his face.

'But how can you be Al?' I whispered as Nicky grabbed my hand. I felt sick. Al was cool and funny, and I knew he must be attractive, and I liked him, more than liked him, and now he was *Nicky*? *Weird Nicky*? How had this happened? This was terrible. I had told him so many things. And all along it was *Nicky*. He tricked me!

Nicky swore he hadn't known it was me, that he hadn't tricked me, and reminded me he had told me a lot of stuff too, but it didn't help.

I realised Nicky was still holding my hand. I snatched it back in fury and glared at him. I'd trusted him! Was this all some hideous trick?

Nicky tried to take my hand again, telling me that he had trusted me too, and that he'd never have had the courage to tell me the things he had if he'd known it was me. 'That's why I told you about "Marisa", why would I have said about that if I knew it was you?'

'Oh my GOD, are you STILL going on about Marisa?' I shouted. 'Why do you think I would even care about your STUPID crush? Who even IS she?'

'You are, of course.' Nicky was smiling at me. 'I've been crazy about you for as long as I can remember.'

I couldn't breathe. My throat felt like it was closing up. Was this a panic attack? Did I need to breathe into a brown paper bag? Why didn't I have a brown paper bag? Did it have to be brown? Would the crumpled Greggs bag someone had left on the desk do? I had to get out, I had to get some air.

I stumbled towards the door as Kate came in, asking if I was ready to go. She looked at Nicky, and suggested he came for a coffee too.

I somehow heaved in a gulping rasp of air, just enough to gasp, 'No. Not Nicky,' and lurched out the room. I was followed by Kate a few seconds later, but I couldn't stop and wait for her. I fled down the stairs, down and down, avoiding the main doors where there would be people, and I'd be easy to find. I burst out the fire escape doors into the blessed cold dark winter's night, where I finally managed to get some icy air into my burning lungs.

'I don't feel very well,' I whimpered when Kate appeared. 'I think I'm going to go home, skip the coffee, sorry.'

Kate put a concerned hand on my forehead to check for a fever, as she fussed that I was white as a sheet.

Perhaps I did have a fever. Perhaps this whole thing was just a delirious dream, and I would wake up in the morning and it would never have happened. Nicky would just be Nicky. Maybe the whole term could be a dream, and Mum would soon be shaking me, saying, 'Wake up, Lila, it's the first day of college!' Yes. It was all just a bad dream. After all, if it was good enough for Bobby Ewing in *Dallas* surely it was good enough for me.

'Kate,' I croaked. 'Am I naked?'

'What? No, you're fully clothed. Though you should really put your coat on, it's freezing.'

Well, that settled it. This wasn't a dream. I'm always naked in my bad dreams. Standing up at assembly, or in the middle of a party, or on a crowded train, or in the supermarket. I had looked up what it meant in a dream book at the library once, and it said it meant I felt vulnerable and or that I was worried an aspect of me was to be ridiculed. I might have my clothes on, but both things were very true right now.

I just wanted to go home, but Kate was adamant that she wasn't leaving me to make my own way home in the state I was in, and said that Kevin would come and pick us both us, and she called him on the state-of-the-art mobile phone Kevin had recently given her, because he was 'worried about her safety' if she 'got stuck somewhere' and which was the envy of the whole college. Kevin's Merc purred up five minutes later, and Kate piled me into it and squooshed up beside me, simply saying, 'Thanks Dad. Lila's feeling a bit off colour.'

I sat in the back and watched the streetlights sliding past. Normally I adored being in Kevin's car and spent the journey making up stories about what it would be like to have a car like this, pulling up to a valet parking lot at a swanky restaurant and chucking the keys casually to a bell hop in one of those funny pill box hats before sashaying inside for martinis and caviar. Because it was only a fantasy scenario, I didn't have to worry about the drink driving implications of the martinis and the Mercedes, or the lack of valet parking facilities in the UK, or that I suspected caviar might be quite nasty, as I simply couldn't comprehend that spoonfuls of cold fish eggs, however expensive, could possibly be nice. I didn't even have the heart to do that tonight.

I pressed my cheek against the window. A few minutes ago I had been so cold and pale I had worried Kate, and now my cheeks burned furiously with shame and embarrassment.

Nicky. All the things I had told him, and it was Nicky all along. This was the worst thing that had ever happened to me.

I decided as soon as I got in, I would ring Dad and ask if I could come and stay with him. Perhaps I could tell him Mum had an infectious disease and I had to quarantine. No, he'd want to talk to Mum. I could say there was an outbreak of something at college, and I couldn't go and must be sent away for fear I caught it, like Amy being sent to stay with Aunt March in *Little Women*. What was she avoiding? Was it scarlet fever? Would Dad believe there was scarlet fever rampaging through the corridors of the college and my delicate constitution couldn't stand it? Probably not. That was the downside to having doctors for parents. Measles then, or mumps. I'd think of something.

Kevin stopped outside the house and turned to me. 'Hope you feel better soon, love. Ooh, how's that clever neighbour of yours? He's such a nice fellow, Nicky. We should've given him a lift home too, Katie!'

I gulped at the thought and mumbled my thanks to Kevin. Kate walked me up the path to the door.

'You know you can talk to me,' she said as I put my key in the lock. 'About anything. OK?'

That was kind of her. But it didn't matter, because hopefully I wouldn't be here much longer.

Mum was out, to my relief, so I went straight to the phone and dialled Dad's number. Anita answered to my dismay and informed me Dad was working.

'Never mind, I was just wondering if I could come and stay for a bit?'

Anita gave a long-suffering sigh. 'This is your father's home, Elizabeth, you are always welcome here.'

YES! Dad would have asked all sorts of awkward parental questions, but Anita, devoted only to Border terriers, did not know she was supposed to quiz me about missing college etc. I suppose because Border terriers don't have to bother with college.

'Thanks,' I said gratefully, before asking if it was too late to get a train tonight and then maybe stay for . . . a while. I left it open-ended, let her and Dad get used to the idea, before I broached the subject of staying for good.

I knew it had been too easy. Anita immediately informed that was absolutely not possible and waffled on for a while about how they were going to Vancouver in the morning. I wasn't really paying attention to the detailed itinerary she felt the need to provide me with (though it might have been nice if someone had told me about this trip before now) until I heard her say something about what a wrench it was to leave the dogs in kennels for so long. I saw a glimmer of hope and offered to dog sit instead of the poor puppers being abandoned in kennels.

Anita hesitated. 'I suppose I *could* cancel the kennels; it would be less disruptive for my babies to stay at home . . .'

I waffled on about coming now, literally being on a train in the next hour. I had her convinced, I was just about to hang up and run for the train when Anita said, 'Oh. Here's your father home. Jim, Jim darling, it's Elizabeth on the phone. She's offering to come and dog-sit while we're in Vancouver. Isn't that a good idea? Then my preciouses can stay at home.'

'WHAT!' I heard Dad explode down the line at me. 'Elizabeth, what is this nonsense?' He ranted that of course I couldn't come and dog-sit, stop being ridiculous, what about college, what would my mother say? 'Anita, I can't believe you even entertained this idea.'

He didn't buy the measles outbreak at college – 'You're vaccinated, you'll be fine' – or scarlet fever, despite my pleas.

According to Dad, it would be incredibly irresponsible of him as a parent to leave me alone in the house for ten days with only a pack of incontinent mutts for company (that made Anita squawk with fury) and then tried to console me by offering to arrange for me to come for the weekend when they got back from Canada.

Why had he had to come home just then? Another few minutes and I would have been on the train and there would have been nothing he could have done. Well, apart from put me on the train back again. Why did no one understand me, or how much I needed to get away?

I trudged into the kitchen and investigated the fridge. I was not hungry. I still had a sick feeling in the pit of my stomach. I wondered if I could call Jas and tell her about what had happened, but she was going out with Mark tonight. And anyway, once again, how would I explain to her how it had all started? How did I explain about Tom?

Oh God. Tom. I had told Nicky about Tom. I had sworn a most solemn vow to Tom (well, pinkie-promised) that I would tell no one, and within a week, I had blabbed to Nicky! This situation really couldn't get any worse.

I left a note on the table for Mum, telling her I had gone to bed with period pains, and went upstairs and crawled under my duvet. Mum came home about half an hour later and tiptoed in to see me with a hot water bottle and some paracetamol. I was grateful for the paracetamol, because my head was aching rather badly by then. I couldn't face talking to her though, so I said I didn't want any dinner, and was just going to try and get some sleep.

I finally drifted off in a doze, and dreamt I was walking back into college, like I had on Tuesday morning, to a throng of people gathered round Nicky's photos of me. I pushed through to the front to see them again and realised I was naked in them. People were elbowing each other and sniggering, and as I looked down, I realised I was naked there in the corridor too. I woke up with a start, with Mum coming back in to say that Nicholas was at the door asking for me.

I pulled the duvet back over my head and groaned I felt too ill.

Mum said she'd told him that, but he said if I didn't feel up to coming down, could she give me a message?

Dear God, what had bloody Nicky told Mum? 'Tell Lila I love her?' 'Please Dr MacKay, would you ask Lila if she'll be my girlfriend?' 'Dr MacKay, I would like to ask for your daughter's hand in marriage?'

'It was a bit odd, but he assured me you'd understand,' Mum went on. 'He said, "Please tell Lila not to worry about the Nigel question, no one else will get her answer from me."'

I hoped the message meant Nicky wouldn't be telling anyone else about Tom. That much at least was decent of him.

SATURDAY 9TH NOVEMBER

Kate rang me this morning, wanting to check how I was feeling, and invite me to sleep over after Kevin's big fireworks party tonight. I had forgotten about the fireworks party. I said I wasn't sure I was up to it, but Kate was insistent. 'Whatever's wrong with you, moping around won't help.'

'It will if it's scarlet fever,' I pointed out.

Kate refused to believe that I had scarlet fever, and said she'd be so disappointed if I didn't come, and so would Tom, *and* she'd never hear the last of it from her dad, he adored me. 'Nearly as much as he loves Nicky. He keeps trying to pair me off with Nicky – a nice clever boy, he says. He's only just got over the disappointment that I won't be marrying Tom!'

'Your dad knows about Tom?' I said, jolted out of my misery.

Turned out it was part of the reason Kevin was so cool about how much time Kate and Tom spent together. And he *really* didn't like Tom's dad and said they spelled banker wrong when it came to him, and it should start with a 'W'. 'And Dad likes almost everyone. So now he thinks Nicky is a most suitable young man for me.'

I tried to laugh along with Kate, but I had to ask if Nicky would be there.

Of course Nicky was going to be there. He was helping Kevin set off the fireworks, because *of course* Nicky had to go and be so blooming clever that he had worked out a way to setthe fireworks off to music without having to run between them with a lighter, so Kevin was delighted with him. It seemed everybody loved Nicky but me.

Maybe that wouldn't be so bad. If Nicky was busy with Kevin all night, there wouldn't be many opportunities for us to talk. Anyway, it would be easy enough to lose him in Kate's huge house and garden, especially if there were lots of other people there. Maybe it would be easier just to go, instead of having to make excuses. Apart from anything else, I knew Jas wouldn't buy the 'woman's problems' excuse because we always got our periods at the same time, even though Mum insisted that girls syncing periods was just an urban myth.

So I said I'd go.

I was deliberately late to the party. Jas had asked if I wanted to go over to hers and get ready and then go with her and Mark, but I said I'd just see her there. I didn't want to get there until Nicky was fully occupied with Kevin and the fireworks. I wished I hadn't agreed to sleep over, because now I would have no excuse to sneak off early. I supposed I could always just claim tiredness and go and hide in Kate's bedroom.

I got there about five minutes before the fireworks started. Jas grabbed me as I came in the door and squinted at me. 'You look a bit . . . tired?' she said.

It is well known that 'tired' is just a euphemism for 'You look like death.' I *was* tired, after a night of alternating terrible dreams and lying awake clenched with shame and horror at all the things I had told Nicky. I had made a minimal effort for tonight as well. I didn't want Nicky to think I had glammed myself up for him.

The fireworks were spectacular. Kevin had excelled himself. Huge speakers blasted out the 1812 Overture, and the fireworks exploded in perfect time to the music. We all stood open-mouthed as the rockets lit up the night, the moment filled with nothing but the music and the glittering stars and flowers tracing their way across the sky. I wanted the kaleidoscope of sparkling joy to go on forever.

Nothing lasts forever though, especially not fireworks. Transient bursting fragments of light and colour, they finish too soon, leaving nothing but cold air and smoke and the drifting smell of cordite. As the music came to its triumphant finish with the last blasts of the trumpets, and the rest of the party started to wander away, I couldn't move, still hypnotised by the sensory overload. But then Kevin and Nicky were standing in front of me, both grinning from ear to ear.

'The best one we've ever had, I think,' Kevin said smugly. 'And it's all down to Nicholas here.'

Kevin bustled off to check on the caterers and I looked round and realised everyone else had gone back inside, or over to the bonfire on the other side of the lawn, and there was just Nicky and me standing there alone.

'I need to go too,' I said and spun around to dash back to everyone else, where Nicky couldn't say anything, where

I could pretend everything was OK. But Nicky caught my arm and said he needed to talk to me. I unwillingly let him drag me over to a seat at the edge of the lawn, where he told me how he had gone to see Tom that morning and explained how he had come to know his secret.

I groaned. 'Why, why did you have to do that?'

'Because it didn't seem right that Tom didn't know I knew.' Nicky had wanted Tom to know there was one more person he didn't have to pretend around, someone else who had his back. Nicky brightly told me that he had explained everything to Tom, and Tom totally understood and wasn't angry with me, and was in fact thrilled that everything was working out for Nicky and me.

'He's really happy for us.'

'Us? US? Nicky, there is no us.'

Nicky stared at me, a look of confusion on his freckled face. He was frowning and pulled away from me to sit at the other end of the bench. The confusion had been replaced with anger as he demanded to know why I had said I liked him, how couldn't I know that he loved me, that he had loved me for years, and why didn't I find this as amazing as he did.

'Why did you come tonight if you didn't want to see me? If you don't want to be with me? You said you liked me. You TOLD me.' he cried. He took a breath, and closed his eyes for a moment, and then asked what he had done wrong. Was it that he hadn't asked me out properly? Was that what I wanted? OK, he would ask me. He grabbed my hand again and said, 'Please will you be my girlfriend?'

Until he said all that, I had been thinking maybe it wouldn't be so bad. Maybe Nicky and I could be friends.

He could be a confidante, someone to bounce ideas off, and discuss the things I couldn't tell anyone else. There was also a small, shallow nasty part of me thinking, 'And no one would ever have to know then, we could keep it a secret.'

Somehow, in all my wild wallowings in woe through the dark watches of the night, it had never occurred to me that Nicky would expect me to now be his *girlfriend*.

I had never ever envisaged myself with Nicky. He was *Nicky*. What would people say if I went out with Nicky? How could I possibly become the sort of person I wanted to be, if I was going out with Nicky? Maybe I was never going to be the cool popular girl, but I wanted to fit in, to be like everyone else. Going out with Nicky was never going to achieve that. No, he wasn't the pant-wetting frog dissector of our childhood, but he was still strange and different. He was still Weird Nicky. Wasn't he?

All I could do was try to explain that I hadn't known it was him, when I said I liked Al, I hadn't known it was Nicky, and even as I heard the words coming out of my mouth, I knew how feeble they sounded, that I wasn't explaining it properly, that I couldn't make him understand.

'But it was me. It was all me. More me than anything else you've seen of me. I was totally honest with you in those messages. I told you everything about me, and you liked me for it. So how can you not want this? This is me. *That* was me. What is the difference?'

I wanted to cry. I wished I could make him see the difference. This was awful. Excruciatingly awful.

Maybe I could just go. Get up and run away. Where would I run away to? London, people always ran away to

London. My Aunt Lucy lived in London, I could run away and live with her and get a job, and never have to finish this conversation or see anyone ever again. How would I get there? How did you get to London? Dick Whittington walked there. I could hitchhike! I could hitchhike to London and live with Aunt Lucy and none of this would ever have happened!

But hitchhikers get murdered. Did I want to avoid an awkward conversation with Nicky enough to risk a psychopath prowling the M6 service stations looking for emotionally repressed teenagers who would rather take their chances with a Ginsters pasty and an axe instead of actually having to face up to difficult truths? And even if I avoided the crazy axeman, I knew I would never be allowed to stay with Aunt Lucy (assuming she would even have me) and drop out of college, any more than I could scuttle off to live with Dad and take up breeding Border terriers with Anita.

A few months ago, I would just have laughed and walked off if Nicky had asked me out. I wouldn't have been bothered about letting him down gently. But now, I didn't want to hurt him. I didn't know what to do, or how to explain things to him. It had been so much easier, talking to 'Al' through a screen, instead of sitting here, with Nicky right in front of me, on this cold dark night, the gunpowder smell still lingering in the air, the sounds of the party in the background, a shriek that sounded like Jas, and Nicky staring at me, waiting for me to say something.

'You're . . . you're not someone I've ever thought of going out with,' I tried.

My hand was getting sweaty clutched in his, as Nicky said he knew I hadn't ever thought of him like that, but it was different now. Oh God, why was he making this so hard?

I had to be brutal. 'I just . . . I can't go out with you, OK?' I said.

He finally let go of my hand. The night air was suddenly very cold against my damp palm. 'You don't *want* to go out with me. Because I'm "Weird Nicky" and you don't think I'm good enough for you.'

He stood up. I wasn't sure if he was furious, or if he was trying not to cry, like I was.

I tried to tell him it wasn't because he wasn't good enough for me, that it was because I just want to fit in, to be like everyone else. And Nicky, Nicky doesn't fit in, and what would people think? I hadn't meant to say that last bit. I had just been trying to explain.

Nicky glared at me. If he *had* been upset, he was now just angry. 'What will people *think*? Who cares? You say you're worried about Tom, but what will happen if you walk down the street holding my hand? People might think "bit of an odd couple" or "he's done well there" and that's it. If *Tom* did that, he could be beaten up, his dad could disown him. In your last message, you asked me if I really knew that girl or if I was just in love with an illusion I'd created. And yeah. I don't know who you are. I do know you're not the girl I was in love with though.'

And Nicky walked away quietly. That was the worst part. He didn't storm off. He didn't stamp away in a rage. He hadn't even raised his voice. Nicky walked away from me in the same way Nicky did everything. Quietly. Unassumingly.

I burst into tears. As I sobbed, I thought about all the small things Nicky had done for me and Mum over the years. Not just cutting the grass. Helping us carry in our groceries every week. Watering Mum's houseplants when we went on holiday. I had forgotten that for years, since we were children, he would always bring me the first rose that bloomed in his garden. A white rose, like the rose of York, I realised now. His mother had dug it up and moved it and it had died, and she had replaced it with some rather gaudy hydrangeas, and so this year he had brought me a wild white rose and I had laughed at him and asked him why he did it, and he had just shrugged. But it had been a beautiful rose and I had kept it on my dressing table till it faded and died. The way he had saved me on the first day of term without hesitation or question. Explaining to Tom that I hadn't meant to give him away. Those beautiful photographs he'd taken of me. And I realised that for some time now, I'd been getting used to Nicky's quiet presence. I had started to like him being around.

If he had only given me a little more time to get used to the revelation of him being 'Al'! If he had let me have a few days of seeing 'Al' in him, as well as just Nicky, then it could all have been so different, because I now knew that I did like him, and that I did want him, regardless of what anyone thought!

Kate found me half an hour later, frozen and still sniffling, and persuaded me indoors to get warm, assuring me everyone was going home now.

Upstairs in Kate's bedroom, thawing gradually, gratefully clutching the mug of hot chocolate she had brought me, I hiccupped out the whole sorry story. The shot of brandy she had added to my hot chocolate might have had something to do with my confession. She told me I had a remarkable knack of creating drama at parties, and I said I didn't mean to, and she said she knew that before adding, 'Imagine the carnage you'd leave in your wake if you were *trying*.'

She didn't understand, though, why I had been so shocked by the idea of going out with Nicky. 'I know he's not conventionally handsome, but he's really cute. I never thought you'd be the sort of person who cared that much about looks anyway. And you like him, you know you do. So what's the problem?'

I tried to explain again, about wanting to fit in, and be the same as everyone else, and how Nicky – Nicky would always be *different*, and how could I fit in, if I was going out with someone as strange as Nicky?

And then I got to the heart of the problem.

I've always been different.

My parents were the first in my class to get divorced. While everyone else was having lovely wholesome family weekends, I was being shuttled between my parents and hearing my mum crying at night about Dad leaving her. Other people's mums didn't work, or they had normal jobs that finished at 5pm, but my mum was a GP on call at nights and weekends and I had a babysitter who had to stay over in case she got called out. And when everyone else was having nice ordinary holidays to Spain or Portugal that they booked in January, Mum forgot the holidays were even coming up, so while Rachel and everyone else was talking about where they were going in the summer, I'd be wondering if Mum even knew when I broke up. And if we DID ever go on holiday, it was always something strange and last minute, or I'd be sent to stay with Dad and Anita, and Anita was never very happy about it, and half the time Dad would be working as well, so nothing was ever *organised* and *tidy* and *normal* the way other people's families were.

'And that's all I want,' I sniffed. 'To be *normal*. To know the right thing to say, not to say stupid things and sound like an idiot.'

'You don't say stupid things, you're *funny*. Like, really funny,' Kate insisted.

I had never thought of myself as funny. I'd always assumed when people told me that, they either were being kind, or meant it in the 'peculiar' sense.

'And anyway, *my* family's not normal, is it?' Kate went on. She was right of course, her mother had died before Kate could even remember and Kevin . . . Kate laughed as she told me how Kevin used to turn up at parents' nights in the loudest suits with the loudest voice, and he didn't look like the other dads and his accent wasn't like the other dads, and then Kate said, 'But do you know what the main thing I have learnt from my dad is?'

I shook my head.

'That it doesn't matter what other people think of me or of him.'

She said her dad used to care. That he used to feel less, because people looked down their noses at him, because he left school at fourteen, because he didn't go to university, because they thought he sounded 'common'. And then he realised, those people who he thought of as 'better' than him – what had they done with their lives, what had they achieved, compared to what he had done? He had thought of having elocution lessons once, so he sounded 'proper'. And then he thought – why? Why not be proud of who he was, what he had done?

'And he's right,' Kate concluded. 'Why try to be like everyone else?'

It was easy for them though. Kevin was rich, and Kate was beautiful. I was just *me*.

Kate pointed out that loads of people loved me for that, and as I shook my head, she listed Jas, Tom, her, Nicky. Her dad. My mum. My dad too. 'Your step mum – well, never mind her. Her dogs probably love you though.'

I knew Kate was right. That everything she was saying made perfect sense. Except it *did* matter to me, what people thought of me. I *did* feel like I was less than they were. Less important, less clever. Their opinions mattered more, because I mattered less. And even as I knew how very stupid that was, I thought maybe it was partly my fault. That the more I *let* people make me feel less than them, the more I *would* feel less than them.

Maybe it wouldn't happen overnight, but maybe if I told myself often enough that I was good enough, then maybe I could finally convince myself that I was? That people like Kate and Rachel were not better than me? Certainly Kate didn't believe she was better than me – she just believed she was enough. Rachel, well – she probably did think she was better than me, and everyone else, but that didn't mean she was right.

I just had to keep reminding myself of all of this.

'Thanks Kate,' I said. 'I don't think Nicky does love me any more though.'

Kate said he would come round, if I went to see him tomorrow and explained things to him, like I had to her.

I gave Kate a hug, and thanked her for always being there for me. And then I had a thought and asked if there was anyone she liked. All of the rest of us were looking for someone, somewhere. Was she? Kate smiled, but it was an odd sort of smile. 'No, there's not. I'm still . . . figuring out who I am. Sometimes . . . I think maybe I'm like Tom. Other times, I think maybe not. I don't know. Not yet.'

God, why is being sixteen so confusing? Do you think we will ever look back on this time and go 'those were the best days of our lives' like old people always tell us we will? Like maybe when *we're* really old too, like forty-five or something?

SUNDAY 10ᵀᴴ NOVEMBER

I took Kate's advice and went to see Nicky when I got home today. Well, after I'd had a shower, and done my hair in such a way as didn't look done and put on just enough make up to hide the effects of last night's tears, but again didn't make me look ridiculous on a Sunday afternoon. And I wore the jeans and top he'd said he'd liked last week, when I thought he was Al.

His mother seemed rather surprised to see me and said he was out at his driving lesson. She didn't know when he'd be back.

I smiled as brightly as I could, as if it didn't matter at all whether I saw Nicky or not, and went home and sat by the sitting-room window looking out for him for the rest of the day, so I could grab him and talk to him as soon as he came home. But Nicky never appeared.

Finally, at ten o'clock, Mum sent me to get ready for bed. I was really quite worried as I washed my face and brushed my teeth. Where *was* he? This wasn't like him.

I looked out my bedroom window one last time before I got into bed and saw Nicky turning into his gate and trudging up the path to his front door. Heedless of my Care Bear pyjamas and make-up-free face, I flew down the stairs and was just wrenching our own front door open to hurtle after him and throw myself into his arms and explain I was sorry and I had made a terrible mistake and I had never meant to hurt him, when Mum appeared and said, 'Lila, what on *earth* do you think you're doing?'

'I need to talk to Nicky!' I wailed. 'I can't stop, I have to catch him!'

Mum was having none of it though, and was adamant that I wasn't going running around the streets in my pyjamas disturbing the neighbours. Whatever it was could wait till the morning. And even though I begged and said I really *really* needed to talk to Nicky tonight because it was, like, life or death, Mum refused to countenance that there could be anything so vital that I had to rouse half the neighbourhood in the middle of the night (I felt that this was something of an exaggeration on her part).

There was nothing I could say to convince her. 'I need to ask Nicky about homework' wouldn't cut it, because it would just trigger a lengthy lecture about managing my time better, being more organised and taking my A-levels *seriously*. And after my many diatribes against 'Weird Nicky', I didn't think Mum would even believe me if I said, 'Well, the thing is, I've sort of fallen in love with him and I have to go round there and tell him before it's too late.' Even if she did believe me, she would still have said that it could wait till the morning. I fear my mother does not have a romantic soul.

If I lived in some sort of proper teenage world like in an American film, I could shin down a tree outside my bedroom window and sneak out and find Nicky who would have done the same and would be sitting under the apple tree in his garden, and he would look up and see me, standing there in a shaft of moonlight (the Care Bear jammies having morphed into something super cool and demurely sexy) and say, 'Oh Lila!' and everything would be OK, and we would kiss and that would be The End.

But of course, we did not live in that world, so I was sent to bed, to lie seething under my cartoon *101 Dalmatians* duvet cover that I had told Mum I was too old for, and she had said was perfectly serviceable while reminding me that I had promised if she spent all that money on it that I would keep using it until it wore out. But that was when I was ten! How was I to know duvet covers lasted so long? And that I would grow up to experience such emotional turmoil and that Pongo and Perdita would not be conducive to my woe?

MONDAY 11TH NOVEMBER

The results of the photography competition were announced today. To absolutely no one's surprise except possibly his, Nicky won both his categories, and the overall prize for the competition.

He walked up on to the stage to collect his awards looking so surprised and happy and overwhelmed that my heart nearly burst for him. Then, as he attempted to leave, Mr Lorrimer stopped him and said, 'One moment, Nicky. There's more.' Mr Lorrimer announced that the judges had found Nicky's photos so extraordinary, 'especially his portrait work' – his portraits of *me* – that they had recommended he enter for the UK's most prestigious photography competition, the Talbot Prize.

Everyone clapped and cheered, and Nicky turned so red that all his freckles vanished and merged into one. He hurried off stage as soon as Mr Lorrimer gave him the nod, and was soon surrounded by crowds of people congratulating him. Even Rachel was hovering, suggesting he might like to take some photos of her, smiling sexily and saying, 'After all, if you can make *her* look that good, just imagine what you could do with a *proper* subject, you'd stand far more chance of winning the Talbot Prize like that.'

I felt quite cross. Nicky was *mine*. How dare Rachel try and muscle in? And it was the photos of *me* everyone had loved. Why should she assume that Nicky would do even better with photos of her, just because she was bloody *Rachel*?

I couldn't even get near him to try and talk to him though, until the bell rang for classes to start, and everyone dispersed and Nicky was left on his own at the side of the lecture theatre, looking quite relieved. I should have gone too, I was going to be late for French, but I had to talk to him, even if it was just for a minute.

He was gazing at his certificates and the silver plaque he had won as I walked down from my seat and put my hand on his arm and he jumped and spun round. All the light and animation went out of his face as he realised who it was. He looked at me with no expression at all.

I congratulated him and waved at his armful of prizes, then I tried to say I was sorry, about the other night, that I was so confused, by everything, that I said all the wrong things, and I didn't mean them. It all came out all in a gabbled rush, as Nicky was still staring at me with that blank look. He raised his eyebrows very slightly.

'Oh, I think you meant them,' he said. 'I think you've only "realised" you said the wrong things because suddenly everyone's interested in me. Am I good enough for you to go out with now, is that what you're trying to tell me? Am I supposed to fall at your feet, and declare my undying love and gratitude? Well, if you'll excuse me, I did that once before, and your response was shame and mortification and, I believe your exact words were, "What will people think?" If you didn't want me then, when I was just Weird Nicky, when I would have done anything, *anything*, for you, then I don't want you now, when you only want me because everyone else does.'

And he turned around once more and walked away from me.

Why does this keep happening to me?

The worst part was that throughout his whole speech, he didn't seem angry, or bitter, or upset. He just seemed to feel nothing at all.

I hurried after him, trying to tell him that this was nothing to do with his prize, that I had wanted to say all this to him yesterday.

For the first time, a hint of emotion crossed Nicky's face, but it was an expression of weariness. 'I'm going to be late for class now.' And he banged out through the doors of the theatre and left me standing alone once again.

I went to the toilets and cried a great deal. I was going to be in trouble for missing French, but I didn't care. Eventually, I dried my face, and went to reception and told them I wasn't feeling well and needed to go home. When Mrs Fitzsimmons, the dragon lady keeper of the college reception desk demanded to know what exactly was wrong, I said, 'Women's Troubles.'

It was not a lie, after all. My Troubles may have been of the heart and not the uterus, despite what I had implied to Mrs Fitzsimmons, but they were definitely Women's Troubles. It is one of the few advantages of being female, that the flip side of vile males assuming any emotion you show must be 'hormonal' or 'the time of the month' is when you need an unquestionable, get-out-of-jail-free card, you can claim the Women's Troubles, and no one can do or say anything about it.

Mrs Fitzsimmons did look sceptical as she rang Mum's surgery to inform her of this malady and she glared at me as she said, 'Your mother has given permission for you to go home yourself as she can't come and collect you. Sign yourself out. I assume we won't be making a habit of this, Miss MacKay?'

I went home and lay in the bath, sobbing quietly to myself for a while, and then crawled into bed. I thought about writing a poem about how sad and distressed I was. I got as far as 'There once was a boy called Weird Nicky, whose habits sometimes made me feel icky,' when I realised that I was writing a limerick and not a poem. No one can take you seriously with a heartbreak limerick. I finished it anyway.

There once was a boy called Weird Nicky,
Whose habits sometimes made me feel icky,
But he turned out to be good,
I'd kiss him if I could,
I'd even give him my very last biccy.

I think it's the name. Nicky, while very useful for things to rhyme with, just isn't a romantic name, suggesting lovelorn yearnings. It's a jolly sort of good everyday name. If only he could be called something heartbreakingly tender like . . . oh I don't know. Tristan? No, Tristan is a bit of a pretentious name. Though then I could be called Isolde, which is a terribly romantic name. Why must I be called the very prosaic Elizabeth, with all its dull shortened versions, instead of something passionate and glorious like Isolde? I feel like my life would be very different if I was called Isolde. But I would have to face a lifetime of spelling it to people on the telephone. I suppose at least people know how to spell Elizabeth.

I tried another poem, using Nicholas this time, but the only thing I could find to rhyme with it was 'arse'. I think I must face the fact that love poetry may not be my milieu as a writer. I wish I knew what was. Is it not enough that I am facing a future of lonely spinsterhood, unkissed, unlovable and unwanted? And now I don't even get to be a tortured writer on the subject? I don't have so much as a windswept moor to wander across with my broken heart.

I thought about going to the park to be broken-hearted, but it's really not the same. You can't be *properly* broken-hearted in a park. Imagine if Emily Brontë and her wretched imagery had tried to set *Wuthering Heights* in a park. What perilous passion could have taken place between Cathy and Heathcliff as they tried to navigate the tarmac path between the ice-cream van and the bandstand?

I gave up on the poetry and just lay in bed and felt sorry for myself until it was time for *Home and Away*, but I couldn't even concentrate on the problems of an Australian soap. I shuffled to my window to stare out despairingly instead. Oh god, I *am* turning into Cathy Earnshaw. Perhaps I *will* die of my broken heart.

I was still standing there sadly when I saw Nicky coming down the road. He was very late. He'd probably stayed behind in the computer labs to find another willing sap to lure in with his Richard III theories, or maybe he'd been working on his photos for the Talbot Prize, probably with *Rachel*. He looked up at my window as he turned in his gate, and I dived back, lest he saw me standing there and thought I was looking for him. Which I was, of course, but I didn't need him to know that.

Mum was less sympathetic than I had hoped when she came home. Instead of immediately recognising that I was having some sort of existential crisis and possibly a nervous breakdown, she simply said that if this sort of thing was going to keep happening, she'd have to look into having me referred to a gynaecologist. Possibly THE LEAST ROMANTIC word in the ENTIRE English language.

Really, it would serve Mum right if I ran off with an impoverished, bigamist poet who seduced me in a graveyard, just to inject a little romance into my life. But I don't want Percy (what a dreadful name) Bysshe Shelley. I just want Nicky.

EMILY

CHAPTER SEVENTEEN

Blimey. Lila was a total bitch there. I know it was a shock about Weird Nicky – it was a shock to me reading it – but she did not cover herself in glory. Really, Lila, there's wanting to fit in, just like I do, and there's behaving like that!

It made it even harder to believe Mum had once been Lila. I just could not see her caring that much about what people thought. That was what she was always telling me anyway. (Hypocritical much, MOTHER?) I know she tried to make it up to him, but I'm not surprised he wasn't interested. She was *mean*. Then again, he did spring it all on her. Maybe it wasn't *all* Lila's fault.

At least I know now why Mum is always on at me about not worrying about fitting in. She doesn't want me to make a huge mistake like she did. Maybe Weird Nicky *was* the love of her life and she has spent all these years regretting him. Maybe that's why it didn't work out between her and Dad, because she was still pining for Weird Nicky. What if she resents me being born, because I am not Weird Nicky's baby?

I was so worried about this, I asked Uncle Tom about it on the way into town. He was sufficiently disturbed by my question that he even turned off his terrible old people's radio station (he tells me Radio 2 is not for old people, that it is where all the good music is) and said, 'Emily, listen to me very carefully. No one else in the world knows your mother as well as I do, except possibly Jasmit and Kate, and I swear to you, and they would too, that Lila may have many regrets about life, but *you* – you are not one of them. She loves you more than anything. That's why she tries to stop you making the same mistakes she made. She does understand more than you think, you know.'

'Would she love me more if Weird Nicky was my dad?' I said in a small voice.

'She *couldn't* love you more. Lila loves you as much as it is possible for one human being to love another. Please believe me,' Uncle Tom said. Then he laughed. 'I had forgotten how she used to call that poor boy Weird Nicky.'

We drove on for a while, and Uncle Tom switched the radio back on. I couldn't even argue and ask to play my music through the Bluetooth yet, but I had grand plans for the soundtrack to our journey home once my phone was fixed. There were other things I needed to ask though, and for some reason it's always easier talking in a car.

'Is it strange seeing Mum like she is now, when she used to be Lila? Don't you miss that Lila? She's so different now.'

Uncle Tom considered for a while. 'Emily, sixteen-year-old Lila MacKay didn't go to bed one day and wake up the next at the age of forty-four with a mortgage and a child and an unfulfilling job. She was seventeen-year-old Lila, and then all the ages in between, and we all grew and changed with her. So no, I don't look at her and think, "Who are you? Where is Lila?" Because to me, she still is that same person. So am I.'

'Yesterday, you said you weren't that boy anymore,' I pointed out.

'I meant I'm stronger and braver than he was,' Uncle Tom said. 'So is Lila. We've grown up. We face challenges differently now. Life changes how we react and behave. We learn and we grow, but ultimately, we're the same people. It's an over-used metaphor, but it's like when steel is put in a fire and tempered and twisted and beaten. At the end, while it might look like something completely different, and it might have a completely new purpose, it's still the same piece of steel that went into the fire. That's your mother. And me, I hope. Sometimes we might forget what we were, but it's still there, unchangeable. And whoever you think your mother is now, she's still Lila MacKay. She'll always be Lila MacKay. You'll see that one day.'

Three hours later, a smiling bearded man in the Apple Store handed my phone back to me. It was a joyous moment. Uncle Tom seemed to find it slightly less joyous, as it had cost him nearly £200, though the Apple man assured him it had been quite a cheap and easy fix. Uncle Tom looked unconvinced, but a promise is a promise after all. There were so many notifications flying up my screen when I turned it on, that I was slightly worried it might melt down and break again.

'You can look at them all when you're home,' Uncle Tom said firmly. 'Come on, let's go and get some lunch. You've managed a week without being surgically attached to that thing, you can wait a few more hours. NO, Emily, turn it off.'

I had some small revenge by insisting on playing Taylor Swift ALL the way home, while Uncle Tom groaned and said all the songs sounded the same, which is totally untrue and all the evidence anyone needs that Uncle Tom is a MASSIVE BOOMER. When I said that to him, he said he could still change the Wifi password and disconnect me from the world again. It just felt so amazing to have my phone back, to know I could message Poppy at any moment and she could reply and to be back in the world of my friends, instead of being alone with my own thoughts, going round and round in my head, with only Lila for company..

I had asked Uncle Tom over lunch how on earth people *managed* in his day, and he was quite huffy about it.

'What do you mean, "in my day"? You make me sound like some Victorian buffer. I think you'll find, young lady, this is very much still "my day"!'

'If you're calling people "young lady", I don't think it is your day,' I argued. 'I heard you earlier complaining about how that policeman we passed was practically a child, I think that's a pretty surefire sign you are officially old.'

'Firstly, that policeman *was* very young,' Uncle Tom insisted, 'and secondly, to go back to your earlier question before you decided to be so very cheeky, we *managed* without phones because we knew no better. We talked to each other in person. Made phone calls. Hung around in parks.'

'Sounds lame.'

'Shut up and eat your carbonara. We had *hobbies*. And inner resources.'

'Ugh. See? Hobbies are for old people. What even are inner resources?' '

Uncle Tom admitted he wasn't sure, but that he was always being urged to cultivate them when he was young, so he was assuming he must have some.

I thought for a minute and then asked if inner resources included things like his poetry and my drawing.

'Yes, probably.'

'Ha, there, you see, I *do* have inner resources,' I crowed. To be honest though, I probably wouldn't have done so much drawing recently if I'd had my phone – not that I was going to tell Uncle Tom that. In addition to the pictures of Toby and Uncle Tom, I had been drawing the views from the house, and I had even attempted to draw one of the old photos of Mum and Tom and their friends, though it wasn't very easy as the resolution on the photo was so rubbish. I had enjoyed it, and there had been times when it was nice to not have the constant distraction of mindlessly scrolling for hours. And I was pretty sure that after the week of sanding and sugarsoaping I now had all the skills required to start that home reno TikTok, so I had a fallback plan if becoming an artist didn't work out.

It had been nice too, chatting in the evenings with Uncle Tom, and even reading Lila's diary had been interesting, once I got over the ick. I was still very disappointed in Lila, both for how she had treated Nicky, and for her problematic views about *Wuthering Heights* and the things she had called

Emily Brontë and Cathy and Heathcliff. I would have to take that up with her. I wondered what she would say if I told her that in my newfound maturity I had noticed there were some interesting parallels between *Wuthering Heights* and *Saltburn* – but she would probably just demand to know how I had even watched *Saltburn* and I didn't want to tell her about Poppy's big brother's dodgy Firestick that he sometimes let us use. I decided I was definitely going to be on my phone less now though. Just as soon as I had gone through all the hundreds and millions of messages waiting for me.

The messages were mostly from Poppy, in increasing levels of desperation as she tried to get hold of me, because the prehistoric Nokia only does old-fashioned text messages and I don't think Poppy even knows what they are. I had sent her an email from Uncle Tom's iPad explaining about my phone, but Poppy only checks her email about twice a year, so I don't think she'd got it.

The gist of the messages were that my worst fears had come true. Toby had asked Poppy out. She had turned him down, and been most indignant on my behalf, even demanding to know what Toby thought he was doing, asking her out when everyone *knew* he liked me, and Toby had denied any such thing, pointing out that he had never even spoken to me, but that is hardly the point, is it?

Poor Poppy had been in an agony of indecision whether to tell me about this or not, but had decided it was better I knew what sort of a person Toby was. And it didn't matter now anyway, because her final messages, sent this afternoon, were to inform me that Toby Cooper was a total slimeball and after Poppy had turned him down, he'd asked out Olivia

Evans, and then after going out with her for two days, he'd dumped her and asked out Amy Price. So, Poppy concluded, I had had a lucky escape, and was not to be upset about him, but where *was* I and did she need to call the police, because she was getting really worried about me, and was I not talking to her to because of Toby asking her out, because Poppy swore that she had done nothing to encourage him and had been shocked and horrified by him and she would never do anything to hurt me like that, I had to believe her.

I did believe her. And even though I had started to wonder about my feelings for Toby, this still hurt a great deal. I had envisioned me going home and being all cool and nonchalant about him, and now – now I was going to have to watch him and Amy Price, or whoever he'd moved on to by then, and know he had just bypassed me altogether because maybe I *was* unlovable and would be alone forever. Like Lila.

Uncle Tom came upstairs to tell me that dinner was ready and saw my face and asked if I was OK and I tried to say, 'Yes, I'm fine,' but all that came out was a sort of sobbing snort noise, and then he sat down and gave me a hug and asked if I wanted to talk about it and all I could manage to say was 'Toby' and then, 'I want my mum.' Uncle Tom was amazing, but he wasn't Mum. We tried calling her and FaceTiming her, but she didn't pick up, and although Uncle Tom kept reminding me that she'd be here on Monday, it didn't help. I wanted her now.

In the absence of Mum, the next best thing was Lila, so I went to bed, and had a good cry, and hoped that whatever Lila did to get over being unlovable and rejected by Nicky would give me some hope.

LILA

CHAPTER EIGHTEEN

The last two weeks have been hideous. Nicky has stomped around college performatively avoiding me. I have done my best to apologise on more than one occasion and he just looks at me and walks away.

Initially he was giving me the same blank empty look that he gave me the first morning after Kate's party in the lecture theatre, but now he has developed what I assume is his attempt at an expression of noble suffering and dignified pain. It makes him look like a constipated duck. I wouldn't have minded that so much, but he is upsetting everyone else as well. He refuses to sit with us at lunch, and slumps alone in a corner looking martyred, so Tom feels bad for him and goes to hang out with him, which means everyone else at our table feels awkward because of Nicky, and we all know that Tom is sitting over there with him because of me, because I'm such a terrible person.

The only people who don't seem to have noticed the atmosphere are Jas and Mark, because they are too wrapped up in their own little love bubble.

I've apologised to Kate and Tom and Luke and Andy for causing all this trouble, and they've all been very nice about it and said things like, 'Nicky will come round,' which Jas has said as well, insisting that of course it will all be OK and Nicky will stop punishing me, and we'll all live happily ever after, but she said the same about Tom. And looked how that turned out.

I woke up this morning and thought how *tired* I am of all this. All of it. Boys. Relationships. Everything. It is all so much effort, and for what? All of my hopes for college, all of my dreams of love, passion, romance, are reduced to me being made to feel awful every day, because of one throwaway comment I made to Nicky, when I was still trying to come to terms with what was happening.

And how is it fair that I am made to bear all the blame for what happened? Yes, what I said was hurtful and unnecessary, but I panicked. And maybe, *maybe* if Nicky had just given me a little bit of breathing space, maybe if he hadn't immediately thrown himself into 'Now you are my girlfriend, even though I've never even kissed you and you don't get any say in this, you just have to wear this big badge for the world declaring that you are my girlfriend whether you like it or not' then I wouldn't have reacted like that. And yet apparently because I didn't instantly shout and bellow, 'Yes, Nicky, I am your girlfriend!' from every rooftop, then I am the biggest bitch that ever there was, and I must be punished every day for the next two years. And I have had *enough*.

Everything we are told – every magazine article, every film, every story, every fairy tale – informs us that we must seek love. That love is the most important thing.

That we must find that love and validation from a partner. And those who don't, especially women, are to be mocked or pitied, or burned as witches (OK, that doesn't happen so much now, but *even so*). So we all pursue love, pretend to be other than we are to make someone love us, to achieve that ultimate goal. The princess is rescued by the handsome prince, and they live happily ever after. We are *literally* fed these lines from the moment we are old enough to grasp the structure of a story – find someone to love you, and everything will be all right.

But at what price? The Little Mermaid loses everything. Cinderella is transformed into someone else. Snow White's stepmother attempts to murder her. Even Rapunzel has to cut off her hair. Every heroine must lose some essence of who they are. And I can't be bothered with it anymore. This is such an important year of my life, and I have been wasting it, daydreaming about love, mooning after Tom, breaking my heart over Nicky. Well, enough. I'm moving on. I *will* be happy. I will find a way, and it will not involve any boy.

I am going to throw myself into my A-levels. I am going to go to an amazing university, and I am going to become a hugely successful writer, and I will write about anything but love, because I am *sick* of love. It is 1996. We are all supposed to be feminists, and how *can* we be, when all we think about is *love*? There is a world to be changed. I don't even care if I die without being kissed now (though I would at least like to know what it feels like, if only out of curiosity) because I am just going to concentrate on all the other things that are so much more important than boys and love and sex.

I walked into college with new resolution. I felt about ten feet tall and was slightly disappointed no one else seemed to have noticed my newfound sensibilities and FEMINISM. Kate did ask why I kept scowling though, and I said, 'Because I am going to OVERTHROW THE PATRIARCHY,' and she said, 'Fair enough.'

At lunch, Tom grabbed Nicky as he passed, like he did most days, and Nicky glanced at me and shook his head and made a dramatic face and trudged off, and Tom then looked over at me and looked guilty and said, 'I should go and sit with him, I feel bad leaving him on his own.'

'Why?' I said. 'This happens every day. He's choosing to sit on his own. You shouldn't feel bad about his choices.'

Tom grimaced awkwardly.

'We were having a really nice chat, Tom. Please stay here. I've tried and tried to make it up to Nicky, and at this point, I think he's just being a bit silly.' I knew this was brutal, but I was running out of patience with Nicky.

Even Kate said she thought Nicky was being childish now, so Tom sat back down but kept looking over at Nicky. I steadfastly ignored him instead of sneaking anguished peeks and instantly looking away when he looked at me. I concentrated on enjoying my lunch, enjoying my conversation with Kate and Tom, and *moving on*.

I did accidentally look up at one point to see Nicky staring over at me, looking puzzled. I was going to do that guilty, furtive look away because we'd made eye contact, but instead I simply smiled politely and turned my attention back to what Kate was saying. And it felt good. Being in control, taking charge of my life, felt *good*. All term I had been blown about by the winds of other people's whims and desires. Now I was going to do things my way.

FRIDAY 29TH NOVEMBER

I had a free period before lunch today, and an essay to finish, so I went up to the computer lab to get it done so I could go out with Kate after college and enjoy the rest of my weekend. I usually try to avoid the computer lab during the day, as it's always busy and I find it hard to concentrate, but today I was determined I was going to get everything done before the weekend, which I think is a sign of how very mature I am becoming, instead of constantly procrastinating and making excuses.

Sure enough, the computer lab was full when I walked in. Mr Everett, the teacher in charge, wasn't sure he could squeeze me in, and then he realised there was a space in the corner where someone had just left and directed me over there.

Too late, I realised the only available space was next to Nicky.

My first instinct was to simply turn and flee, making excuses about suddenly remembered appointments and other more important things I needed to be doing. But Nicky had looked up at me, and if I left now, I would let him win.

I could feel my cheeks burning as I took my seat, and I felt quite sick, but I simply ignored him, logged on and opened my essay and attempted to focus on Arthur Miller.

Out of the corner of my eye, I was aware of Nicky fidgeting. Really, it was very difficult to concentrate on the travails of Willy Loman when Nicky appeared to be doing a passable impression of sticking his fingers in the socket behind him. I looked round in exasperation to make sure he hadn't done that, and Nicky whipped his head round to look back at me. We stared at each other for a second, then I turned back to my screen and put my Walkman headphones on and cranked up the volume. (I had taped the charts last Sunday night and was currently listening to my guilty pleasure of Robson and Jerome, though if anyone asked, I claimed it was the Prodigy.)

Nicky continued to squirm and writhe beside me, until I was tempted to pause Robson and Jerome and enquire solicitously if he had wet his pants again. Before I could give in to my baser nature though (I suspected referring to *that* incident was the one thing that could make Nicky hate me even more than he already did), he leapt up and grabbed his books. He managed in the process to knock over *my* pile of books. I couldn't help but think he had done this out of some sort of childish spite, and turned to him angrily as he scrabbled my papers off the floor. He slammed them on the desk and then dived after one final piece of paper, which he glanced at briefly and then placed on top of the jumbled heap at my side before stalking off.

I looked at what the offending piece of paper was. Oh good. It was my poetry attempt about him that had turned into a limerick. I flushed again, with anger and mortification. It's not a crime to write a limerick, is it? All the same, I was relieved that my poetic endeavours had turned out so poorly. It was utterly cringe-making that Nicky had read my limerick – it would no doubt make him hate me even more – but thank God it had not been some heartbroken outpouring of blank versed misery bemoaning my tawdry pointless existence in a Nickyless world. At this point, I was simply resigned to his scorn and dislike.

I wish it was different, but it isn't, and so I just have to get on with it.

♡ ❤

SATURDAY 30TH NOVEMBER

I was lying in bed, watching *Live and Kicking* and wondering if I should get my hair cut like Zoe Ball when the doorbell rang. Mum was out (if she'd been here, she would have chased me out of bed to Do Useful Things, while chuntering I was too old for programmes like *Live and Kicking*). I heaved myself downstairs in my jammies, wondering idly if maybe it was the postman with an exciting package for me. I always hope the postman will have something exciting for me, even though he never ever has, not once in my life. Well, occasionally he has, for my birthday or Christmas, but never out the blue. I live in eternal hope though.

It was not the postman. It was Jas, and it was her turn to be snotty and soggy and sobbing.

'Mark dumped me!' she wailed as soon as I opened the door.

I couldn't believe this. Just yesterday lunchtime they had been entwined round each other like bindweed. It had quite put me off my jacket potato. Jas had refused the invitation to come out with Kate and me after college last night, because, as she whispered conspiratorially, she had a *special* date lined up with Mark. I had whispered back, equally conspiratorially, 'Remember what *Just17* said and don't do anything you don't want to and remember to *stay safe*.'

How had they gone from that, to this, in less than twenty-four hours?

I dragged Jas inside and made us tea and got the ordinary ice cream out the freezer. Then I put it back and took out the mint Viennetta and two spoons. This was an emergency after all. I plonked the Viennetta down in the middle of the kitchen table and pushed a spoon as Jas, who was still sobbing, and said, 'Tell me what happened.'

I was feeling very sensible and elder-stateswomanly at this stage, having been through so many of my own emotional traumas recently. I felt I was probably in a good position to dispense much sage advice. Perhaps that is my calling. I may never find love myself, and may shrivel and become crone-like, but I will be famed for my wisdom. I could be an agony aunt, like Claire Raynor on *TV-AM*, or Irma Kurtz in *Cosmopolitan*. I don't want to advertise sanitary towels like Claire Raynor though. You could not pay me enough to stand there and be on TV telling everyone the towels now have 'wings'.

I wrenched my mind back to Jas, who was sniffling and shovelling in Viennetta at an extraordinary rate, and grabbed myself a spoonful before it was all gone, as Jas hiccupped out her short but sorry tale, which was basically that she had gone round to Mark's last night because his parents were out, expecting a romantic evening of snogging on the sofa in front of Blockbuster Video's finest new release, only for Mark to let her into the hall and stand there shuffling his feet awkwardly before dropping his bombshell in front of his mother's Laura Ashley bowl of pot pourri.

Jas paused in her sorry tale and bellowed for a bit.

'He said he needed *space*. And when I said what did he mean, he said space *from me*, and he didn't think we should go out with other any more!'

Jas stuffed the last spoonful of Viennetta in her mouth and collapsed face down on the table. I rubbed her back, and attempted to slide some tissues into the pool of snot and tears that was spreading over the table.

Jas sat up suddenly and said, 'Do you think it was because I said I didn't want to do it yet?' and then went face down again, this time with a distinct splash in the snot pool.

I assured her if it was, then Mark wasn't worth it, and she was well shot of him.

'But I love him,' Jas whimpered. 'I really really love him, what am I going to do?'

I had to be stern. I could understand and sympathise with Jas's pain. It was not so long ago that I was sobbing to her that *I* really really loved first Tom, and then Nicky, and what was I going to do. But I was older now (well, by a few weeks) and much *much* wiser. I had to make Jas see that we had been so very wrong in our headlong pursuit of boys, and that there was much more to life.

'Jasmit!' I used my most grown-up tone of voice. 'Stop it.' And when Jas asked why I was talking like that, I said, 'Because I am being a wise elder woman of the village. You do not love Mark. You are better than that. You are too good to love someone who treats you like that.'

It took some time, but eventually I persuaded Jas of my epiphany: that we needed to focus on ourselves and not boys, that we had wasted our precious first term of college on our headlong pursuit of love, and that there was more to the world and we simply had to discover it, and in the process, turn ourselves into the independent modern women we so longed to be.

'And then boys will like us?' Jas asked.

'NO, Jas,' I sighed and began explaining it again.

Finally, Jas said, 'That's all well and good, Lila, but what about the Christmas Dance?'

I had forgotten about the Christmas Dance. People were already starting to pair off, or eye up potential partners. At least four people had already asked Kate and been turned down.

I was currently alternating between two different fantasies. In the first, an incredibly hot new guy started at college next week, everyone fell in love with him but he asked *me* to the dance, and we walked in both looking insanely gorgeous and Rachel turned into a puddle of bile on the floor out of sheer jealousy, while Nicky gnashed his teeth in rage at what he could have had, before attempting to declare his undying love and it was my turn to regretfully inform *him* that he was too late. In the second, I did not go to the dance. I stayed at home, wistfully adorable in a pair of striped pyjamas, gazing sadly out the window as the snow fell gently. Suddenly, someone would bang on the door, and there would stand Nicky, in a dinner jacket, with a limo waiting, declaring undying love etc etc. I would just *happen* to have the dress of my dreams hanging upstairs and somehow my hair and make-up would already be perfect and off we would go.

Dammit. It really is harder to swear off boys and get over Nicky than I had perhaps indicated to Jas. No matter. I needed to rally and be strong.

'We will go together.' I hoped I sounded more convincing than I felt. 'We don't need boys.'

Jas was doubtful and declared that everyone would think we're losers.

But who cares what other people think? Also – feminism. Smash the patriarchy!

'Yeah!' Jas was half hearted in her cheer. 'Is there any more ice cream?'

WEDNESDAY 4TH DECEMBER

Lunchtimes have been even more awkward this week, as Mark no longer sits with us, although everyone assured Jas that he had been totally in the wrong and he was the one who deserved to go and sit somewhere else. This was incredibly kind of them, as Mark had been friends with Tom and Kate and Luke and Andy far longer than Jas and me, but Tom confided that none of them had really liked him. Of course, then Jas and I had become part of the group, and he'd started going out with Jas, so it seemed he was here to stay. But now he had behaved like a scurrilous cad, none of them were sorry to have an excuse to distance themselves.

However, this lunchtime, Kate very neatly solved the problem of *not* being thought losers for our lack of partners to the Christmas Dance. She suddenly said, 'Why don't we all just go to the dance as a group?' She pointed out how silly it all is, this having to have a partner business, which is true – Craig Morden and Amanda Beckett are only still going out together so they've both got a partner for the dance, Amanda said she'd have dumped him weeks ago if the dance wasn't coming up and she's going to bin him as soon it's over. (Poor Craig.)

Going as a group would be much more fun, Kate said.

Tom wasn't there, as he has started going to the gym at lunchtime on Wednesdays, which is definitely nothing to do with Giles Atkinson also going to the gym on Wednesdays, but Kate said he was up for her plan. The rest of us all agreed enthusiastically too. It wasn't so different to what Jas and I already had planned, but the bigger the group, the more it looked like a *choice* rather than desperation.

It was poor timing on Kate's part though. As I was leaving my French class, Jake Henderson fell into step beside me. I liked Jake, he was a sweet and jolly boy who had let me copy his notes on more than one occasion when I had been too busy daydreaming about Tom, or dashing French Comtes, or eating my heart out for Nicky.

'Hey Lila!' he said with that nice open smile of his. It wasn't the sort of smile that lit up a room, like Tom's, but on the other hand, it was much pleasanter than the scowls Nicky cast in my direction these days, and so I beamed back and then Jake stopped smiling and looked awkward.

Oh God, what now? What had I done now? I attempted to look enigmatic and mysterious.

It turned out I hadn't done anything. Well, not anything terrible, because Jake wanted to ask me to the Christmas Dance which was lovely and sweet and marvellous and splendid. Shame it was a few hours too late. Not too late, I reminded myself sternly. Even if Kate hadn't already put forward her masterplan, I'd still have had to turn Jake down. I could hardly abandon Jas in her hour of need. I couldn't deny that, patriarchy or no patriarchy, it was wonderful to be asked though.

I gave Jake my most dazzling smile as Nicky barged past us, muttering, 'Excuse *me*' and stomped off into the science block.

'What's wrong with *him*?' asked Jake, looking perplexed. 'Anyway, Lila? The dance?'

'Oh Jake, I'm so flattered to be asked, and honestly,' I crossed my fingers, 'if you'd asked me before lunch, I'd definitely have said yes.' It was not really a lie, I told myself, I would have *wanted* to say yes, which was practically the same thing. I explained though that we had all agreed to go as a group, and then as Jake's face fell, I suggested he joined our group too. He still looked a little downfallen about his rejection, but he said if that was OK, then yes, he would like to come with us.

I tried not to smirk to myself as I walked away from Jake. It *was* nice to have been asked. Bad feminist, BAD, I chided myself. Oh, so what? the bad feminist part of me snapped at the good feminist inside me. Aren't I allowed to be at least a little flattered, even if I don't depend on male attention for validation? The good feminist, I suspected, merely raised her eyebrows in judgement about this remark.

EMILY

CHAPTER NINETEEN

Lila did give me some hope. Both that there is more to life than stupid boys, and that although Toby is a skank who doesn't deserve me, maybe someone nice, nicer than him, might come along one day. In the meantime, I too am swearing off boys. I informed Uncle Tom of this over breakfast, when he asked how I was feeling, and he burst out laughing.

'Oh my God. You look *exactly* like Lila did, every single time she swore off boys.'

'What? How many times did she swear off them?'

'Oh, so many times. So, *so* many times.'

'Well, I'm only going to swear off them the once. Men are pigs!' I declared, as Uncle Tom reminded me that he was a man, and some of them were OK, and I insisted that I was not taking that chance and henceforth I would be devoting myself to Higher Things.

Uncle Tom was still laughing at me and saying he'd remind me of this vow in a few years when the doorbell rang and he went to answer it, and then there was Mum in the kitchen.

'But you're not meant to be here till tomorrow!' I said in astonishment.

'I know, I was going to stop off and stay with Kate tonight, but I just really wanted to see you, so I called Kate, and she's going to come here tonight instead. You don't mind, do you?' Mum added to Uncle Tom. 'You did say you had plenty of room?'

Uncle Tom assured her he didn't mind in the slightest, and then, very disloyally, *proving* that men cannot be trusted, announced, 'Emily has sworn off boys by the way, Lila. I'll leave you two to talk.' And he wandered off saying something over his shoulder about fixing the guttering.

'Have you really?' said Mum, laughing. 'What happened?'

I told her about Toby, because she was my mum and I just wanted her to hug me and tell me everything would be all right, and she did, and I felt much better, and then she suggested we wrote Toby's name on a piece of paper and put it in a drawer, because she had read somewhere that if you did that, it cursed the person and they would die within the year. I was quite shocked, and pointed out I didn't think Toby deserved to *die*, he just maybe needed to get a rash in an embarrassing place, or have his trousers fall down at an inopportune moment.

'Well, both those things are likely to happen to him if he carries on like that,' snorted Mum. 'I'm not sure the curse thing works anyway, I tried it with Lily Hunter after she didn't invite you to her birthday party, and she's still alive.'

'Mum, Lily was seven then! That's a bit psycho?'

'Huh. That's what happens when you wrong my daughter. I will make sure there are consequences. I'm here to protect you darling, and I'm always looking out for you. I know you think I'm overprotective and I don't understand but I do, I really do. I just want to keep you safe and I don't want anyone to hurt you. Or at least, if I can't stop you ever getting hurt, I just wanted to keep you from being hurt for as long as possible. Because I love you.'

I was very taken aback. Mum and I didn't really do these deep and meaningful 'I love you' conversations. We said 'I love you' when we said goodbye in the morning and things, but we didn't *talk* about it. It was nice to hear, of course, but also embarrassing. And I couldn't help but wonder how many of my classmates and friends she had tried to hex over the years. I decided perhaps it was best if I didn't know and then I could feign innocence if any freak accidents to happened to anyone, so I just said, 'I love you too, Mum,'

I still couldn't reconcile Mum and Lila though. They seemed to be two separate people. But later that night, after Kate had arrived, and all the grown-ups were drinking wine in the kitchen and FaceTiming Aunty Jas who was at some very important scientific conference in Colorado and they were all crying with laughter about something, I caught sight of the photo of them all that Uncle Tom had pinned up on the kitchen noticeboard, and just for a second I saw it. I saw them. Young Tom and Lila and Kate and Jas in the faces of my mother and her friends before me.

Uncle Tom was right. Those laughing hopeful young people were still there somewhere. Lila was still there somewhere. Which reminded me, I hadn't finished reading her diary.

Mum had been looking through it this afternoon before Aunty Kate had arrived, and had looked horrified at some pages and had laughed at others, and had looked suspiciously like she was crying in a few places. She had anxiously asked me if I had been all right reading it, and had said she really hadn't been sure it had been the right thing to do. She still wasn't.

'I'm mortified at some of the things I wrote in there,' she had said to me.

'So you should be,' I told her. 'You were very rude about Emily Brontë. I take it I am definitely not named after her then, however much I hoped I was?'

'No,' Mum had sighed. 'I told you before, you were named after your father's mother. And I always liked the name Emily. Secretly I thought of you as named after Emily Dickinson. She's a poet,' Mum added as I looked confused.

'In a few years,' I said, 'probably all the girls called Emily will be named after *Emily in Paris*.'

I went and got the diary from the kitchen dresser where Mum had left it, and took it up to my bedroom to read, while Mum and Aunty Kate and Uncle Tom continued to tell totally cringe anecdotes about their youth.

LILA

CHAPTER TWENTY

FRIDAY 20TH DECEMBER 1996

The long-anticipated day of the Christmas Dance finally dawned. Kate and Jas and I had spent the previous weekend shopping for our dresses, accompanied by Mum and Jas's mum, who vetoed anything that they deemed too 'grown up' or 'too sexy' or 'too revealing' to our immense disappointment.

It was precisely because of Mum and Mrs Chatterjee's rather Victorian views on dresses that Kevin had rolled up to our house and enquired of Mum if she would take Kate with us when we went dress shopping, explaining that he did not feel equipped to take Kate himself.

He told Mum he didn't know what was suitable for a young girl to wear to a dance, as his idea of 'suitable' and Kate's were apparently very different. 'And then she twists me round her little finger telling me it's fashion, so I would be so very grateful, Dr MacKay, if you and Mrs Chatterjee could help her pick out something you'd be happy to have your own girls wearing.'

Mum, who had seemed rather taken by Kevin, had agreed that of course, she would be *delighted* to take Kate with us, and so a heady day was spent traipsing around John Lewis and Monsoon, seeking the Holy Grail of three dresses that Mum and Mrs Chatterjee deemed to meet their standards, and we did not think would spell instant social death.

Eventually, Jas found a glorious midnight blue taffeta storm cloud in Monsoon. Kate, so tall and willowy that everything looked marvellous on her, decided on a deep red silk halterneck dress in John Lewis, in which she managed to look both understated and dramatic at the same time. And I acquired the most beautiful long slinky black velvet number on our third visit to Monsoon. It had taken that number of visits to wear Mum down about it, as Mum did not approve of young girls wearing black. To my relief, Mrs Chatterjee eventually took my side, possibly because she just wanted to call it a day and go and get a cup of tea, saying, 'It does look marvellous on her, Helen, you must admit. And it meets all our other criteria. It's not too short, or split too high, or too low cut.'

'That's the trouble,' sighed Mum, thinking I couldn't hear her in the cubicle where I was changing back into my jeans. 'It makes her look an absolute knockout. I don't think it's the dress, actually. I think she's growing up.'

'Well, we both know there's nothing we can do about that,' Mrs Chatterjee said, and then she told Mum she should let me have the dress, because your first grown-up dance dress should be something special that you should remember forever.

I was so thrilled when I came out the changing room and Mum said I could have the dress that I kissed her right in the middle of the shop floor.

College finished at lunchtime today, and Jas and I went back to Kate's so we could all get changed for the dance together. Kevin had provided us with some Bucks Fizz while we got dressed, which was *much* nicer than the warm beer or cider we were accustomed to at parties. By the time we were ready, we were all stunned by the almost unrecognisable girls staring back out at us from the huge mirrors in Kate's bedroom.

The boys were coming to Kate's for a drink before the dance too, but as we trooped downstairs before they arrived, Kevin appeared brandishing a large camera.

'Not so fast!' he yelled, demanding photos, lots of photos, as it was his little girl's first grown-up dance and Kate groaned despairingly about how embarrassing he was.

But Kevin refused to back down, as he had promised Mum and Mrs Chatterjee that he would get plenty of photos for them too. Then the boys arrived, including Jake, and Kevin insisted on more photos with them, in every possible combination – 'Never let it be said I failed in my role as the evening's official photographer' – and there was more Bucks Fizz and then it was time to go.

Kevin had been keen to hire a limo to transport us all, but Kate had talked him out of it, to my disappointment. He had arranged a couple of the local taxis to take us instead as there were so many of us.

Most excitingly, the dance was being held in the ballroom of a hotel, and an actual real live ballroom seemed like the most impossibly glamorous thing I had ever heard of. It did not disappoint, with glittering chandeliers and marble columns aplenty. I clutched Jake's arm as we went in, as much in wonder as because I was slightly wobbly on my new and unaccustomed heels.

Jas hissed as we sat down, because Mark had just walked in with Rachel. Then she produced a quarterbottle of vodka from her bag which she proceeded surreptitiously to add to her Diet Coke under the table.

I asked if that was a good idea, given that she had already had quite a lot of Kevin's Bucks Fizz.

Jas was unrepentant. 'I might have to sit and watch him with her, but I don't have to do it sober.'

An hour later, after a lot of dancing, I was so glad we had gone with Kate's plan of us all just coming as a group. This was much more fun than being stuck with one partner, and not being able to dance unless they wanted to, as we had observed when Rachel started berating Mark for refusing to dance to The Proclaimers, which was cheesy but *fun*.

I was very hot, and I decided I needed some air. Jake offered to come with me, and we stepped out the French windows on to the little terrace outside. Something moved in the shadows, and I realised it was Tom and Giles Atkinson, sitting very close together on the wall at the end of the terrace.

I hurriedly turned to Jake, who was behind me, and implored him to fetch my pashmina, as I was afraid of catching a chill in the night air, and once he was out the way, scuttled over to Tom and Giles. Giles looked terrified.

'Go round the corner,' I murmured to them. 'Then you can see anyone coming before they see you.'

Tom was holding Giles's hand. 'But then we can't hear the music,' he said. 'If we can't dance together, I wanted at least to listen to the music together.'

Luckily Jake was taking his time finding my pashmina. I dashed back inside, kicked off my heels for speed, ran down a corridor off the ballroom, opened the windows on to the lawn below the terrace, flew back to Tom and Giles, cramming the beastly shoes back on and beamed. 'Now you can hear the music *and* you can dance if you want to.'

'Lila, thank you.' Tom hugged me. 'Maybe next year, we won't feel like we have to hide.'

I hugged him back and said I hoped this would do for now.

They dived down the steps as Jake finally came out with my pashmina. After putting him to all that trouble, I had to pretend I wanted to stay out a bit longer, even though I was freezing by now. I finally reckoned I had lasted long enough, and we shivered back through the doors, just as Nicky was passing. I had resolved to be icy and distant if I saw him, but I couldn't help it. I smiled at him. For a moment he smiled back, and then his smile died before it had even properly begun, as he saw Jake coming through the French doors behind me.

Jake announced he was off to the loo, and I went back to our table. Everyone was dancing except Jas, who had finished the vodka and was looking rather odd. 'I feel . . . sicky yuck,' she mumbled. 'Think I need to go outside.'

She lurched unsteadily to her feet, listing decidedly to

starboard. I attempted to pull her back to centre, but the list was determined, and in these heels, she was liable to pull me over. I kicked off my shoes once again, leaving them under the table this time, and started trying to manoeuvre her towards the doors back out on to the terrace. It wasn't easy, rather like trying to steer Bambi on ice. Someone appeared on Jas's other side and propped her back upright.

'Oh, thank you!' I gasped and then realised it was Nicky.

Jas groaned that she really felt very pukey. We managed to get her outside and pointed at the flowerbeds before she began to heave.

I ordered Nicky to hold Jas's face while I got her skirts out the way, because her dress was dry clean only. Nicky seemed nonplussed that I was more concerned about Jas's dress than Jas herself, but he didn't know how much she loved that dress. Jas made unladylike noises for a while, and I felt a pang of remorse, as Jas spewing vodka and Bucks Fizz was not the soundtrack Tom and Giles had been hoping to accompany their romantic moment on the lawn, but there was not much I could do about it now. It wasn't exactly how I had seen my evening going either.

Finally, Jas straightened up and said she was feeling better now and had she got any on her dress? I assured her the beloved dress was *fine* and Jas suddenly noticed who had been her other ministering angel of puke.

'OH!' she said. 'I'm . . . I'm going to go to the loo and fix my face and eat, like, half a tube of Polos now.'

I suggested I should go with her, but Jas insisted she was *fine* and just needed five minutes on her own and she tottered off back inside.

'I suppose we should go in too!' I said brightly to Nicky, who was still standing at the edge of the terrace, his hands in his pockets, looking pensive. There was something different about him. 'Thanks so much for your help.' And I started to walk towards the doors.

'Lila?'

I turned back to Nicky.

'You look so beautiful tonight,' he said. 'I know I shouldn't say that to you when you're here with Jake, but you do. And I've been horrible to you and I'm sorry. That's all I wanted to say.'

'I'm not here with Jake,' I said. It was the first thing that came into my head. 'We came in a group. Didn't Tom tell you?'

'Tom did say, but then I saw you, and I thought . . . so you're not with Jake?'

And then it was Nicky's turn to gabble wildly, about how he had been so hurt and angry, but even though he tried to hate me, he couldn't. He still loved me, he said, and could I forgive him? And then he said, quite hesitantly, 'And . . . can you not be my girlfriend? Can we just . . . like each other and take it slowly? Please?'

Nicky took a step towards me, looking hopeful, and extended his hand towards me. For a moment, just a moment, I put my own hand out towards him to take it, and then both fury and the good feminist inside me prevailed, and I pulled my hand back.

'You were horrible to me,' I said furiously. 'I tried and tried to explain, but you wouldn't let me, YOU just stomped around sulking. And *actually* I've sworn off men and I'm devoting myself to my studies and giving serious thought to my career and I'm thinking of ways to dismantle the patriarchy and be a better feminist, so I don't *need* you.'

HA! I waited for Nicky's impassioned speech to woo me back. I was pretty sure it was going to be a good one, and I was hoping for a lot more 'I love you's and maybe even a few 'I am so unworthy of you's before I magnanimously forgave him. But he just said, 'Oh. I'm sorry I bothered you then.' And turned around and slouched dejectedly over to the doors.

I couldn't believe it. He was actually going to leave it at that and walk away? Didn't he know how any of this worked?

'Wait!' I cried. 'You're not meant to just walk away. If you're not going to try to talk me round, you are at *least* meant to once more express your heartbroken, unrequited, undying, eternal love and passion for me- maybe throw in a line about "Whatever our souls are made of, yours and mine are the same", you can't just say "OK" and *go!*'

Nicky walked back to me, looking at me oddly. 'Are you trying to say maybe there is a chance for me if I quote *Wuthering Heights* to you?'

I tried to look dignified as I informed him I hated *Wuthering Heights*, actually, and he said well why did he see me reading it all the time then, and I pointed out it was on the curriculum, and I had to, and could we please talk about something other than my English set texts!

So Nicky pulled me into his arms, and murmured, 'If I loved you less, I might be able to talk about it more.'

Oh. *Emma.* NICE!

Nicky held me tighter and asked if it would still count as swearing off men if I let him kiss me? I agreed it would probably be all right, and then, as he leaned in towards me, I suddenly noticed something.

'Nicky, your eyes,' I exclaimed. 'They're *sea-green*. Have they always been sea-green?' How have I never noticed this?

He said he'd got contacts. 'And yes, they've always been green, obviously. Red hair, green eyes, it's not that unusual a combination, though red hair is a recessive gene, of course, that will eventually die out, and green eyes are recessive to brown, but dominant to blue so –'

'Shut up and kiss me!'

'Lilaaaaaaaa!' A wail came from the doorway and Jas lurched back out into the night, looking a less than healthy colour.

Nicky let go of me with a sigh, and we both grabbed an arm and steered Jas back towards the flowerbeds and went through the same drill again. She was sitting on the wall feeling sorry for herself when Mark rushed out to her and was all apologetic saying he wanted to make her jealous by coming with Rachel, 'but I miss you, I'm sorry.'

Jas regarded him scornfully and then said, 'I'm gonna be sick again,' and stood up looking for her favourite flowerbed.

'Look after her, it's the least you can do,' said Nicky, thrusting Jas at Mark. Jas retched as Mark solicitously held her hair, and then straightened up and told him she would not go back out with him if he was the last man on Earth.

I suppressed a snigger at Mark being chucked after the upchucking, as Nicky grabbed my hand and pulled me down the steps on to the lawn. I wondered if this was the moment to point out that I didn't have any shoes on and my feet were very cold, but I wasn't sure I could cope with any more interruptions.

We ran on, past some bushes where I heard what sounded suspiciously like Tom laughing, and Nicky stopped under a big tree and wrapped his arms around me again.

'You're shivering,' he said in concern, and I was forced to point out that while he was cosy in a DJ, I had on a sleeveless dress and *no shoes* in December, so he took off his jacket and wrapped me in it. I wondered if I would ever be adequately clad in a romantic situation, or if I was eternally destined to borrow clothing from sensibly dressed men. This was so much more delicious than the encounter with Tom under Nicky's apple tree though.

'Now can I kiss you?' he asked.

'Yes, but wait! What changed your mind?'

'Your limerick. I knew it was pointless to try and pretend I wasn't still hopelessly in love with you when I saw it. How could I not love a girl whose response to heartrending events is to write a limerick? So, then I thought maybe I could just ask you to the dance, but I heard Jake asking you, and then I considered joining the French Foreign Legion.'

I was confused as to how we had gone from limericks to the Foreign Legion via the Christmas Dance. Nicky patiently explained that that's what people used to do to escape doomed love affairs. And then he said, '*Please* can I kiss you now?'

'Yes, but it won't change anything and I'll still be a feminist and –'

And then Nicky kissed me, and the stars were shining above, and the breeze was gently rustling the trees, and I could hear the music from the ballroom faintly drifting towards us, and it was perfect.

EMILY

CHAPTER TWENTY-ONE

I sat there, stunned. It was a happy ending, but it *wasn't* an ending, was it?

I could hear Mum coming up the stairs, and I needed to know what had happened, how Lila MacKay had gone from standing under the stars with her head full of dreams being kissed by a boy with sea-green eyes, to becoming *Mum!*

She came in and asked if she could sit down, and said, 'Did you finish the diary?'

She wanted to know if it had helped. 'I wasn't at all sure about this plan of Tom's. Even less so, looking back through that diary this afternoon, and then I realised, reading how I felt back then, all the times you've told me I just don't understand what it's like to be a teenager, well. You were right. I didn't.'

'But you *did*,' I said in confusion. 'Lila did, she totally understood it.'

'I know, I know, but I think I had forgotten,' Mum said. 'The agony, how serious everything felt, how *awful* it is being a teenager. All these years, I've been telling myself of course I know what it is like for you, but I didn't, not till

I was reading it all back, and I remembered how convinced I was that no one understood. Just like you are. So I'm sorry if I've made you feel that way, or not taken your feelings seriously.'

I was taken aback. 'Thanks Mum. Thank you. But . . . what happened next?'

'You know what happened,' said Mum. 'I grew up. I met your father. I had you. Life happened.'

I shook my head. 'No, I mean with Lila and Nicky. What *happened*? Where is he?'

'I have no idea,' Mum said sadly. 'Like I said, we grew up. We moved on, that's all.'

'There has to be more than that!' I was indignant. 'I am *invested* in their story now, you can't just say, "We grew up" and expect that to be enough! Tom said there were more diaries. Do you still have them? Can I read them?'

Mum looked startled 'I really don't know if that's appropriate, Emily.'

'Please.'

'Let me think about it. And read them first to see if they are suitable. And think about it some more!'

'Is that a yes or a no?'

'It's a maybe!'

Oh my God! Why are grown-ups so ANNOYING!